THICK AS THIEVES

A LESBIAN ROMANCE HEIST

CARA MALONE
ANNA COVE

1

CASS

This job would be significantly easier if there were a man on the other side of the table.

Or even a woman who was a bit, let's say, curious. If there was even a crack of uncertainty in the woman sitting across from me, a queen on her throne, I would have been all set. My nut-brown hair was smoothed into a French twist. I'd put on mascara and eyeliner to highlight my most striking feature—my eyes. And I was wearing a dress, for goodness' sake.

But there were no cracks in Mildred Fillingham. I checked everywhere cracks would usually appear, but the woman's beady eyes never flickered, never deepened in color to betray carnal desires. Her body never softened from its slate-stiff position. Her words remained dull and flat, without deeper meaning. She was as locked up as the vault right down the hallway.

Yet just like the vault, there was always a way in. I just had to find it.

"And you worked as a teller at the Porterfield National Bank for five years?" the woman asked.

Well, I robbed the place five years ago, but... I smiled pleasantly, remembering my breakfast from that morning to add disinterest to the look. French toast, smothered with syrup, strawberries and whipped cream. It was always important to lend credence to your facial expressions. I smoothed out my skirt to add to the blandness. "Correct," I said, folding my hands, the picture of innocence—a picture helped by the fact that I looked twelve rather than twenty-two.

Mildred would check my references, no doubt, but not until tomorrow and by then I would have obtained what I needed.

"And why did you leave that position?" Mildred asked, peering over her glasses.

She would have been so much more attractive without them, and if she let down her hair a little... My mind snapped to an image of her shaking out that gray, curly hair, a naughty Helen Mirren.

Stay. On. Task. Cass. What did a woman like Mildred want to hear? Charm hadn't worked, nor my subtle flirting. Perhaps... "How long did it take you to move up to bank manager in this organization?"

Mildred blinked once and paused, and I thought I might have been off-base in my question. It was getting late, and I still needed her to take me on a tour of the place. Fifteen minutes before closing. There was still time. But only if we got through the rest of the interview quickly.

"Thirty years," she answered.

I sat back in my chair. A row of windows lined the wall behind Mildred and I let my gaze drift over her shoulder, where my crew, Spider and Talia, were waiting in a van outside. Then I refocused. "And I'm guessing you had a lot of pushback on the way."

Mildred scoffed. "Like you wouldn't believe."

"But you worked hard, and you earned your position here."

"Yes, nothing better than a good day of hard—"

I slapped the table, making Mildred jump a little. "That right there. That's why I want to work here. I want to come to a place where I'm inspired to do better every day. I'm sorry to say it, but the top brass at Porterfield just wouldn't cut it for me. I want a strong leader to look up to, a strong... woman."

Mildred narrowed her eyes, though her cheeks colored a bit under her caked foundation.

"I really shouldn't say this." I paused, letting my own cheeks grow warm with the memory of my last conquest. Where had that been? California? Life was such a whirlwind lately. "But I've admired you for a long time, Ms. Fillingham."

Mildred glanced down at her desk. Did she have one of those panic buttons? Had she figured me out and already pressed it? Her finger tapped once on the desk, then a smile spread across her face. "Call me Millie."

Bingo. "Millie. What a pretty and unique name."

At my words, whatever faint blush had appeared on Mildred's cheeks vanished. She stood, her hands tee-peed on the desk. "Well, it looks like I have everything I need here. It was lovely meeting you, Ms. Stone."

"Cass, please," I said, standing up, offering her my hand and my real first name, although I'd given her a fake last name. My stomach turned, but I pushed the feeling away and made sure to smile large. *I need that damn tour.*

"I'll be in touch," Mildred said, coming around the desk.

Momentum dictated she would be guiding me out the door. But she couldn't do that, not yet. I wasn't ready. "I actually have a few more questions, if you don't mind."

"Oh." Mildred seemed surprised, but she stopped moving and perched her spindly form on the edge of the desk like a flamingo. "Go on."

Now, how to ask my questions without seeming suspicious? *Where do you keep your most valuable items?* wouldn't work. Nor would, *Could you show me how you get into the safe deposit vault?* Mildred checked her watch, and I thought I felt the hardwood floorboard under my foot vibrate faintly with an impatient tap of her foot. She wanted to end the interview so she could close up the bank. *Quick, Cass. Think.* "Do employees get a discount to store valuable items here?"

Mildred raised her eyebrows.

"My mother just passed—"

"I'm so sorry."

I was sorry, too—sorry I had to lie to this nice woman. My mother was alive and well, or at least as well as someone could be sitting in a jail cell, with a disappointment of a daughter like me on the outside. "She left me a valuable heirloom that I'm scared to keep at home. Porterfield lets me keep the item in their vault, but I was wondering if... well... you know how precious these items are and you know the salary of a bank teller. I was wondering if I could bring it with me and store it at a discounted rate."

As Mildred shook her head, I thought I'd gone too far. But then she said, "Of course, depending on the size of the item."

"It's about... well... this big." I gestured vaguely in the air, marking out the size of a large dictionary.

"That should be fine. We have the capacity for something like that." She paused. "Here, why don't I give you a tour of all our facilities?"

Score.

But the tour was only a side benefit. My real goal was to get close to Mildred Fillingham, to swipe her keycard for the vault. Spider had provided me with a replica and, as long as I could replace it, Mildred wouldn't figure it out until the next morning. Hopefully, the tour would take me through closing, past the time where Mildred would have to use her keycard again. By tonight, we would have what we needed and we'd be off.

Mildred gave me a wide berth as she led me out of her office, but I couldn't steal the keycard then, anyway. I had to wait until after she'd used it at the vault. Timing was everything.

And my timing, as usual, was perfect. As Mildred brought me through the teller space, the last customer of the day finished his business and cleared out. As she introduced me to the two young tellers, I smiled and quipped, and told them I hoped to join them soon. Then they started cashing out their tills and Mildred checked her watch.

"Well, it's getting late but I can show you the deposit lockers if you like."

"Sure," I said, trying to act casual, though my heart sped in anticipation.

I followed her through a narrow hall to a pair of vault doors—one to the money and the other to a large room with rows of lockers. A guard stood between them. Mildred pulled out a lanyard from under her jacket, leaned forward and scanned a card on the door on the left. She opened the door and then stuffed the lanyard back into her bosom.

Great. Of course she kept the lanyard on one of the more sensitive parts of her body. At least the old bank hadn't yet implemented fingerprint technology, but I was going to have to do some crazy voodoo to get that keycard out of there. But I could. I was Cass Hartley, after all. Small, scrappy, resourceful. Loved robbing banks and counting her money on deserted beaches.

Focus.

Mildred nodded to the guard as we entered the vault, explaining to me, "We have extra security here this weekend—the construction outside was wreaking havoc on our vibration sensors and we had to turn them off."

"Ah," I said. I knew this. It was part of the reason the pickup had to happen tonight. The guard would be easy enough to handle, though. I assessed the area quickly. Three rows of lockers with a long, rectangular table along the back. So many potential treasures locked in their cages, ignored by their owners, ripe for the picking, but I only cared about one.

"Items the size you indicated would go over here," Mildred said, striding toward the left-most row. As we went, I noticed a hint of something, no more than a brief movement in the shadows—a feline swish. We weren't alone.

"Is it climate-controlled?"

"Of course."

"Do you mind if I see the size of a locker? Of an empty one, of course."

Mildred nodded and moved to the locker at the end of the row. She pushed a key into the lock and opened it up. Then I heard it again, a shuffling. Something about it made me twitch. Why would someone move so softly? They could have been shy, I supposed, but I hadn't exactly *seen* this person. Were they trying to hide? If so, why? The two tellers were getting ready to leave. Maybe it was a janitor or something?

Mildred was talking about the padding the bank could install in the box for my item, but my ears were finely tuned to the soft clicking of heels and the swish of fabric on fabric.

"You know what?" I said, tapping my dress pockets. "I think I dropped my glasses at the door. Be right back."

I said the words and slipped away before Mildred could respond. I rounded the corner and saw a flash of dark fabric disappearing behind the far row. Three more steps brought me to the other side of the row where I came face-to-face with a woman, which I had expected.

What I *hadn't* expected was the curly blonde wig, or the blue-gray eyes, or the dark purple lipstick out of place on her fair skin. I also didn't expect how fast she smoothed her wrinkled forehead and narrowed her widened eyes. Most people wouldn't have even noticed the initial surprise, but I wasn't most people. She was *surprised* to see me.

Why? Did she recognize me?

I certainly didn't recognize her, though I wouldn't

be *opposed* to recognizing her in the future. And more of her, too.

"Excuse me," she said and brushed by me. She smelled like lilacs and coconuts, a gentle cloud of loveliness that kept me from chasing after her. It kept me from doing anything until Mildred called my name.

"Coming," I said.

I had to focus. I had to get that keycard from Mildred, replace it with the fake that Spider had made, and get out of there. That was the easy part. We had planned for all of that.

What we hadn't planned for was company. And I was reasonably sure, by the look of that woman, we were going to have some tonight.

2

MADISON

There was something familiar about that girl.

I didn't have time to pause and think it over—I was only interested in high-tailing it out of that bank before the manager or the security guard got a good look at my face. I was wearing a blonde wig over my natural dark red hair, as well as a matte, plum lipstick that really wasn't my shade. But none of that would help me if that stiff, unflinching woman really took a good look at me.

I was already pushing my luck, lingering in the deposit room to size up my mark, when I overheard that girl's ridiculous line of questioning.

Officially, I was there to "examine some personal effects from my grandmother's locker" and it was supposed to be a simple task—get in, gather some intel, locate our target for later tonight, and get out again.

Instead, I was wondering just who this chick thought she was fooling with those questions. *Do you mind if I see the size of a locker?* She might be fooling the bank manager—a minor miracle—but I saw right through her. *I dropped my glasses?* Please! She was up to something.

I had to know who was poking around *my* mark on the eve of the most important heist I'd ever pulled, and doing it so brazenly. When I *accidentally* bumped into the girl at the end of the aisle, I wasn't surprised to discover how young she looked—her technique said she was new to the game.

What *did* surprise me was the familiarity of her features.

She had rich brown hair pulled into a neat twist that paired perfectly with the professional look of her clothes—a sleeveless dress that hugged her petite frame without being too revealing. Her almond-shaped eyes were what really caught my attention—I knew those eyes from somewhere.

She smirked as I brushed past her, the girl's shoulder skimming along the fabric of my blouse, and my breath caught momentarily in my throat.

It wasn't until I was marching down the sidewalk outside the bank, ducking under some scaffolding left up by a road construction crew, that I finally put aside my annoyance at the girl's presence—and her brash confidence—long enough to realize who she was.

Cass Hartley.

She was the daughter of Bill and Brenda Hartley, a couple of con artists who were pretty well-known in my line of work. They pulled some incredible cons in their day: jewelry heists, bank jobs, big-time stuff that eventually landed them in the big house. They got greedy and it was a damn shame.

I knew the Hartleys had a daughter, but I had no idea she was pulling jobs on her own now... or that she'd grown up so pretty.

All the more reason for this to be my last job.

As I marched down the sidewalk, turning at the end of the block and making my way back up the street on the back side of the buildings, I wondered how much trouble she would be. At first, I'd discounted her silly questions to Mildred, assuming she was a small-timer, maybe a pickpocket ready to try her hand at a more challenging game, but a Hartley wouldn't walk into a bank and show her undisguised face without having a plan in place.

Oh God, I thought. *What if she's after the book, too?*

What were the odds? They had to be miniscule, right? Sure, Cass had the familial connections to find out about the sale of the rare first edition, leather-bound copy of *Twenty Thousand Leagues Under the Sea* that I had my eyes on, and she could use her parents' network of friends to find out it was currently being held in locker number 231 at the First United

Bank of New Vernon while the funds were being transferred. But the statistical probability that Cass Hartley had her sights set on *my* final target was incredibly low.

Right?

I had a sick feeling in my stomach as I reached the rear entrance of Pets Unlimited, which had, in fact, run out of pets about six months before and gone out of business. I let myself into the office area of the abandoned pet shop, which I'd been using as my headquarters for the last week. I was met by the broadshouldered, frowning figure of my muscle, Tank.

"What took so long?"

"Just a little foot traffic," I lied. "How's the breach going?"

"Good," he said. "Your demo guy says we're down to about half an inch of steel between us and the vault, and it won't take long to cut through that when the time comes."

"Good. Show me," I said, following Tank to the front of the shop, where mounds of broken concrete lay in front of empty cages and the windows were covered with multiple layers of newspaper.

My demo guy, Nelson, was kneeling in a cavity situated along the side wall about twelve inches deep. I'd used him on a few other jobs before and there was nothing he couldn't break into—or out of. All day, he'd been slowly making his way through the concrete pet shop wall, timing his drilling with the construction noise outside on the street. Now all that was left was to penetrate the adjoining, thick steel wall of the bank.

The road repair was nearly done and once the construction crew left, the bank would reactivate all the vibration sensors they'd been forced to turn off this week. It was one of the sweetest instances of serendipity I'd encountered in my fifteen years of high-stakes theft, and if we didn't make our move tonight, it would be a beautiful opportunity wasted. It really was the perfect end to a flawless career.

Whatever Cass Hartley was planning, I just had to hope she moved slower than me.

It was a few minutes past midnight when Nelson put on a welder's helmet and asked, "You ready, boss?"

"As I'll ever be," I said. "Bree?"

"Ready," my hacker said. She'd been monitoring the bank's security systems ever since Nelson started chipping away at the concrete, and she was standing by to disable any alarms that might go off as he breached the last half-inch of steel. I moved with her and Tank into the empty manager's office to give Nelson room to do his work, and he then flipped down his helmet.

Bree sat down cross-legged on the floor, her computer in her lap and a look of intense concentration on her face. Tank poked his head out the door to give Nelson a thumbs-up. *Go time.*

My stomach was still tied in knots and I'd spent the last six hours running through all the possible scenarios that could play out with whatever scheme Cass had up her sleeve. *She beats me to it and the locker is empty when we get there. She fucks it all up and the cops are waiting when we cut through the wall. The cops catch her and she rats me out to save herself.*

I'd been planning this for weeks, controlling every detail down to the three identical black ski masks and three sets of gloves sitting on top of an empty ferret cage outside the office. I should have been savoring a familiar surge of adrenaline right about now—not worrying about the myriad ways Cass Hartley could screw me over.

I was frowning as I heard Nelson fire up his oxyacetylene torch to cut through the last inch of steel separating me from my treasure, and it didn't escape Tank's notice.

"Hey, what's wrong?" he asked. "Are you worried it's not gonna work?"

"No," I said curtly, hoping to shut him up.

"Because I think even if Donnie doesn't understand why you took the book, it'll still—"

"I said *no*," I snapped and Tank got the hint. We stood in silence while Nelson cut through the steel and Bree tapped furiously at her computer, disabling the security system.

The very first time I broke into a bank, my heart felt like it was trying to claw its way up my throat and I was utterly convinced that the alarms would start going off the minute we breached the wall. I thought the police would be yanking my hands into cuffs behind my back within minutes.

Tonight I just watched the sparks flying through the small office window, thankful for this distraction from the subject of my brother. If Cass was turning out to be a buzzkill, thoughts of Donnie certainly wouldn't improve my mood. I needed this job to go perfectly, and I needed to commit it to memory—my last heist. Giving up this life was going to be worth it, but I already missed the adrenaline.

"Bombs away!" Nelson shouted as he finished the job and a large steel circle the size of a manhole cover fell to the ground inside the bank with a loud clank.

No alarms sounded, but that was expected. Banks used silent alarms more often than not now, so I just waited for Bree to give me the thumbs-up. She typed away for a few more seconds, verifying that the security system was down, then gave me a nod. I stepped out of the office and distributed the ski masks and gloves to Tank and Bree.

"Nelson, you're done—get out of here," I said as he gathered his welding equipment. "Everyone else, let's go—it's showtime."

I pulled a ski mask over my head, put on my gloves, then crouched and stepped carefully through the newly formed entryway between the pet shop and the bank.

Aside from the bits of concrete and steel debris scattered all over the floor, and the fact that the overhead lights were off, it looked the same as it had this afternoon—*thank God*. Faint blue lights ran along the walls at the floor and ceiling, just enough to light our way, and I used a flashlight to read a few locker numbers and orient myself in the room.

Locker number 231 was in the second row near the back wall, and I waved Bree and Tank into the room.

"231," I whispered to them. "Bree, how long do you think we have before the bank security notices their systems are down?"

"Maybe five minutes, and another ten for the police to—" she started to say, but I held my fist up.

"Shh!"

My ears were pricked and suddenly that adrenaline surge I'd been craving caught up to me. The room was completely silent and I turned my head to the vault door, where I heard a distinct metallic clicking sound as the enormous steel tumblers turned.

"Cops?" Bree hissed behind me, terror on display in her voice.

Tank wasted no time stepping in front of us, using his enormous stature to shield us from any bullets that might be about to rain in our direction.

"Should we run?" Bree asked.

Maybe, I thought, but before I had a chance to get

angry at myself for insisting on pulling this heist even though I had a bad feeling about it this afternoon, the vault door swung open and Cass Hartley waltzed in.

She had her hands on her hips and everything, like she thought she was Superwoman, and she was grinning at me.

"I thought we might see you here," she said as she stepped into the deposit room, two crew members in tow.

"How did you get in?" I asked, my heart rate rising as Cass came closer to me.

In all my years pulling jobs, I'd never run into another crew in the middle of a heist and it sort of felt like we were about to rumble. That, or Cass was about to kiss me—she was walking purposefully toward me and giving me a very challenging look. She was practically daring me to back down.

"We came in through the front door," she said, flashing a keycard at me before slipping it into the pocket of her tight black pants.

I rolled my eyes. I couldn't help it, her confidence was aggravating. "And you probably set off every silent alarm from here to the police station."

"At least we didn't cut our way in," Cass said with an arch of her eyebrow. "We could hear that steel drop all the way on the other side of the door. You're lucky we took care of the guard already or he would have been all over you."

Her lips rose over her sharp canines as she said this

—she was *definitely* toying with me and I wondered how she could read me so easily. How did she even know she *could* toy with me like that?

I cleared my throat as I turned to Bree and Tank and said, "Come on, let's get what we came for before we all get arrested."

3
___

CASS

Even with the ski mask, I instantly recognized the suspicious-acting woman from the deposit room earlier in the day. I'd pretty much been expecting her, and the eyes outlined by the holes of the ski mask tipped me off. Those gray eyes were a color I hadn't seen anywhere but in storm clouds and asphalt.

But we didn't have the luxury of getting acquainted right now.

Talia, my oldest friend and crew member, had been triggered by the chaotic noise the other crew made cutting their way through the vault wall, and she was muttering a set of numbers under her breath to calm herself. Confrontation would only make it worse, so I decided to cut through it. I marched over to the woman with the storm cloud eyes and tore the stupid ski mask off her face.

"This is a bit cliché, don't you think?" I said in a hushed voice, pointing at her before tossing the mask against the row of lockers to my left. "Who are you?"

"Who are *you*?" The woman asked, though she knew exactly who I was. She'd known earlier that day, too. What kind of game did she think I was playing?

I decided to ignore her stupid-ass question and admire her face instead. Even though she wasn't smiling, her lips were set in a little smirk that belied something interesting underneath the boring predictability of her attitude. She wasn't bad to look at, that was for sure, especially now that she'd wiped off that garish purple lipstick.

"What are you here for?" I asked.

"That's none of your business. Bree, how's the security looking?"

She was talking to one of her crew members, standing off to the side with a laptop balancing on her forearm. Petite. Glasses, her eyes magnified by her lenses, wide as an owl's. "Still good. We should hurry. The police could be here soon."

"No thanks to you," the woman, a redhead, muttered in my direction.

Oh, so snobby robber was her game. "If anyone set off the alarms, it was *you* and your freakin' demolition derby. What a stupid idea."

"Don't talk to me like that, Cass Hartley," she snapped.

"So you *do* know who I am."

Talia's string of numbers rose in pitch. She had a finely tuned memory and an eye for details, which was great for pulling jobs but it also happened to magnify whatever was going on around her, so she hated all forms of fighting. Tense voices? Bad enough. Steel-cutting and drilling? Forget it. We were lucky we'd been on the other side of the vault door when the steel fell. Otherwise, I'd be dealing with a crew member trembling in the corner while trying to pull this off. Even so, if I wasn't careful and this woman provoked me, Talia would get worse and I'd have to drag a book *and* a woman out of this place.

The book was going to be hard enough.

It was my terrible luck that our two crews were trying to rob the same bank on the same night—the Hartley luck, of course. My parents were in prison because of it, because of me. I shook my head, forcing the temptation to strangle this woman out of my mind. I had to stay on task.

I'd been so distracted by the redhead that I hadn't spared a moment to take in my surroundings, and it was a good thing I did before I tried to strangle her. She didn't just have her hacker—there was a man with her, too.

Usually, three against three wouldn't bother me. My crew could outsmart just about anyone. But the redhead's third crew member was the size of *two* men. He was a full chest and head taller than me, and his biceps were the size of both my thighs put together.

And with Talia out of commission, there was no way we could take them, even if we could outsmart them.

Which I was sure we could.

The other crew seemed distracted by Talia, who had blocked her ears and squeezed her eyes shut, shouting numbers—but my only real option was to be nice.

My least favorite option.

I walked to Talia and placed a gentle hand on her arm. I pitched my voice to yoga teacher calm for her, too, though my words weren't only for her. "Why don't we go to our respective corners and do what we came here to do, okay?"

"What's wrong with her? Is she slow?" Bree asked.

"That's not nice," the man the size of King Kong said. "It's obvious she's scared."

"She'll be fine," I said in my calmest voice. I had to get this back on track. "Okay, we'll all go on the count of three, get what we want, get out, and we never have to see each other again. Ready? One, two, three."

I let go of Talia, who had calmed somewhat, and we all started moving at once toward the same spot. Since I was a little behind, I slid past the giant dude and shouldered my way next to the redhead. It was such a close space our bodies touched, jostling against one another. She shot me a look. I'm not going to lie, it gave me a little thrill, more than a heist normally would. These days, they were almost boring, like brushing my teeth. Something I did because it was what I did, or to prove that I could. But this little twist, this attractive, infuriating woman, was making my skin tingle in ways it hadn't in a long time.

We both stopped at the same time. In front of the same locker. Locker number 231. Her eyes met mine.

"You've got to be kidding me," she said.

I chuckled, running my fingers over my lips. Yes, this could be fun—more fun than I had anticipated. Especially because the woman looked so damn pissed off. So serious. This was what was wrong with newbies. They were so precious. So serious. "I'm guessing you've never been in this situation before?"

"Have you?" the woman asked.

"What's your name?"

She rolled her eyes and turned her back to me. "Bree, bring me the lock picking kit and let's get out of here."

But Bree wasn't listening. She'd taken off her ski mask and she had her back against a row of lockers, looking up into Spider's eyes. He had his hand on a locker above her head, hemming her in, and she didn't seem to mind too much. *Turning on the charm—one of his strongest skills, second only to making damn fine forgeries.*

"Bree," the woman said sharply.

Bree giggled, ignoring her.

I had to suppress my own laugh at the ridiculousness of the situation. "Spider is charming her with Java-

Script or something like that. We're in it for the long haul, sister. Want to have a picnic?"

It looked like the redhead's eyes were about to smolder right out of her head, and there was no sign of that smirk left on her mouth. "This is not the time to joke."

"It's always a time to joke."

"The cops could be here any minute."

She was right. Even I wasn't stupid enough to push that limit much further. I listened for Talia's numbers —she always counted seconds—and it sounded like we were up to about seven minutes since we walked into the place. If the alarms had gone off, or if the guard had managed to chew through his restraints, the police wouldn't be far behind. But... it wasn't *too* dangerous to goad this woman a little longer. We could all escape through that hole her crew had cut in the wall. But I only had a few moments to play.

"Is this your first heist?" I asked, moving close enough to whisper to her.

She reeled back. "Does it look like my first heist?"

"Honestly? Kinda." I pretended to examine my nails, but watched her out of the corner of my eye as her face turned red.

She stomped over to Bree and Spider, shoving herself between them. "Why did you take your mask off?"

"I took the security system down," Bree objected.

"It doesn't matter," the woman said. "I'm not

paying you to flirt. I'm paying you to do a job. *So get me the lock picking kit.*"

"Damn woman, that side of you is hot," I said, just to keep the mood light, hoping it would calm Talia, wherever she was. Where *was* she? She and that giant dude were missing.

But I didn't have time to worry because the redhead had gotten her lock picking kit and she was in the process of laying it out on the floor. She was about to pick at *my* loot. When I came closer to her she scowled, as if anger alone could get things done, her fiery nature indicating she'd have the book in no time.

My team was losing the game.

And Cass Hartley didn't lose.

I gestured subtly to Spider, who moved silently to my side, bending so his ear was in front of my mouth.

"Talia's missing. Do you think you can distract those two? I think the redhead is all bark, and it's obvious Bree is smitten with you," I said.

He nodded once.

A total flirt with other women, but with me? A man of few words. We knew each other well enough that we didn't have to talk much and I was happy for it. He was solid, never a distraction, my right-hand man.

Talia was just as important to me and usually more useful than she was acting today. She was my computer, my memory bank. Most of the time, anyway. She'd been responsible for keeping the information we'd dug up about the guard's family—complete with names, ages and addresses—in her head so we could distract him enough to tie him up. It was my job to get her out.

"Whatever you do," I said, "don't let them get the book. I'm going to find Talia so we can make our escape quickly. When you see me, go. Run."

He didn't acknowledge this, but I could sense he agreed with the plan. Meanwhile, no one seemed to notice as I slipped down the aisle and out of the deposit room. It was a relatively small bank, so it didn't take long for me to find Talia and the giant man standing at the end of the hallway, illuminated in blue. He'd removed his mask, too, and tucked it in his belt. He had his paws on Talia's shoulders.

Something primal clicked within me and I ran to him, tugging on his massive arm. "Let go of her!"

He flicked his hand, his fingers stinging my cheek. I stifled a scream of surprise, then his hands were on *me* and I knew I was in trouble. I couldn't talk my way out of this. I struggled, but it was all in vain. Every movement was stymied by his massive bulk.

But then he said, "I'm so sorry." His voice was softer, gentler than I was expecting. "I didn't mean to hurt you. Please don't be mad at me."

My mouth tasted coppery. "Let go of me, you ogre," I said through gritted teeth.

"Fine," he said, and I was free. I took in a huge breath and leveled a searing gaze at the dude.

"What were you doing to her?" I demanded.

"I wasn't trying to hurt her," the giant said. He reached out to touch my arm, but pulled away as he noticed my fiery gaze. "You've got to believe me."

"Why did you bring her out here?" I asked. "Alone. Talia, did he try anything with you?"

"I saw she was upset, and I thought I'd bring her over here away from all the noise. It seemed to help," he said. He wasn't letting her talk, but she *did* seem calm, even calmer than when we had come into the vault, and she'd stopped counting.

But there was no way that was due to the giant standing before me.

"You're a liar," I said, grabbing Talia's hand.

"He's not a liar. His name is Tank," Talia said.

I looked at Talia. She had one of the most brilliant minds I'd ever encountered, but she didn't always have a grasp on reality. But those words were said so clearly they shocked me in place. I couldn't believe that after everything that had happened, she'd had the presence of mind to get his name and then state it, especially in seeming rebuttal to what I was saying. It was so... logical.

Not many people understood Talia, and the fact that this Tank had, and had taken her to a quiet place, well, if I weren't in the middle of robbing a bank, I would have sat right down and thought about that miracle for a moment.

Instead, I had to hurry things along. "Come on,

Talia. Let's get the hell out of here," I said. I turned to Tank and said a gruff, "Thanks."

"You're welcome," he answered.

I took Talia's hand to take her back into the vault, but before we went back inside, I turned around and asked, "Hey, Tank, what's your supreme leader's name?"

"Madison," he said, then put his hand to his mouth. No doubt, he wasn't supposed to tell me that key piece of information, but I knew I could catch him off guard.

"Thanks," I said. *Madison*. That was all I needed.

"Hey, Madison," I shouted.

She spun around, lock picking tools in hand, just as the locker popped open. I didn't have to gesture to Spider that it was time for him to do his thing. He knew it, and he was already hovering over her, ready to snag the book. Keeping a tight hold on Talia, I marched toward Madison.

"How do you know my name?" She asked. "Where's Tank?"

Such a rookie mistake. You always had to know the room and its players. She had been so focused on the locker that she hadn't noticed a crew member disappearing. And now it was three against two—the odds were in our favor.

"He heard cops outside. He was going to check it out."

"What?" Madison said, getting up from the floor. "Shit. He's going to get himself arrested doing a thing like that." She groaned and stormed out without looking behind her at Spider and Bree. And with that, she broke another rule: Always keep your eyes on the loot, no matter what an incredibly attractive girl—*moi*—says to distract you.

I pulled Talia over to Spider. "It's time."

It happened fast after that. Bree was gathering the lock picking tools and Spider reached over her to try to grab the book. I was expecting it and watching and I *still* didn't see the movements. But somehow, Bree did. She snapped out of her admiration for him as if it had never been real, elbowing him and knocking his hand away from the locker. I let go of Talia and was reaching to pull them apart when a stray elbow knocked the locker door shut again.

Then the sound of boots echoed down the hall. Madison and Tank ran into the deposit room, and someone shouted, "Stop! Police!"

We didn't stop. We knew better than that.

We were still a block of lockers away from the hole when a bright light flashed and a loud bang went off. I stopped short and staggered back toward Talia, who had frozen in place, wide-eyed and shaking again.

"Come on, Talia. Please. Not now."

Talia didn't budge. Smoke filled the room.

"Please move. We need to get out of here."

Madison and Tank ran toward us from the other side of the vault. They were all moving toward the hole with only seconds to spare, but Talia had us both frozen to the spot. Spider had thrown the flash bang to buy us a little time, but only seconds. No matter how I tugged or pulled, she wouldn't come.

"It's just smoke and noise, Talia. Spider did it to help us get out of here, but you have to move," I begged her. Through the increasingly dense air, I could just make out two shadowy figures coming toward us. The smoke stung my eyes and clogged my throat. I coughed, unable to hold back, and then Talia was ripped from my hand like a BAND-AID and I felt myself pulled onward.

"Talia!" I tried to shout into the smoke, but it was no use.

I let myself be dragged out, too, ready to face whatever consequences awaited me in order to get Talia out of this situation. Part of me hoped Spider had miraculously circled back to the locker and swiped the book, but that was a high-flying wish for a cursed Hartley.

But this wasn't my fault. If this heist had gone as planned, we would all be skipping down the street at this moment. Instead, we were being dragged out by the cops.

And it was all because of Madison.

4
_____

MADISON

The room was filled with smoke. As I ran for the exit, all I could see were bands of light from the police flashlights, and a couple of stoic figures standing in the aisle.

What the hell were Cass and her crew doing?

No matter how flippant her attitude was toward the job, *clearly* the time for lollygagging was over. *Whatever—she can do what she wants with her crew,* I told myself. I squinted, trying to keep the smoke out of my eyes and lungs, and looked around for my own people.

I thought I saw the silhouette of Bree's small frame, heading for the hole in the wall. Good. And Tank had been at my side since we'd met the police in the hallway. And then he wasn't.

"Hey!" I hissed as he ran away from me, trying not

to draw attention to our location. Lord knew how many guns were pointed at me in that moment. "Where are you going?"

"They need help," Tank whispered over his shoulder and I knew right then where he was going—to that bundle of nerves that Cass called a crew member. *Liability*—that's what I'd call her.

"Bleeding heart," I muttered.

Tank could handle himself so I wasn't worried for his safety, although his judgment seemed a bit questionable at the moment. But then, he'd always been like that, as long as I could remember—he looked out for the underdog, and that was what made him good to have around.

Me, on the other hand... I was getting the hell out of there. Helping someone who'd just spent the last ten minutes ruining my final job and repeatedly insulting my professionalism was *not* on my priority list.

Your crew's the one that requires babysitting, I thought. *Honestly, the nerve of that girl.* Her merry band of idiots were the ones who must have tripped the silent alarm. There was no question in my mind about that.

"Freeze!" a cop shouted into the smoke. "Everybody put your hands up!"

I couldn't see much as I turned the corner and headed toward our improvised exit door, but it seemed like the police were being cautious, inching their way into the vault and fearful of having such low visibility. For all they knew, we were armed to the teeth, working together, and ready to fight back.

So I guess Cass's crew isn't completely *useless. My thanks to whoever threw that flash bang.*

I came to the end of the row and where I expected to find the hole, but instead my hand touched cold metal—more lockers. *Shit.*

My heart started beating a little faster. I must have gotten turned around in the smoke. I was in the wrong corner of the room. *It's okay, you'll get out of this. You always do.* I turned around and headed back up the aisle, walking fast and staying on my tiptoes to keep the police from zeroing in on my location. I didn't have a lot of time, but there was enough.

At the other end of the aisle, there was a female figure. Cass. She looked lost, disoriented in the dark, and none of her crew members were around. *That's what you get for working with such amateurs,* I thought.

I should have just left her there. I was going to—it would serve her right to spend the night in a police interrogation room when she'd cost me so much. But she was a Hartley. I couldn't just leave her there. I edged my way toward her, and just as my fingertips grazed the sleeve of her shirt, Cass let out a shout, strangled by the smoke. "Talia!"

That's just great—scream so the cops can take better aim. Sure enough, I heard the distinctive click of a gun cocking near the other end of the aisle and the thin red beam of a laser sight filtered through the smoke.

"Son of a bitch," I muttered as I threw my arm around Cass's waist and dragged her as fast as I could toward the exit.

Goodbye, first-edition, signed Jules Verne book. Goodbye, my ticket to retirement.

Cass was deadweight in my arms, not helping at all as I dragged her over the ragged metal threshold into the pet shop. I felt like dropping her if this was all the gratitude she was going to give me for saving her ass from a felony conviction, but even if Cass didn't have a problem calling me an amateur ten times in ten minutes, I still had a sense of professional courtesy.

Not for her, but for her parents. I wasn't about to let Bill and Brenda Hartley's daughter go down right in front of me.

The smoke was beginning to fill the pet shop, too, but it wasn't quite as thick there and as soon as we were out of the bank, Cass jerked away from me. "Madison?"

"Who'd you think I was, Santa Claus?"

"I thought you were the cops," she said, brushing loose bits of concrete off her pants.

"You're welcome," I said through clenched teeth.

Lord, she knew just how to push my buttons. Those almond eyes were on fire as she looked back at me, telling me wordlessly that I shouldn't hold my breath for a *thank you* note. If I wasn't in such a rush to get out of there, I might have noticed how familiar the sensation was. My little brother used to give me that look all the time—irritation that I'd felt the need to impose myself, rather than gratitude for helping him.

"Come on, we have to go," I said.

The rest of my crew had already made themselves scarce and we were alone in the pet shop. Cass let me lead her out to the street through the rear exit, where the nightlife from a couple of bars nearby was in full swing.

There was live music floating down the street and people congregating near the doors to smoke and shoot the breeze. All of this was by design. If the heist had gone according to plan, my crew and I would have had time to change into street clothes inside the pet shop and then stroll casually outside to a waiting getaway car, the sounds from the bars disguising our activity.

The car was here—an unassuming late-model Chevy parked across the street—but Tank was nowhere to be seen and he had the keys in his pocket.

I should have insisted on carrying a spare set. Never mind the fact that I'd never learned how to drive —life had gotten in the way of that teenage milestone, along with many others. I would have learned pretty quickly if I had to.

And the book had never made it out of its locker. All of this—for nothing.

"Fuck!" I said, kicking an empty cage on my way out of the pet shop.

"Calm down," Cass said. Her tone was casual, as if I were overreacting to her eating the last slice of pizza and not the fact that every single thing about this heist had gone horribly, horribly wrong the moment we met inside the vault. And now I didn't have a getaway plan.

"The cops are going to catch up to us any second," I said. "We have to run."

"Run?" Cass asked incredulously. "Where?"

She motioned up and down the street and she was right—without a car to speed us away, we'd be the most conspicuous bank robbers on the planet, running down the street at one in the morning in all-black clothing. At least Cass had ripped the ski mask off my face—in all the chaos, I might not have remembered to take it off before we hit the street.

"What, then?" I asked. Why was Cass still sticking around, anyway? And where the hell was Tank? His one and only job was pretty simple—*get me out of sticky situations!*

I heard the heavy footfall of boots on concrete behind us, and as I was turning my head to look back into the pet shop, I felt Cass's hand slide into mine.

"Wha—"

Before I had a chance to question her, she was dragging me across the street. *Toward the crowded bar, seriously?* There was no way she looked old enough to

CARA MALONE & ANNA COVE

drink—even if she was, we'd get stopped at the door and that'd give the cops just enough time to...

Cass threw me up against the wall in the shadowed doorway of the bar and I sucked in a surprised breath, then her body was pressed against mine and her lips were on me. My eyes went wide as Cass's mouth opened, her tongue gliding over my bottom lip.

My heart stopped.

My body awakened.

My hips rose automatically to meet hers and I inhaled the subtle earthiness of her skin.

As she kissed me, a few bar patrons walked past us, sneaking amused looks at our public display of affection, and a half dozen cops poured onto the sidewalk across the street. A commotion rose from the bar as people took notice, then Cass pulled away from me, her hand still in mine.

She led me inside the bar. We threaded our way through the crowd, moving against the current as people inside the bar got wind of the excitement going on outside it. In the chaos, Cass led me behind the bar and into a small, empty kitchen, then out the back door to a dirty alleyway. I followed like a puppy, my head still swimming from that kiss.

Then as the night breeze hit my face, Cass released my hand and said, a sly grin touching her lips, "Later, newbie."

I opened my mouth to object—although there

really were no words that would suffice—but Cass was already jogging up the alley.

Later, newbie?! And what was that kiss all about? I collapsed with my back against the wall and pulled out the burner phone in my pocket.

"Tank, you better be less than five minutes away and ready with another getaway car."

_____

5

CASS

That *was a close one.*

When my parents were in the game, they always went in with an ironclad plan. That's what they taught me to do, but... No amount of planning, not even their connections on the inside, got them out of their arrest, trial, and ultimate jailing.

Criminals were always destined to fail when they became too predictable. And I had made them predictable when I'd trusted an outsider to become part of our lives.

When I started running my own jobs, I did it with that in mind. I moved on instinct rather than with a plan. At first, Talia, who had been my room-mate our freshman year of college, was the only person I trusted to go in with me. Spider came along two years later, once Talia and I had dropped out to dedicate our time to increasingly complex jobs. He was actually trying to break into my hotel room when we met. It took about a year for me to trust him, but he figured out pretty quickly that he was better off with me. And ultimately I decided I was better off with him.

We'd been on dozens of heists since and had experienced close calls in the past. But we'd never—*never* —come so close to arrest as we did in the vault.

I would have died before I let Madison see, but I was shaking like a leaf after we left the bank. My heart was beating so hard I could have sworn I was leading the police right to us on a path of beats. I kissed Madison, partly to calm myself down... and it worked. The look on her face afterward, the confusion, made everything right in the world. I was in control again for a brief moment, unpredictable, and I left before I could lose hold again. The feeling of control didn't last long.

Talia was nowhere to be seen. I called her and she reassured me she was fine and with Tank, and she would see me soon.

That was a relief, but still, something felt off. I spent most of the night walking the streets, spiraling out from downtown New Vernon and the heist, images of Madison, Talia, and Spider flashing before my eyes. I needed to get away from the tangled mess.

I kept coming back to the same thought. If I had to do it all again, I would. Maybe if I'd been a little more ruthless with Madison, I could have gotten that stupid book... but it would have set Talia off even worse, and seeing her wrenched away from me in the smoke was terrifying.

I wasn't going to be responsible for putting another person in jail. So what if we didn't get the book? So what if it would be months before we had another opportunity like that? So what if I had to dip into my savings for a while? At least we were all free.

I returned to the hotel room I called home only once a ring of light emerged along the skyline, when the normal people started stumbling out of their homes for the newspaper or a walk with the dog. Too many eyes then. And I needed some rest.

———

Sleep didn't come easily. I snatched a few minutes here and there before eventually getting up. When I was like this, I had to *do* something. And that something was going to see Henry. He'd been the one to tell me about the Verne book in the first place. Henry could help me untangle the mess currently swirling in my mind. Henry could make me some of the most delicious hot chocolate in the universe.

Henry's restaurant, The Wooden Spoon, was one of those bright, airy places in the hipster part of town I would never have frequented if not for him. White tile covered the walls and floors, and the tables and chairs looked like Henry had hewn them out of oak himself. A giant ink-drawing of a cow head lorded over the room. I squinted as I entered the place. How was it brighter inside than outside at eleven in the morning?

A few solo foodies were scattered at the tables, eyes and thumbs trained on their phones as they munched on organic pastured bacon omelets. Henry was in the back corner at the register, dressed in a crimson vest and button-down, not a silver hair out of place. He was writing something and he smiled when he saw me, but he knew better than to draw attention.

He had been in the business for many years, after all. Even though he was out now, old habits never died.

He set his pen down and opened the swinging ranch-style door, coming around the counter. "What's up, kiddo? How did it go?"

I pursed my lips, unsure where to start. My brain was still that tangled mess of thoughts.

"That well, eh?"

"Worse."

Henry placed an arm around my shoulders, giving me a half-hug. "Why don't you sit down and I'll make you a cup of my famous hot chocolate?"

As I sat at an empty table, careful to avoid splinters, my mind wandered to what my parents would have said in this situation. First, I wouldn't have told them. But let's just say I had. They would analyze everything that had gone wrong, pointing out every place where I had made a mistake. *You shouldn't have brought Talia. She's not cut out for this work. And you let that redhead distract you. Don't you ever learn from your mistakes?*

My mother, especially, wouldn't have let up on the *shoulds* until I was in tears. It was one of the reasons I hadn't visited them in jail yet. I hadn't cried since I was twelve.

Even before they went to jail, Henry had always been the one who gave me hugs and kind advice. He was always around when I was a kid and I considered him more of a father than my own father. He at least *acted* like he cared more about me rather than the million-dollar necklace or the rare opal ring or the *whatever* they were about to steal.

Henry came over with two steaming mugs, setting one in front of me, and took the seat kitty-corner to mine. "Tell me what happened, kiddo."

I kept my voice low even though we were far from the other restaurant patrons. "There was another crew there for the book." A crew with an uptight, but intriguingly attractive woman at the helm, I did not add. Another woman. Another distraction. Story of my life.

"No way."

"Yeah."

He leaned forward. "I had it on good authority no one else knew about that bank locker."

"Well, your authority wasn't so great after all," I said more sourly than I meant.

Henry didn't seem to mind. "So, what did you do?"

I took a sip of the chocolate. Maybe it was because I'd barely gotten any sleep, or because Madison had thrown me off my game, or because I had failed, but a river of words poured out of my mouth. "Well, I didn't know they were going after the book at first, so I kept at it. But they'd cut through the steel lining of the vault and Talia had one of her episodes and... I know I should have abandoned the plan, but I just couldn't."

Henry reached out a hand. "It's hard to make decisions in a high-pressure environment. You're doing fine as a crew leader."

Henry's kind response made me bristle. This was weakness. I *deserved* whatever rebuke was coming for me. I'd almost gotten Talia arrested, and if anyone else had done that, I would have given them a severe talking to... at best. Not to mention I'd been distracted by Madison. *Did I ever learn?*

I pulled my hand away from Henry's warm one and folded my arms across my chest. "Well, I'm pretty sure the other crew cutting through the steel set off the silent alarms, and the cops came. We didn't get the book."

Henry nodded, his silver brows furrowing a bit. "That was the easiest spot to pick it up."

"I just *left* millions of dollars in that deposit locker. Maybe my parents were right about me."

Henry sat back, folding his own arms. "Your parents aren't perfect either. I remember your father tripping an alarm once when those silent alarms first came into use. We had to hide in an air duct for twelve hours after that. Do you know how small those things are?"

This wasn't helping. What would it take to make Henry tell me I had messed up? "We almost got arrested," I whispered.

Henry just shrugged. "Risk of the trade."

My God, this man... why wasn't he angry like I was? He shifted his chair closer so he could whisper, his spicy cologne invading my space.

"Who was the other crew's leader?"

"Madison," I said shaking my head, still thinking about what I could say that would trigger him to give me the tongue lashing I deserved. "I didn't get her last name."

"Never heard of her."

"Me either." I hovered my face over the hot chocolate steam. Now that I thought about it, that was weird. Why hadn't I heard of her before? "I know I've been out of town for a while, but I thought I had a good handle on the scene."

"There are always newcomers who think they can make a quick buck."

"Right." But she didn't *seem* new. I had called her a newbie, but that was just to piss her off. She had her stuff down. Well, some of it, anyway. She certainly didn't have the frazzled nerves of a newbie.

"It's like I always say. You can't control other people, you can only control your—"

"No, but I can show them who's boss," I said,

sitting up straight and mowing right over Henry's words. "And in case that's not clear, it's me. This job is *mine*."

"Cass," Henry said, the tone of his voice the same as one he might use with a child.

"What? She wants that dusty book bad, and if I get it first, she'll never challenge me again. What else do you know about the sale?"

"Forget the book, Cass. It's too high-profile now. There are other—"

"Nope. I *need* the book. She needs to know I'm top dog here." I stood, the energy suddenly coursing through my legs. This was how I would redeem myself. I would show Madison who ruled, and then the bank job wouldn't be a failure. I was feeling more like my confident self by the moment. "What else do you know?"

"Just that it's going to a rare books collector who lives in Mandy Lake."

"What's his name? What street?"

"I don't know. My contact only knew about the stop at the bank because he was related to the seller. It was an anonymous deal, hence the stop at the bank. All I know beyond that is Mandy Lake."

"Thank you," I said, smiling. "I can always count on you, Henry."

The bell above the front door jingled and two men in trench coats entered the restaurant. Compared to the rest of the clientele, they stuck out like three-hundred carat diamonds in a pile of coal. No amount of jamming their hands in their pockets and looking around casually would hide them. As if I needed any other indication that they were up to no good, Henry stiffened.

I placed my hand on his bicep and laughed like I was enjoying one of his jokes. *Relax, Henry. You'll give us away.* My first thought was the police that had stormed the bank vault early this morning, but these two were in plainclothes—the cops might be looking all over the city for me right now, but they'd be doing it in uniform. Still smiling, I asked under my breath. "You expecting company?"

"You better get going."

"No way. I'm not leaving you."

"Go."

"Henry," I said, pulling on his shirt as he stood. "What's going on?"

"It's none of your concern."

None of my concern, my ass. That was ridiculous. Henry was the only family I had left. "I'm not leaving until you tell me."

The men were closing in on our table and Henry's face fell as he spoke to me out of the corner of his mouth. "They're trying to take the restaurant," he said, never moving his lips.

My jaw almost dropped open, but I caught it before I could make a scene. "How? Why?"

"I don't have time to tell you now. Please go. It will

be better for both of us." He seemed to quickly recover himself as he leaned over and gave me a quick peck on the cheek.

"Does it have to do with my parents?" I whispered as I stood to go.

Henry didn't answer, just pursed his lips and directed his attention to the men. I swallowed down the nausea stirring in my gut and managed a smile as I passed them on my way out of the restaurant.

Outside, the drizzle stung my cheeks. I ignored it. Those guys looked familiar. I dug at a memory from a long time ago. Why did they look familiar? Then it clicked. They were involved in my parents' last heist— the one that got them arrested.

6

MADISON

True to his word, Tank arrived less than five minutes after I made my extraction call.

The first droplets of an early morning rain were just beginning to fall as he pulled up at the end of the alleyway in a little silver coupe that I'd never seen before. He always was resourceful—one of his best qualities—so I wasn't surprised by that.

What did shock me was the passenger in the seat beside him.

"What's *she* doing here?"

That bundle of nerves who had distracted Tank from his one and only job—having *my* back—and who'd nearly cost all of us our freedom was in the car, her knees tucked up to her chest. She winced when I raised my voice and Tank said, "This is Talia's car. She offered to help."

I couldn't believe the protective tone I was hearing in his voice—for another thief's crew member, no less.

The rain was coming down harder now, sticking my hair to my face and making me shiver. It was obvious that this was a situation where honey would get me farther than vinegar, and there were still cops swarming all over the neighborhood.

I rolled my eyes and said, "Fine, let's go. But I'm not sitting in the back."

I crossed my arms over my chest and waited for Talia to climb over the center console and into the back seat of the coupe, then I got in. Tank was packed into the driver's seat of the tiny car like a sardine in a can. He shifted into drive and I turned the rearview mirror toward myself, eyeing Talia.

She was thin, with olive skin and dark brown hair, and she and Tank must have gotten caught in the rain, too, because she looked like a half-drowned rat. She locked eyes with mine when she caught me looking, though, and refused to look away.

I flipped the mirror back to Tank and said, "I can't believe you ditched me right in the middle of a job. *This job* no less. What the hell happened?"

"I didn't ditch you," Tank said. "I was keeping an eye on you, and you got out safe like you always do, right?"

"Barely," I said. "But we didn't get the book, so all of it was for nothing. Cass Hartley and her band of misfits probably sent a silent alarm to the police station the moment they smashed through the front door."

"We had a keycard," Talia said from the back seat.

I scowled at her. "And?"

"Cass swiped a keycard off the bank manager earlier today," she explained. "If anything, your crew probably tripped an underground sensor when you cut through the vault wall."

"Nice try," I said. "They turned off all the underground sensors because of the construction."

"Okay," Tank cut in. "We'll probably never know, so let's agree to disagree."

Agree to disagree? Jesus. In fifteen years of pulling jobs, I'd never seen Tank lose his composure. That was why I called him Tank. He was immovable. And here he was playing mediator.

I looked out the window for a while, trying not to shiver as the rain dried on my skin. When he pulled up in front of my building, the rain was still coming down hard.

I turned around in my seat, narrowing my eyes at Talia. "I don't know what you and Cass did to get him to give you my name, but it's out there now and there's nothing I can do about it. What I *can* do is make your life a living hell if I find out the name *Madison* has passed your lips after tonight. See that building?"

I pointed outside and Talia leaned toward the window to look up at the towering high rise. It was one of the oldest buildings in town, ornately decorated with marble inside and out.

Talia nodded and I said, "I own the entire top floor. Believe me when I say I have the resources to find out if you, Cass Hartley, or that Casanova-wannabe on your crew are talking to anyone about what happened tonight."

"Got it," Talia said, a surprising irritation edging into her voice. I got out of the car and she climbed over the console again to sit in the front passenger seat, then she added, "You're welcome for the ride."

Sassy. I didn't know she had it in her.

"You going to be alright, boss?" Tank asked.

"Don't worry about me," I said. I glanced one more time at Talia and then told him, "Watch your back."

———

I couldn't sleep. I couldn't even think about sleeping.

It was four a.m., the rain was beating against the windows of the penthouse, and I couldn't shut off my mind. I was supposed to be *celebrating* by now, but instead I was pacing up and down the length of my living room, trying to figure out the moment when it had all gone horribly wrong.

Was it when I recognized Cass in the bank? Or when we both reached for locker number 231? No doubt, I messed up when I saved that foolish girl, and I couldn't even begin to dissect that kiss.

Just who the hell did Cass Hartley think she was, pushing me up against a wall like she knew she could have me?

I felt a sting in my palms and realized that I'd balled my hands into tight fists, leaving four half-moon impressions in each palm. One thing was for sure—the girl knew how to push my buttons, and she seemed to enjoy it.

"Never again," I muttered, going to a large, glass-top desk in one corner of the open floor plan. It was pushed up against a large bank of windows and the rain pattered on them as I sat down and opened the fat Manila envelope that was my intelligence file for the job. I'd spent weeks compiling it, including every detail I could gather, from the black market sale of the stolen book to its temporary stop at the bank before going on to its new owner.

That copy of *Twenty Thousand Leagues Under the Sea* hadn't been seen for twenty years. It was stolen from a museum in New York City in the nineties and even though the museum curators were offering a reward—to the tune of $9 million—the book seemed to have vanished.

I only knew about it because my little brother, Donnie, was obsessed with it back when it was stolen. The theft had been on the news for weeks and it was a big mystery—it had none of the trappings of a typical heist and a lot of people speculated that it had been an amateur job. Security wasn't much back then and all signs pointed to a patron or a docent simply walking off with the book.

Of course, that wasn't what got my brother's gears turning. As a six-year-old boy, he was enthralled with the legend of the treasure map that Jules Verne had supposedly drawn on top of the atlas printed on the first page of the book. Donnie, along with quite a few other interested parties, was absolutely convinced that whoever had stolen the book was going after Captain Nemo's treasure.

Complete bullshit, of course, but the legend meant that particular copy was a highly valuable collector's piece.

When it resurfaced on the black market a month ago, I was watching. As soon as I heard about the sale, I wanted that book—not for me, but for Donnie. I wanted to give him a shot at the treasure, and I was going to get him a copy of that map.

The book's buyer and seller were anonymous, of course, but Bree had been able to work her technological magic and find out which bank they were using to hold the book while the funds transferred. That had been my best chance at getting the book and it was just my luck that Cass Hartley had the same idea.

"What does she even know about it?" I grumbled as I spread my papers across the desk. "Must have only been a fetus when it went missing."

Everything there was to know about that book—and its recent activity—was right there in my files. It should have been a simple in-and-out job, and that book, plus a copy of the map, should have been sitting in my safe by now, waiting to be valiantly returned to the museum in a gesture of goodwill that I could show to my brother to prove I wasn't such a bad big sister after all.

At this point, the possibility of it rotting away in a police evidence locker was not out of the question and for all I knew, the book was out of my reach forever. *And along with it, any hope of reconciling with Donnie.* Nothing in my notes could change that.

"Damn your cavalier tactics, Cass," I growled, then I got up and went into the kitchen. Since everything was ruined, I might as well treat myself to a glass—or a bottle—of wine.

I grabbed one of my favorites—an expensive Bordeaux that I had been saving for after my final *successful* heist. It didn't matter now, though, so I got a glass from the cabinet and sat down at the large marble island to open the bottle. I let my mind go to an ugly place as I drank, and instead of enjoying the smooth licorice tones of the wine, or even wallowing in the failure of the job, I was thinking about that damn kiss.

The fact that I couldn't forget about it stung even more than leaving the book in that vault. That kiss had felt so real at the time, so urgent and passionate. It wasn't just a clever distraction tactic to evade the police —it had stirred something deep in my core.

And then Cass had smiled and disappeared up the alley like it meant nothing to her. That was because it *didn't* mean anything—and that was what nagged at me the most. Was she a better con artist than me?

I drained my first glass and got out my phone. I dialed Bree, who sounded sleepy when she answered.

"Madison? What time is it?"

"I don't know," I said. It must have been around five a.m. by then, but that was of no consequence to me. "Are you near your computer?"

"Always," Bree said. "What's going on? Are you in trouble?"

"No, but I need you to do some digging for me," I told her. When she objected, sounding like she was still clawing her way back up from sleep, I snapped, "Look, I didn't say anything when you turned into a giggly school girl in front of that flirtatious creep, but you work for me and I need your help."

"I'm sorry," Bree said. That got her to wake up. "What do you need?"

"I need to know what went wrong tonight," I told her. "Get me some information on that Hartley girl. I need to know how she knew where to find the book... and where I can find her."

Once upon a time, I let my vagina take over my brain.

It was all over a woman. A beautiful, saucy, and mature redheaded woman who was twenty-five. I was seventeen and lusting after her like a cat in heat, and I wanted to spend every waking hour with her.

Unfortunately, some of those waking hours were dedicated to running jobs with my parents. Long story short, I was careless, the redhead was playing me, and my mistake in judgment got my parents arrested.

Five years later, I was still paying for it. Those trench coated men in Henry's restaurant had looked familiar and as I walked the late night streets of New Vernon, I became more convinced than ever they were connected to my parents' last job. I'd spent the whole day feeling aimless, wandering the city and looking for answers where none could be found—about the failed heist, and about those men.

Henry said they wanted to take the restaurant. If he was in trouble because of my parents—a debt of some sort—then this was my fault, too. It killed me to think of Henry losing something as important to him as the restaurant, and because of me. It was bad enough I had put my parents in jail.

The rain stopped. The sidewalks glistened with moisture under the streetlights, pools of light in the darkness of the cloudy night. I hopped from light to light, barely seeing where I was going as I thought through how I could help Henry.

He would reject pity money.

Then it came to me. The more I thought about it, the more I couldn't believe I hadn't thought of this solution right away. Henry had given me the information about the book. I would pay him for it. It was a simple transaction. Not charity. Not a gift. I would present it that way to him and he would have to take it.

Now, I had two reasons to go after the book. First, to show Madison *I* was boss, and second so Henry could accept my help and keep his dignity. And, to top it off, this all had to happen fast... because those guys in the trench coats didn't exactly look patient.

I sensed her before I saw her. She was just a shadow lurking in the alley next to the hotel. It wasn't uncommon for people to pass through that area, though they usually didn't linger. The door security of the hotel generally kept them moving. But this shadow was still, leaning against the wall, small. She turned her head and the light caught one side of her face, and I knew it was her. Madison.

I marched right up to her and grabbed her hand, dragging her deep into the alley, away from prying eyes.

"What are you doing here?"

Her lips parted, and though in the dark I couldn't make out the color of her eyes, my mind filled with them. A flash of gray with flecks of silver when I'd leaned in to kiss her in the doorway of that bar. I let go of her hand and stepped back from her so I wouldn't be tempted to kiss her again. Could never be too careful, after all.

"If you're here to tail me to the book, you're doing a horrible job of it," I said.

"Do you know where it's going next?" Madison asked.

There was something odd about her speech, but I couldn't put my finger on it. We had only spoken a few words overall, and it had been a heightened situation, so maybe this was just a way of speaking for Madison that I hadn't witnessed.

I folded my arms. She wasn't going to get information that easily. And if she was trying to flirt by leaning closer to me, it wasn't working. "No," I lied. "Do you?"

"No. It's in a police evidence locker for all we know."

Probably not. I was cursing Spider and his stupid elbow when he accidentally slammed the locker shut, but it might be for the best now. How could the police know which of the hundreds of lockers our crews had been after?

"Then why are you here?"

"To... to... admire the architecture." She looked up and the light caught her face once again. She must have been out wandering for a while because the wispy hairs framing her face had curled in the humid air. The hood of her raincoat framed her face. I had the absurd urge to smooth that hair back. It was almost as absurd as Madison's excuse.

I looked away from her. "You're spying on me, aren't you?"

"No."

"Then what are you doing here?"

"I told you. I'm just... out for a walk."

My lips parted and a little gasp escaped. She had pronounced "walk" as *wah-lock*. How hadn't I picked up on this before? I could see it clearly now. The leaning, the slight slur of her words. "You're drunk."

"I am not."

"Come here." I once again took her hand and

dragged her, not too gently, out of the alley and into the light of the street. "Follow my finger."

"This is ridiculous," Madison said, looking away and looking sort of adorable in her raincoat. "I will not."

"I'm not letting you leave without doing this. Follow my finger."

Madison crossed her arms and harrumphed. Her gaze remained fixed on mine as I ran my finger in front of her face. God, she was sexy when she was pissed off. I tilted my head. "Do it."

"Fine, I don't know what you think you'll find, though."

She let her arms down by her side and focused on my finger as I drew it back and forth in front of her eyes, a few inches from her face. Her eyes stuttered a bit as they went. Yup. There it was. To piss her off even more, I bopped her nose while delivering my verdict. "You're drunk."

"How do you know?"

"Field sobriety test. I know. Plus, you just admitted it."

Madison scowled. "I've been drunk for two days thanks to you, trying to forget about what happened. What are you, a cop or something?"

A deep laugh bubbled from my stomach and out of my mouth. "That's funny, sweetheart. Why don't you come in and I'll make you a cup of instant coffee to sober you up before I send you home again?"

And maybe I can pull some information from that drunk, sweet mouth of yours.

Madison started shaking her head lightly, then shook it more vigorously. "No. I came here for a reason. What do you know about the book?"

"So you *didn't* come to admire the architecture or for a random walk, hm? There isn't much to admire."

Madison's cheeks puffed out with a little burp. She covered her mouth, but didn't acknowledge it otherwise. I'd only just met her but it wasn't hard to see it was very important for her to be perfect little Madison, always in control. Except perfect little Madison wasn't so in control right now. She was *drunk* and a little sloppy.

"Just admit it," I taunted. "You're here because you like me. You want another kiss?"

"No," she said, loud enough to draw the attention of the doorman. I waved a few fingers at him.

Given Madison's state, it wasn't safe to talk out here. What if someone overheard? What if Madison accidentally blurted out the name of the book, or mentioned the bank? I took her arm, gently this time, and tucked it into the crook of my elbow. "Why don't we go inside and warm up a bit, hm?"

Madison didn't answer this time, and let me take her inside. The doorman winked at me as we passed. I winked back. *Just another woman I'm bringing up to my room. That's right. Nothing to see here.* Madison leaned on me as we walked to the elevator and went up

CARA MALONE & ANNA COVE

to my room. Thankfully, she said nothing during our trek.

"You really did a job on yourself," I said under my breath as I eased her into the spartan desk chair near the door. It was the only seat in my small room other than the bed and I was *not* putting her on the bed. Once upon a time I'd thought about upgrading to a bigger suite, but I'd spent so much money on my parents' appeals, and I didn't need a whole lot, anyway.

"You really did a job on me," Madison slurred.

I froze, not expecting her to answer. "What do you mean?"

"Why did you think you could kiss me like that?"

The police were after us. It was a cover. That was the truth, but there was something about the way Madison leaned on the back of the chair, chin resting on her arm. Something about the way she peered up at me through her eyelashes. Something about the parting of her lips that encouraged me to work this angle.

As I thought over the perfect turn of phrase, I went to the kitchenette in the corner and poured coffee grounds into a cup, then started heating the water. Then I came over and leaned on the desk next to her chair. "I've never met another female crew leader who was so young and capable. Can you blame me for being a little turned on by you? I'm sorry if you're not into women—I took a gamble and I thought I'd guessed right."

"I am," she said, and I was sure the words were

coming out easier than if she'd been sober. "It's not that."

Redness flushed her cheeks again. In this light, I could see a slight orange tinge to her complexion under a cloud of faint freckles. So she was a natural redhead. Hot. And a lesbian after all. Even hotter. I pushed off the desk and went to the kitchenette again, pouring hot water into the mug of instant coffee grounds, suddenly wanting Madison to be sober. When I handed it to her, she sucked it down surprisingly quickly, wiping her mouth delicately with the edge of her sleeve when she was done.

I smiled in spite of myself. *Stay on task, Cass. The book. Not the woman—the book.*

Before I could ask another question, she asked one of her own. "How did you know the book would be at that bank, on that night?"

I shrugged. "Connections."

"Figures. It's because you're a Hartley."

"Excuse me?"

"You're Bill and Brenda's kid."

Madison seemed less drunk now. Either that coffee worked fast, or maybe she'd been playing me the whole time? Trying to seduce me? Get me vulnerable so she could work me for information? Well, it wasn't working. Nope. "Bill and Brenda have nothing to do with this."

That wasn't strictly true. The information *had* come through Henry, who I knew because of my parents. But if Madison was trying to make me feel bad about that, it wasn't going to work. Not only did I already feel bad enough on my own, but I wasn't going to let a woman make me vulnerable again.

"Come on, they're two of the best grifters in the country," she said. "They must have taught you something, though the professionalism obviously didn't transfer."

Madison didn't know the first thing about growing up with Brenda and Bill. They hadn't taught me anything about real life, or relationships. My idea of professionalism might not be the same stuffy version Madison subscribed to, but my parents *did* teach me how to run my own jobs. How to avoid fingerprints and cameras and sensors and...

There it was again.

I was letting Madison get under my skin. But this explained how she'd found me. It was hard to be anonymous when your parents were as well-known as mine. She must have had her tech whiz, Bree, get to me through what was known about my parents. The *how* didn't matter, though. I had to find out what Madison knew about the book's movement... if she knew anything. How close was she on my tail?

Or maybe she was just a crazy stalker, thirsty for me after that kiss in the bar doorway. It was a fifty-fifty chance and I felt like gambling.

"Do you want to know where to find the book

next?" I asked. "I bet even if I told you where to find it, I could still get it out from under your nose."

There was fire in her eyes again, like she was about to lunge across the desk, but I couldn't quite tell if she wanted to fight me or... kiss me. I liked it, and my arrogant declaration had exactly the effect I wanted—she was getting riled up. It really bothered her when I questioned her abilities.

"We both failed in the bank," she pointed out bitterly.

"You're right," I allowed. The way she was looking at me stirred something deep in my core and the full effect of my exhaustion suddenly settled on my shoulders. I hadn't slept since before my interview with Mildred and I needed to get Madison out of my room soon, before I did something stupid.

It was time to jump the shark.

"I know where the book is going," I said.

"Me, too," she said. *Liar.* I could see it in her storm cloud eyes.

"Where?" I challenged.

"I'm not telling you."

I came a little too close to her—for effect, of course —and gazed straight into her eyes. *Time to do a little fishing.* "I'll tell you what I know. I know the buyer's name."

I studied her expression. She didn't flinch.

"*And* the address," I added.

Nothing. If she'd known any of it, her face would

have betrayed her knowledge. I was excellent at reading microexpressions, but I didn't see any flash of recognition in Cass's eyes.

Before I had a chance to try again with the city—the only piece of information I actually had—Madison stood abruptly. She looked around as if she was just now taking in her surroundings and said, "I need to get out of here. I never should have come."

"It's okay. Stay until you're ready," I said. This was the last thing I wanted, but I hated the idea of her wandering drunk down the street. "I promise I won't ask you any more questions."

Or try to seduce you...

"I don't trust you," she said, narrowing her eyes at me.

Smart girl. Madison walked to the door and opened it before I could find what to say next. What was it about her that made me hesitate? I should have just let her go. Instead, I followed her into the hallway.

"Wait," I said. "I'll call you an Uber."

"And give you my address?" Madison asked. "Not on your life."

She got to the elevator and pushed the call button, and my pulse was beginning to race. If I let her go right now, there was a chance she could find the book before I figured out who my target was in Mandy Lake. Madison might not have the power of the Hartley name behind her, but she was resourceful and she obviously wanted the book bad.

She'd come all the way here, drunk as a skunk, just to do a sloppy job of reconnaissance, hadn't she?

The elevator door slid open and I put my hand on the frame to block her path. "Wait. What do you say we work together on this?"

"What?" Madison asked, shocked. "No way."

I had to be smart with my next words or I'd miss my opportunity. If I let her get into that elevator still thinking of me as the enemy, my chances of getting the book—and saving Henry's restaurant—dropped to about half. With Madison on my side—or at least believing we were on the same side—there was no way I could fail again.

"I know the name of the town where the buyer lives," I said.

The elevator door slid shut and Madison didn't stop it.

I kept going. "Between what I know and that Bree girl you have, it'll be easy to find the book. We'll split the money. Think about it—two crews working together, easiest job either of us has ever done."

In the silence of the hallway, I could hear her breathe. A little quick. A little heavy. It matched the rhythm of my heartbeats.

"What do you say Madison? Come on. You need me."

She took in a sharp little breath, her eyes filled with fire again. "I wouldn't work with you even if you presented the Verne book to me on a platter. You may be Bill and Brenda's daughter, but you're cocky and loud, and you don't have a fraction of their skill. Now, thank you for the coffee and goodbye."

She turned on her heel and marched down the hall, deciding to take the stairs rather than wait for the elevator to return. The stairwell door closed behind her with an echo down the hall and a smile crept across my lips.

I always did love a challenge.

8

MADISON

Cass Hartley sure had a way of getting under my skin.

I never should have given in to the ridiculous urge to scope out her hotel after I made Bree find the address, but I was on my second bottle of wine in so many days at that point so what could I say? My inhibitions were lowered.

Whatever else I had to say about Cass and her methods, the girl was good at reading people and getting them to do what she wanted. She got me into her room, after all, and inebriated or not, she made me want to talk to her.

I got out of there as soon as I'd sobered up enough to realize the colossal stupidity of what I was doing—a few more minutes and I could very well have been sleeping with the enemy. She'd given me enough indication that she was interested—unless it was all a part of her manipulation game. *That* thought made me a little sick to my stomach as I woke up the next morning in my overstuffed king-sized bed and realized what I'd done.

What *was* last night except a pitiful display of weakness?

I slid to the edge of the bed and sat there for a moment, wondering if I was going to be sick. My head was throbbing from the wine—a thousand-dollar Bordeaux was *not* something to guzzle during a pity party for one—but mostly, I felt sick over that interaction with Cass.

I'd been pulling cons and heists ever since I was a fourteen-year-old kid stealing groceries and school clothes for Donnie, and in all that time I'd *never* let a situation get so far out of hand as this one. In the harsh light of day, it seemed so much worse.

She knew my name. She knew my crew. She'd seen me drunk and vulnerable to her prying questions. I just *knew* I'd given myself away to her—not in words, but in the expressions of my stupid, drunken face. And worst of all, I had no idea where the book was going next. And *she* did.

I stood, swaying slightly as a wave of lightheadedness washed over me, then I clenched my fists.

If there was anything I hated more than a botched job, it was an abandoned one, and Cass Hartley was not going to win this battle. I pulled a silk robe on over my pajamas and shuffled into the kitchen to put on a strong pot of coffee, then called Bree and Tank.

"Are you done with that bundle of nerves yet, or is she lying in bed next to you as we speak?" I asked Tank when he answered.

"Aww, come on, Madison," he said. I could hear the embarrassment in his voice and I felt immediately guilty for teasing him. "You know I'm not like that. I got her home safe and that was it."

"Good," I said. "Then you're available to talk about phase two of the Verne heist."

"Phase two? We don't even know where the book is anymore," Tank said.

"Exactly," I said. "That's phase two. Phase three is beating Cass Hartley's crew to it because she's still going after the book and I can't let her have it. Come over. We need to start immediately."

Thirty minutes later, Tank, Bree and I were sitting around my large marble island, sipping my favorite Jamaican fair trade coffee and plotting our next move.

"What makes you think Cass is still going after the book?" Bree asked. "Or that she has the resources to find its next destination?"

"Please," I said. "She's a Hartley. She had resources handed to her on a platter from birth. Last night I... did a little recon mission." Bree arched her eyebrow, but that was all these two were going to get out of me about last night's unfortunate adventure, and it was all they needed to know. "Cass definitely knows something, and I have a feeling if she wants the book, she'll get it."

I decided to also omit her insulting notion that I *needed* her, as if my crew and I weren't a well-oiled machine capable of digging up the information on our own. No need to relive *that* moment.

"So what do you want to do?" Tank asked.

"We have to get to it first," I said firmly. "Bree, did you make any headway in your research?"

After she'd given me Cass's address, I told her to do whatever digging she could to get me information on the book's movement. Mostly, I needed to know if we were going after the buyer, or if our little snafu at the bank meant the book had been moved into police custody. That would make things a lot harder.

"Not yet, but I brought my laptop," she said.

"Good," I said. "I need you to get me the location of that book. It's out there. Cass got it somehow."

"And me? What can I do?" Tank asked.

I smiled at him. "Since you and that girl seem to have bonded, I thought we could use that to our advantage. Get close to her. Keep an eye on what Cass and her crew are doing."

"Madison, no," Tank objected. "I don't want to use Talia like that."

"What are you, dating her already?" I snapped. "This is business and she's our competition. Plus, Cass seems pretty close to her—for all we know, that girl could lead us straight to the book."

Tank looked into his mug, swirling his coffee, and said, "Okay, but I don't like it."

"You don't have to," I reminded him. "You're being paid to do a job and that's what I require of you. Now get to it."

He nodded and finished off his coffee, then I walked him out of the penthouse. Bree was completely absorbed in her laptop when I came back into the kitchen. She had a habit of becoming single-minded when she poured herself into a task—I probably could have stripped naked right there in the kitchen and she wouldn't have noticed.

I went into the bedroom to change out of my pajamas, putting on a pair of designer straight-legged jeans and a blazer that accentuated and complemented the curves of my hips. I stepped into a pair of flats—comfort before fashion—and headed back into the kitchen.

"Anything yet?" I asked as I slid back onto my stool at the island.

"Yeah, actually," Bree said. "I was able to hack into the police evidence database and I searched the intake forms for the last seventy-two hours. They got your ski mask, but there's no mention of the book."

"So it's not at the police station?" I asked, trying not to focus on the irritation rising in my chest at the mention of the ski mask—the one Cass had pulled off my head and recklessly tossed to the vault floor.

If the police found a hair on it...

I was practically a unicorn—fifteen years in the business and never once had I been arrested. My fingerprints weren't even in the system, let alone my DNA. And now that I was one job away from going legit, Cass Hartley had to ride in on her high horse and jeopardize everything. *Great.*

"Nope," Bree said with a smile. "The book is still out there."

"Well, that's good news," I said, taking a deep breath. There was no sense in fixating on things I couldn't control. "Keep digging—we need to know everything Cass knows."

It was a couple hours later when Bree put her hands up in the air and shouted, "Bingo!"

"You have the location?" I asked, perking up from where I was sitting at my desk, attempting to aid in the search. We both knew that Bree's superior hacking skills would bring her to the information first, but I hated feeling helpless.

"No," she said. "But I've got a name."

"Let's hear it," I said, coming over to her eagerly. But Bree liked a little showmanship in her work and she always held me in suspense and insisted on explaining the *how* of her craft before she spat it out.

"Once I figured out that no relevant information had been discovered by the police, I started digging into the bank's records," she said. "That was actually *harder* than hacking into the police database—they really had things locked down. It took me about an hour just to figure out how they'd set up their tangled web of encryption protocols, and another hour to break through it."

"You're a genius, Bree, and it's tragic that your work will never be appreciated by the world at large," I said, talking fast so we could get to the point. "Tell me the name."

"The deposit locker was registered to," she said, pausing for dramatic effect. I could have freaking strangled her, but then I'd *never* know what she'd found. "Michael Rutherford."

I threw my arms around Bree in a rare show of affection and her widening eyes told me that I'd startled her.

Or maybe it was the sound of the toilet being flushed.

I let go of Bree and we whipped our heads toward the bathroom.

"Is someone else here?" Bree whispered.

My heart was hammering in my chest too hard to answer and I glanced at the knife block on the kitchen counter. I wasn't the violent type, but if it came down to self-defense against an intruder, I guess I'd have to try.

The bathroom door opened and Bree and I were clutching each other like scared prey animals. Then out stepped none other than Cass Hartley, wiping her hands on my decorative hand towel.

"What the fuck are you doing here?" I snapped, my hands on my hips. In the back of my mind, I was replaying my conversation with Bree. How loudly had she said that name?

"Hey, Maddie," Cass said as she strolled into the kitchen. "Bree, how's it going?" She set the hand towel on the island and walked casually over to the coffee maker. She helped herself to a mug from the glass-fronted cabinet above and poured herself some coffee, then said with a friendly smile, "I hope you don't mind —you partook of my coffee last night, after all. Damn, this is good."

"I buy good coffee," I said through clenched teeth. "How did you get into my bathroom?"

And how long have you been there?

"A magician never reveals her secrets," Cass said with a coy smile as she continued her tour around the penthouse. She walked around the end of the island, slowly sipping her coffee as she went, and looked around the living room. She whistled and said, "You buy nice *everything*. I like your digs."

I clenched my fists. A small part of me was still thinking about the knife block—that was how much Cass Hartley messed with my mind.

Cass circled back to the island and set down her coffee, leaning her elbows casually on the counter. Bree quietly closed her laptop—as if the damage hadn't already been done—and finally, Cass said with a smile, "I don't know how much you remember from last night —you were pretty drunk. But I was serious about working together. You rejected my offer because you doubted my skills, so I thought I'd just pop by and show you my talents."

"Remind me to have words with my doorman," I said.

"Oh, I didn't come in through the lobby," Cass said with a wink. "Anyway, I figured you would want to reconsider my offer now. I mean, I'm pretty sure you don't have a city to narrow your search, and I do. How many Michael Rutherfords do you think there are in the United States?"

Well, there it was—she'd heard the name.

"Four hundred and forty-three," Bree answered, her laptop open again. She just couldn't resist the urge to answer that question.

I narrowed my eyes at Cass, ignoring Bree. "You have his name now, and you're telling me you have his location. Why would you work with me instead of going to get the book yourself?"

"I don't know," Cass said casually. "Maybe I'm intrigued by you. Maybe I get bored running with the same crew heist after heist. Maybe I'm tired and I just don't feel like competing with you. The clock *is* ticking, though. If you say no again, make no mistake—I'll be going after the book one way or the other."

I shot a look at Bree—I'd give anything to read her

mind because I had no idea what to make of Cass or her offer. Was she playing me like she had last night?

But a leader makes decisions quickly and decisively, and I could *not* lose that book, even if it meant sharing it with Cass. So I turned back to her and stood a little taller as I put on my professional tone of voice. "Fine. We'll work on this together, but I'd be willing to bet I have at least ten more years of experience than you do. That makes me your superior and I'm going to be leading this job. I will not compromise on that— either you agree or we race each other to the book."

"As much as I like the idea of a race," Cass said, standing upright so that our eyes were level, "I need that book more than I need to beat you to it. Split the profit fifty-fifty?"

Fifty-fifty. No doubt, my crew and I would be doing eighty percent of the work, but fifty percent was better than nothing, and all I really needed was the map. If Cass knew the town *and* the buyer's name, she would get to the book first and I'd be left with nothing.

"Fine," I said, holding out my hand.

Cass slipped her palm into mine, her skin soft and her handshake firm. She didn't break eye contact with me, holding my hand for several beats longer than was comfortable. Was it just me or was the air in the room sweltering?

"Get your crew together," I said, taking my hand back. "We'll meet tomorrow to formulate a plan."

"Sounds good," Cass said, her tone as casual as if

we were planning a bowling night with our friends. "I've got a meeting place where we'll have privacy. I'll text you the address."

I glanced at Bree, still not sure what to make of the train called Cass Hartley that had just rolled over me. As Cass took one last sip of coffee and stepped around the island, I said, "You don't have my phone number."

She passed close enough by me that I could feel the fabric of her shirt against my blazer. My heart jumped into my throat as Cass winked and said, "I have my ways. I'll be in touch."

9

———

CASS

"So, what's next?" Spider leaned his beanpole body against a brick pillar in the middle of what I liked to call our command center, examining his fingernails like he just didn't care. The spot was perfect for us, an abandoned textile factory where we could store our tools and meet in peace. We had set up camp on a raised platform that was once used by the factory foreman so I could see everyone who came in and out. Not that anyone ever did, except today.

I shrugged. "We go after the book."

"Do you know where it is?" Talia asked, sending a particularly focused glance at me. Ever since the bank vault, she seemed calmer. Any other time she would have been upset about how the heist had gone, but this time... nothing. I wasn't going to question our good fortune, but it was certainly a curiosity.

"Not exactly," I answered.

"What do you mean not exactly?" Spider asked.

I appreciated that Spider wasn't harping on the details—he hated a failed heist almost as much as I did—so I tolerated his attitude. "I know it never made it out of that deposit locker, Henry gave me the name of the town it's going to, and I... *found out* the name of the buyer."

I didn't tell them exactly how, and Spider didn't ask. He just said, "What's the hold up, then? Sounds like we have everything we need."

The time on my phone said I had fifteen minutes until Madison and her crew arrived. I'd purposely waited until the last minute to tell Spider and Talia what I was up to, that way Spider wouldn't have too much time to object.

"We can't ignore the fact that our first attempt went so wrong," I said. "We need to nail down why that happened before we can go after the book again."

"It went wrong because that redhead showed up—" Spider started to say. I ignored him.

"Spider, the way you handled their hacker was perfect. Great job. Talia—"

She started shaking her head faintly, her eyes on a peeling tile of the filthy linoleum floor. She thought I was going to yell at her for what happened, and to avoid a meltdown, I went to her and put both hands on her shoulders. "It wasn't your fault we lost the book. You did something wonderful."

The shaking slowed and she pulled a strand of dark

hair out of her mouth, tucking it behind her ear. Then she looked at me with such innocence that I doubted myself for ever including her in my schemes. "I did?"

She's stronger than she looks, I reminded myself. Every time I had thought of dropping her from my crew, she saved the day. By now, five years later, I wouldn't dream of dropping her. In a situation like this, I needed her photographic mind to help me keep tabs on all the moving parts. "Yes. You and Tank. You really hit it off, didn't you?"

"Yeah, I guess we did," she said, a smile flickering at the edge of her mouth.

"That'll work in our favor. Spider, come here. There's something I need to tell—"

I froze, a tingling sensation riding my spine. I released Talia and turned to the door just in time to see Madison waltzing in like she owned the place. Flanked by Bree on one side and Tank on the other, she looked like the leader of a band of misfits. It almost made me laugh.

I heard a click to my right and spun to face Spider, unholstering the gun that he wore against his ankle. I always begged him to leave that dangerous thing at home, but that was the one thing he wouldn't budge on. "Wait!" I whispered, pushing the barrel of the gun down to the floor. "I invited them here."

"You what?" he hissed.

"There's not enough time to explain." *Thanks to Madison's early drop-in.* I threw a look over my shoulder at the advancing crew, nearly fifteen minutes premature. I only had a few seconds before they came within earshot.

"Try," Spider said through gritted teeth, his eyes narrowed on the other crew approaching the platform.

"Tank!" Talia exclaimed when she saw him, heading for the stairs to meet him. She was completely oblivious to the gun in Spider's hand and the tensions rising between us, and I winced as she stumbled on the bottom step. Tank was there, though, catching her like an elephant hugging a mouse.

"Put that thing away," I said to Spider in the sternest tone I could manage.

"Not until you start talking."

Why was he doing this? Sure, he often made surprising choices during jobs, but they were always in the best interest of the group, and he listened to me... most of the time. I turned away completely from the other crew at the base of the stairs and faced Spider. "Are you threatening me?"

"I do what I need to do."

Was he was doing this to piss me off? Or maybe it was some weird tough guy hang-up? The latter didn't make it any less annoying. Madison and her crew were far too close for me to really explain anything, so I had to settle for, "You need to trust me—I have a plan. Now put that damn thing away before I take it from you and shoot your balls off. You know I can. And I will."

Spider's face hardened as he slipped the gun back

into the holster, then Madison and her crew headed up the stairs. Tank went first, with Talia trailing behind him, Madison and Bree bringing up the rear. I barely kept my jaw in place as I watched Talia slide her hand into Tank's big paw. He must have really put her under his spell. Had they...? I shook my head. No. Not Talia. It wasn't possible.

"Hello, Madison." I smiled at her like we were neighbors meeting in a supermarket.

She didn't acknowledge me. Her eyes were fixed on Spider. "If we're going to do business, he needs to get rid of that gun. No guns. That's the deal."

"No problem," I said. Truthfully, I didn't much like having it around, either.

Spider folded his arms, the muscles of his forearms flexing. There wasn't much to him and he didn't look like much of a threat compared to Madison's hulking beast, but Spider was abnormally strong for his size. "I'll do whatever I damn well please."

Tank stepped up behind Madison to back her up and I positioned myself in the space between them, a hand outstretched to both Spider and Tank. "We will get rid of the gun, as long as you let Spider search all of you for weapons."

After a long moment, Madison gave a tight nod. Everyone waited in silence while Spider gave all three of them a quick and efficient pat down, Talia still clinging to Tank's hand despite the search. He looked like he could crush her with one finger, but his grip on her hand was tender and Talia betrayed no signs of pain.

Spider finished and reluctantly handed me the gun, which I locked in the drawer of the desk. The lock was broken, but Madison's crew didn't need to know that.

Spider spoke first. "You here to botch another job?"

A frown line appeared between Madison's brows. "That had *nothing* to do with us."

"You cut your way in," he said.

"Your girl was busy having a panic attack—"

"Okay, okay," I said, interrupting them before things got too vicious to move forward together. "Madison, your early arrival interrupted the conversation we were having."

Madison lifted her chin. "Punctuality is important."

"Yeah, well, you could have given me a warning," I said.

"Like you did at the bank?"

Was that a smirk? I had to hand it to her, she had rebounded nicely from that night in my room. She was *very* put together this time. Though simply dressed, I could tell her ensemble was more expensive than my entire wardrobe, and not a hair or stitch of makeup was out of place. Which told me her sloppy drunkenness had been an anomaly—perhaps *I* had ruffled her that much. That would make my plan much easier to execute if I could get past this awkward moment. To do that, I had to get Spider on board.

I turned to Spider, sending him a telepathic message. *Trust me.* "Spider, you asked what was next for the book. We're going to work with Madison and her crew to get it."

I tried to put everything that wasn't in my words into my eyes, but Spider, even after all these years, couldn't read my mind, in spite of how much I needed him to. "No, we're not."

"*We are*," I said, keeping my tone even. "We all have the same information about the book, and after the bank, we know we're pretty evenly matched. We can either compete against each other and make things a lot harder than they have to be, or we can work together to ensure our success. Besides, two brains are better than one."

"But six is a shitshow."

"Spider—"

"I'm not doing this."

"Come on," I said, my tone finally growing edgy. "Stop being a baby."

"Stop being a doormat. She's conning you."

"No, she's not." *We're conning her.* I couldn't say more to counteract his argument because it would reveal my plan, and it needed to stay secret in order to work.

Spider brooded for a moment, then brushed past me and took the stairs two at a time. "I'm out of here.

Way to let your pussy make decisions for you *again*," he shouted over his shoulder.

I steeled myself, trying not to react. Spider could be hasty sometimes. His quick reactions helped in high-pressure situations, but in others it was extremely frustrating. His boots clanged on the metal stairs, echoing in the vast space of the factory.

Madison was watching me carefully. There was a little disparagement in her tone when she said, "You better go deal with that."

Without a word, I followed Spider down the stairs, jogging to catch up with him. I finally caught him at the entrance to what used to be the head offices of the factory. I grabbed his skinny arm and pulled him inside. "You idiot," I hissed.

"You're the idiot."

"Spider." Gripping his worn button-down in my fists, I shook him. "Get a grip on yourself. What's wrong? Why don't you trust me on this job?"

"Because of how you are with her."

"What are you talking about?"

"Do you think the rest of us don't notice the way you look at her? This is Laura all over again."

I froze. The fact that he would say that name to me was a slap in the face. I hadn't even allowed myself to think it in years. "What the fuck, Spider? If you would just shut up for a single minute I could explain it to you."

Spider's dark eyes roved over mine. His body relaxed and I released my grip on his shirt.

I gave myself a moment to let go of the hurt—that never helped anyone—before telling my story. "Madison showed up at my place the other night, drunk. I thought she might have information we didn't have about the book and I tried to pull it out of her. When that didn't work, I broke into her apartment and overheard her and Bree doing research. They had the name of the buyer."

Spider's eye grew hard again. "If that's all, why should we work with her now? Why not just use her information and get the book ourselves?"

"Don't you see? This is the next level," I told him. "She's obsessed with that book, *and* she's hell-bent on taking the lead. We could either compete with her, or we could sit back and let *her* do all the work, and then swoop in at the end and snatch the book from her."

Only Spider's eyes moved, as if he was reading something in my face. "What about Talia? She's obviously infatuated with Tank. We can't trust her if that's the plan."

"So we won't tell her." I shrugged, but it felt bad to say that. Spider was right, though. If Tank had hooked Talia so quickly, who knew where her loyalties would lie when push came to shove. Plus, she didn't *need* to be involved in that part of the plan. We could use her brilliant mind while we were retrieving the book from the buyer, sure. But when the time came to steal it away from Madison, all we needed were wits and cunning, and Spider and I had that in spades.

"And you think it'll work?"

"I know it will," I said, keeping my voice low so it wouldn't carry across the high factory ceiling. "I've got her in the palm of my hand."

Then Madison's voice carried to us as she shouted, "We don't have all day!"

I closed my eyes. Well, my plan would work if I didn't kill her before we were done. When I opened my eyes, Spider was walking back down the hallway.

"Where are you going?" I asked, running to catch up.

"Back upstairs," he said, then added in a whisper, "But if this fails, I'm done, Cass. Forever."

During the wait, Madison had draped herself over my chair. Bree had set up her laptop on the desk, and Talia and Tank huddled close to her. They all looked at Spider and me as we reached the top of the stairs. Madison was no longer smirking.

"Are you two done?" she asked, all the amusement gone out of her expression.

"Yes," I said.

"And you're still in?"

"Of course," I said. "Right, Spider?"

Spider nodded, only a shallow nostril flare betraying his real feelings on the situation.

Madison glanced between the two of us. Her mood had darkened in the time we'd been gone. Did she suspect something? Or was she just annoyed that I was wasting her time? Probably a combination of both since she wasn't stupid. At least, I didn't think she was.

"Now that we're all on the same page," she said. "Let's get something straight. I'm in charge here."

She was doing exactly as I expected—exactly what I wanted. I took a seat across from her in one of the broken desk chairs Spider and I had gathered from the offices. "Of course. Would you like us to call you Your Majesty? Supreme Leader?"

The smirk reappeared. "Queen Madison will do," she said.

This woman constantly surprised me. Whenever I *thought* she was a hardass perfectionist, she come out with something like that, or got sloppy drunk and showed up outside my hotel. "Okay, queenie. What's next?"

"We start with scoping out the buyer's house."

10

MADISON

ueen Madison. It was ridiculous and I hoped Cass noticed the snark in my tone when I said it, but on the other hand, in order for this ill-advised teamwork situation to work out, I needed her—and the rest of her ragtag crew—to think of me that way.

A little bit older.

Definitely wiser.

In charge of this heist, or else it didn't happen.

And I didn't mind the idea of Cass bowing down in front of me, either. But that was neither here nor there, and I wanted to get out of *there* as soon as possible. How had she even found this place? It was cavernous, and the fact that I could see the entire empty production floor from our perch on the foreman's platform did nothing to ease the unsettling feeling of being exposed.

I much preferred the low-profile conference rooms

I rented around town to do my planning—never the same one twice, never any risk of being caught trespassing or suspected of doing anything other than some very boring, unremarkable business dealings.

This place was downright brazen, just like Cass herself.

"Let's get this over with," I said, nodding to Bree. "Did you find the address?"

"Yes," she said, turning her laptop around on the desk for everyone to see. "While I'm sure we all would have preferred to end this in the vault, the bank actually helped us out. I was able to hack into their client database and find the name attached to the deposit locker we were after—Michael Rutherford. Coupled with information that Cass gave us about the book's destination—Mandy Lake—I was able to find an address. 1834 Carraway Lane. The book was not entered into evidence at the police station, so we have good reason to believe we'll find it at that address as soon as the transfer happens. With any luck, Rutherford will have no idea his deposit locker was even tampered with and he'll go on with his plans to move the book."

I watched Cass and her crew while Bree made her long-winded explanation. She could never resist the chance to explain her methodology, and that gave me the opportunity to study my opponents—err, *allies*.

Cass looked a little bored with it all. She was leaning casually back in her chair, arms folded under her chest and exaggerating her cleavage in a V-neck shirt. She locked eyes with me and I looked away.

Talia was still holding Tank's hand—I had *no* idea what on earth was going on there. I'd have to deal with that later.

And Spider—I didn't like the guy. He was still giving Bree seductive looks and her cheeks reddened when she noticed. He was a playboy and I knew he was going to hurt her if given the chance, and that was enough reason to dislike him. But what the hell had he and Cass been talking about for so long in that office? And that gun... that was not a good sign.

I narrowed my eyes at him when he looked at me and raised my chin in a show of dominance. *It's Queen Madison to you, and don't forget it.*

"I looked at the house using a street view map," Bree continued. "It's big, but nothing we can't handle. I think the best course of action will be to put video surveillance on it for a couple of days so we know when the book arrives, and that'll give us a chance to observe the routines of Rutherford, and anyone else who might live there."

"Bree and I will go—" I started to say, but Cass cut me off.

"And do the job while you're there, then disappear with the book?" Cass asked, pushing out of her chair and coming closer to me.

She stopped with her hands on her hips right in front of me and I felt my heart flutter momentarily—it was just the adrenaline that always came with the promise of a new job. Right?

"Do you really think I was born yesterday?" she asked.

"I'm undecided," I said, not backing down.

"Well, you're not going to that house alone," Cass said. "In fact, from now on, everything we do includes at least one member from each crew."

I rolled my eyes and let my irritation show in my face. It had been all of about fifteen minutes and Cass was already going back on her promise to let me take charge—but I had to admit this particular idea was a good one. That was the only way we could make sure neither crew double-crossed the other. I folded my arms over my chest and said curtly, "Fine, that sounds fair."

She grinned at me, her almond eyes lighting up like she'd just won a significant victory—one that had nothing to do with double-crossing. "Good. I'm going with you to place the cameras."

"Umm." My first attempt at speech came out as a stutter that I resented very much. I was going to have to be alone with this girl?

I glanced at Tank, whose expression was unreadable as always. Beneath the surface, though, he must have been wondering what the hell had gotten into me. We'd been working together for so long, and before that, we were friends. I *never* let emotion come into play when it came to pulling jobs—it was dangerous to allow it.

I released my arms, letting them hang casually at my sides so they wouldn't betray defensiveness. Then I straightened my posture a little bit more and tried again. My voice was strong and commanding, just how I liked it. "Fine. We'll meet at the bus station at eight o'clock sharp tonight and take public transportation so no one can track us. *Don't* be late."

7:57 p.m., and no sign of Cass.

I was sitting alone on a bench that was damp from all the rain we'd been having and I could feel it soaking through the seat of my yoga leggings. At least they were black and the wetness wouldn't show too much, but my irritation was mounting with every minute and Cass wasn't there.

The buses around New Vernon ran punctually— something I very much liked about them—and Cass had exactly three minutes or I'd be going to Mandy Lake without her.

I closed my eyes and took a couple deep breaths. I pushed Cass out of my mind and thought about *Twenty Thousand Leagues Under the Sea* instead. I hadn't spoken to my brother in ten years, but I was sure things would be different after I got him a copy of that treasure map. I

CARA MALONE & ANNA COVE

would bring the book back to the museum and show him that I was done with the life of crime, trading it for a relationship with the only relative I had left. *Eye on the prize.*

"You asleep?"

I startled and opened my eyes to see Cass gliding past me on a skateboard. She popped the board up and caught it with some footwork I tried not to be impressed by, then I checked my watch. "One minute to spare."

"But not late," Cass pointed out, and then like clockwork, we heard the diesel rumble of the bus as it approached the bench.

Cass tucked her skateboard under her arm and made a little *after you* bow as the bus door opened. I rolled my eyes as I stepped aboard and paid the fare for both of us. The bus was nearly empty and she could have sat anywhere, but when I sat down, she slid in beside me, using her hips to push me into the window seat.

Arrogant.

And smelling of warm vanilla.

Stop it, Madison.

"You do that a lot, you know."

"What?"

"Roll your eyes," Cass said. "What makes you so annoyed with the world?"

"I'm not annoyed with the world," I said. Then I glanced at her thigh pressing up against mine and said,

"I *am* kind of annoyed at your clothes, though. Who wears ripped jeans to a covert mission?"

"Someone who wants to look inconspicuous," she said, then grabbed the fabric of my leggings and gave it a stretch, letting it snap back on my thigh. "Unlike you."

"I'm wearing yoga pants," I said. "They're versatile."

"You're wearing black from head to toe," Cass answered, her tone rising to an incredulous register. "You look like a bandit. Please tell me you don't have that ski mask in your backpack."

"No," I said, "Thanks to you, that's been entered into police evidence."

"Good," Cass said with a smile. "You look enough like a goon as it is. *I* look like a teenage girl out for a skate—perfect for the college town we're going to."

I resisted the urge to roll my eyes again. She wasn't going to get the better of me tonight like she did when she'd let herself into my apartment. And in her hotel room. And at the bank. This woman was going to be the death of me... but not before I got that book.

M andy Lake was an hour bus ride from New Vernon. That gave us plenty of time to plan our strategy, and I showed Cass all the technological goodies that Bree had packed for us in the backpack I was carrying. She had included everything from simple button cameras to high-tech night vision goggles.

Cass grabbed a pair and let out a laugh. "What are these for?"

"Surveillance," I said. *Duh.*

"What are we supposed to do, strap them to a raccoon?" she asked, still laughing.

I snatched the goggles back and tucked them carefully into the backpack. "Okay, so maybe Bree and I are guilty of being a little over-prepared at times. That's better than under-prepared."

"With all this tech at your disposal, why don't you just fly a drone through an open window and get the book that way?" Cass asked. "Then we wouldn't even need to come all the way out here."

"And deprive myself of this bonding opportunity?" I asked. My voice was dripping with sarcasm, but Cass's thigh was still pressed against mine and I was acutely aware of it.

"You're right," Cass said. "I *am* worth an hour on public transportation."

She was looking at me, those beautiful light brown eyes boring into mine, and a lump formed in my throat. I opened my mouth to say something—anything—to fill the silence, and then the bus stopped short and I had to put my hand out to keep from slamming into the seat in front of me.

"We're here," Cass said with an effortless smile, then stood and waited for me to go first.

It was fully dark as I stepped off the bus with Cass in tow. Mandy Lake was a small college town with a long main street, the pristine campus of an expensive private school at its center. There were a smattering of middle-class neighborhoods coming off it like the branches of a tree, and at the edge of town, a fifteen-minute walk from the bus stop, was the lake that provided its namesake. Circling the lake were about a dozen large, expensive houses.

Bree had done some research into the area and given me a primer on Mandy Lake before she'd handed over the bag full of cameras. While Cass and I walked, I told her what I'd learned.

"This was a railroad town. It popped up on account of the tracks that still run through its center," I said, pointing down Main Street to where the tracks were. "For the first century of its existence, Mandy Lake was a working class town and everyone who lived here made their livelihood thanks to the trains. It wasn't until the turn of the 20th century that a couple of rich industrialists discovered the beauty of the lake. They founded the college and began building their houses here."

"Is that what Michael Rutherford is?" Cass asked. "An old industrialist with a penchant for even older books?"

"Bree said he's young—in his forties," I answered. "I think he's old money. It was probably his father who was the industrialist."

"A spoiled rich kid," Cass said. "My favorite."

The houses—no, *mansions*—around the perimeter of Mandy Lake were breathtaking. Cass and I walked down the winding Carraway Lane, away from the town and into a neighborhood that felt opulent and secluded. There were streetlights illuminating our path, but not many. Each house was larger and more ornate than the last and as we looked for house numbers in the dark, searching for 1834, I lowered my voice and said, "Do you still think your ripped jeans and the skateboard under your arm are inconspicuous?"

Cass didn't answer my question. She just said, "There—that's it."

Her voice was low and breathy, and in the dark, it made the hairs on the back of my neck stand up.

The house was set back from the road, its perimeter lined with a large iron fence that had intimidatingly sharp finials at the top of each spire. Lit with spotlights hidden in the meticulous landscaping, the large Victorian house loomed like it was straight out of a horror film. Thick moss grew over large portions of its stone walls.

"Wow," I said.

"Yeah," Cass breathed.

We stood in admiration of it for a moment—and, at least on my part, in fear of the spikes on top of that fence. There were no lights on in any of the many windows facing the road, and no cars in the long driveway—not that I expected a person of means like Michael Rutherford to leave his car exposed to the elements. But a quiet house was good news for us, and I wasn't in the habit of looking a gift horse in the mouth.

I asked, "So, up and over?"

"Looks like our best option," Cass said. "Unless you want to try the intercom at the gate."

I smiled at the idea, then said, "It doesn't look like there's anyone home. I see a couple good climbing trees in the side yard where we can put our cameras out of view. Let's do this quickly."

Cass and I jogged from the road to the fence and crept along it for about a dozen yards, looking for the best place to enter where we wouldn't be spotted by the neighbors or—God forbid—Rutherford.

"Here," Cass said as we passed under a large oak tree with thick branches that extended over the fence. "When we're done, we can crawl along the branches and jump down on this side of the fence."

"Good thinking," I said. The branches were too tall to use on our way into the property, so I asked, "If I give you a boost, do you think you can clear the fence spikes?"

"I better," Cass said with a nervous chuckle.

I knelt down and cupped my hands together, then Cass set down her skateboard and put one foot into my hands. "On three, okay?"

She nodded and I counted down, then launched

her as hard as I could into the air, praying that it was enough. The last thing I wanted to do was impale Bill and Brenda Hartley's daughter on a fence—they might be in jail, but I was pretty sure they still had the means to destroy me.

But Cass easily cleared the fence, grabbing onto the crossbar at the top and gracefully avoiding the spikes. It wasn't until she landed on the other side that the prospect of scrambling up the six-and-a-half-foot fence all on my own became daunting.

"I don't think I can do it," I said. Boy, were those difficult words to push past my lips—and rare, too. "You're going to have to place the cameras yourself. I'll keep a lookout, and I'll contact Bree so we can confirm each camera is working."

"Okay," Cass said. I took off the backpack and passed it through the bars to her. It was a tight squeeze, but with a little jostling, we got it through the fence.

Cass winked at me, then took off at a sprint across the lawn. It was too bright—there was an abundance of decorative lighting incorporated in the landscaping and my heart sped up for each second that I was on one side of the fence and Cass was on the other.

"Hurry, Cass," I muttered, looking around.

I was standing in the shadows between two streetlights and the nearest house wasn't for at least a quarter of a mile, curved around the shape of the lake. The chances that a busybody neighbor would spot us were slim, but I wouldn't be doing my job as a lookout if I wasn't considering every possibility.

I watched Cass throw the backpack carelessly over one shoulder and I winced as she leaped up and grabbed a low branch on a tree near the house. *If she drops those expensive cameras...*

She swung one leg over the branch, making it look effortless, and because she was a good thirty feet away from me, I allowed my eyes to linger on her partially shadowed body.

Cass pulled herself upright and took the first camera—safe and sound—out of the backpack, her strong thighs gripping the tree branch for balance. She twisted and reached over her head, her shirt rising slightly and exposing her midriff. She was careful of the branches that might obstruct the camera's view as she mounted it to the tree trunk, and I tried not to stare at her exposed belly.

She threw me a thumbs-up and I texted Bree, who was standing by. After a moment of waiting that felt like an eternity, Bree texted back—*Camera one is online*—and I let out a long sigh of relief.

I gave Cass a thumbs-up in return. *Okay, time for camera two,* I thought. She dropped out of the tree like it was nothing, then started strolling across the lawn, looking for her next vantage point.

What is she doing? "Hurry up," I growled, too quiet for her to hear, and gestured for her to get on with it. Cass just kept walking at that jaunty pace, like she owned the damn house, and then out of the corner of my eye, I saw something move.

I snapped my head to the source, a small flap in the bottom of a side door about a hundred feet behind Cass. It moved again, and then a white blur burst through the doggy door and started tearing across the lawn.

"Cass!" I shouted. "Dog—*run!*"

So much for inconspicuousness. My heart was pounding, but definitely not faster than Cass's. Her eyes were wide as she broke into a sprint, powering her way across the lawn. When she got to the big oak tree, she scrambled up the trunk like she was more cat than woman, with the dog barking and snarling behind her.

I went to the branch extending over the fence, much higher than the small tree she'd just hopped down from. I was completely useless on this side of the fence, and the only thing I could do was attempt to break Cass's fall.

"Hurry," I hissed as she made her way over to the branch. Small twigs broke off and fell to the ground behind her. I closed my eyes for a moment and prayed. *Don't let the branch break.*

"Look out," Cass said as she crossed over the fence.

"Jump," I said. "I'll catch you."

"Yeah, right," she said, but then her footing slipped and she fell out of the tree. She was a windmill of flailing limbs and I felt one of them connect with my right eye just before we both fell to the ground and the wind was knocked out of my lungs.

When I regained my breath, Cass was crawling off me.

"That's a fucking poodle," she said, her voice at full volume.

"Huh?"

"That," she said, pointing at the dog, who was at the fence, still barking and baring his teeth at us. "...is a French poodle with the prissy, shaved fur and everything. That's what I jumped out of a tree for?"

"It's a mean poodle," I said as Cass extended her hand to help me up. She pulled me to my feet, using a little more force than necessary as I collided with her chest, then got my balance and stepped back. "And you punched me in the eye."

"I'm sorry," she said. "Let me see."

I tried to push her away, but she cupped my face in her hands and tilted it to catch the light of the moon. Her face was just inches from mine and I couldn't help thinking about what happened the last time we were this close. The dog stopped barking and I was falling into Cass's gaze.

"Yep," she said. "You might end up with a shiner. That's okay though—it'll make you look like a badass."

"*More* of a badass, you mean," I said.

A badass would kiss her right now. *Just saying.*

Cass released my face and stepped back. "We should get out of here before someone hears the dog."

He was still barking after all. I realized he'd never stopped, and it was Cass's proximity that had made me stop hearing it for a moment.

"What about the rest of the cameras?" I asked.

"It's too risky to go back in now," Cass said. She grabbed her skateboard, then took my hand and dragged me back to the street. While I wasn't exactly eager to linger near a barking dog, I was frustrated that we'd botched yet *another* mission.

"Is one camera going to be enough?" I asked. We'd brought ten of them and the house was enormous. I couldn't see this as anything but a failure.

"It'll have to be," Cass said, letting go of my hand when we got to the curb.

"And you're sure you got it mounted properly?"

"Yes, Queen Madison," Cass said, then she dropped her skateboard on the pavement and pushed off, gliding along beside me.

11

CASS

Turns out, Madison wasn't so bad once you got past the holier-than-thou attitude and that eye roll of hers. Sure, she had a stick up her ass, but the plan she was developing—*we* were developing—made sense.

Our teams gelled well, too. Though I tried, I could barely separate Talia and Tank, and after a few days, I realized it was easier to keep them together than to try to wrench them apart. As long as their relationship didn't interfere with my plans, I didn't really care anyway.

Bree came in handy with all her technology, and even Spider came around to the idea of working together when Bree made quick work of bypassing Rutherford's security system. Then Spider discovered the blueprints for the house, plus a building permit for a climate controlled addition, and it was like our crews had always been working together.

Even Madison and I got along. It was kind of like vacation. Who wouldn't want to sit back while someone *else* barked the orders for once? Especially when that someone was as easy on the eyes as Madison. Not that I would ever tell her that. Who knew what kind of damage that would do to the operation? But looking and thinking never hurt anyone.

We waited seven days, watching the house and waiting for movement. There wasn't much. The poodle would appear every day at seven in the morning, one in the afternoon, and five in the evening. The lights inside would come on for a couple hours once the sun went down, and then blink out around ten. And that was where our luck really kicked in. A brand new Maserati would leave the house every night like clockwork and return early the next morning, leaving the house empty and waiting for us. Whatever he was doing—gambling or visiting a girlfriend—-Michael Rutherford was a creature of habit.

It was almost too easy. And extremely boring. The only excitement came when we saw what must have been the book being delivered on day two. Around noon, a black SUV with tinted windows pulled up to the gate, was promptly buzzed in, and parked on the circular drive in front of the house. A man in an expensive suit got out of the passenger seat carrying something approximately book-sized, disappeared into the house, and emerged just a few minutes later empty-handed.

After that, Rutherford was back to his normal routine.

On the final night of our surveillance, all of us were gathered in my command center viewing the feed. We lounged in our broken chairs, eating popcorn, and we watched the Maserati pull out of the driveway at ten o'clock sharp.

I turned to Madison. "Do you think it's time to go?" I deferred to her judgment and I noticed her mouth take on a sideways smirk when I did it. I wanted more of it. Well, that and I realized the more relaxed I could make her now, the more buttered up she would be when we snatched the book right out from under her.

Madison popped a handful of popcorn in her mouth and chewed, then primly wiped her hands. "Tank, are you ready to go?"

"'Course, boss," he said, straightening from his curled position next to Talia.

Madison nodded. "Spider and Bree, how about you? Are you *sure* you have the security system nailed?"

"Yep." Bree nodded, her glasses slipping with the movement. She pushed them up her nose.

"Ready," Spider said.

I already knew we were ready. We'd been working on our plan for days and delaying would only bring us closer to the time that Rutherford returned home in the morning. We had to be long gone when that happened. Our plan was in place, the target was out, and it was time. But when Madison turned to me, I couldn't help but feel a flutter in my stomach.

"How about you?" she asked.

Was that a purr I detected in her question? A honey-laced tone from the ice queen? It made me tingle to the tips of my fingers and I shook them to make the sensation go away.

Focus.

"I'm ready, Your Majesty," I said.

I stood and turned away from her so she wouldn't see the look on my face because what Madison didn't know was that both plans were ready. Spider and I had made a plan to steal the book once we got to our post-heist rendezvous situated in a motel a few towns over from Mandy Lake. I glanced at him and he nodded, almost imperceptibly.

Bree made a quip that I missed and Madison laughed, and part of me shriveled. It was the weak part, of course, the part that always fell for the wrong woman. I couldn't help but throw a look over my shoulder, to see the ice queen's rare smile. She winked in my direction and it sent a dart of uncertainty through me.

No. The plan is the plan.

This week had actually been kind of fun and Queen Madison had actually been loosening up a bit toward the end of our surveillance party. But this was it. Our fun was ending. In just a few short hours, the only thing Madison would feel for me was hate.

———

"I can't believe you insisted on bringing *her*," Madison stage-whispered to me in the empty house.

Thankfully, Talia was in her own world, walking ahead of us and examining every crevice of Rutherford's house. Bree had turned off the alarm systems and unlocked the door, and she was in the car with her laptop open just in case we came upon any more digitally locked doors. Spider was with her, and Tank was outside, somehow blending his bulk into the topiaries.

"You won't regret having her," I said to Madison.

"You could have warned me beforehand, at least," she said, her snappy tone back. "You know I hate changes of plan."

"You would have fought me on it and you wouldn't have let her in."

"Can you blame me? She freaked out at our last job. She's a liability, Cass."

"Shh. Please just trust me on this—we need her. She's got the layout of the house memorized from the blueprints, and she has an eye for detail," I said. "And keep your voice down."

If Talia knew she wasn't wanted, she *might* be a liability. I needed her mind to stay clear and her perception sharp. That was where she was most useful. It was bad enough that she was obviously falling in love with Tank. Love messed people up and I couldn't help wondering whether it would eventually cloud her perfect memory.

Madison took a breath as if to double down on her arguments, but I stopped short, placing a hand on her arm and letting Talia move noiselessly up the curving mahogany staircase. "Can you believe the architecture in this place?" I asked, letting my voice go a little seductive. "I mean, the house can't be *that* old, but the detailing is just... you don't see this in modern houses."

"What?" Madison asked, her eyes still on Talia.

"I just thought I'd point it out, since you have an appreciation for architecture." I smirked, remembering fondly the night Madison showed up at my place drunk. It seemed so long ago, and maybe she'd been too drunk to get the joke. I let it slide. "This guy must have tons of dough. Maybe we should—"

Madison turned her gaze on me, stirring up all kinds of dust that had settled on my heart. She was beating me at my own game. "Don't even say it. We're sticking with the plan. Get the book, get out. Don't touch anything else."

"I'm just kidding. Gosh." I rolled my eyes. She continued up the stairs and I followed.

"Good."

"Though I'd love to see this guy's bedroom. What

do you think? Canopy bed? Or one of those Viking ships? A sleigh bed?"

"Will you shut up for three seconds?" Madison snapped. "I can't remember the layout of the house with you babbling in my ear."

"That's what Talia's here for," I said. "Relax."

I didn't mention that I had also memorized the floor plan, or that the house wasn't *that* big. We had hours if we needed them, and we'd find the room eventually. I just did as she asked, and when she reached the top of the stairs and Talia was no longer in sight, Madison hesitated. "Where did Talia go?"

I stopped behind her. The hallway was empty and the silence of the house throbbed in my ears. The darkness was only lifted by shafts of blue-tinted moonlight streaming in through the windows at both ends of the long hall. Talia was nowhere to be seen and all I could do was hope she wasn't having another breakdown in one of the many rooms.

"She's just scouting ahead," I said. For all I knew, that was true, and I didn't need Madison questioning Talia's right to be here again.

"Should we wait here?" Madison asked. She was buying it.

"Yes," I said. If Talia didn't come back in a minute or two, I'd go looking for her. In the meantime, I would stand here and let Madison think she was still in control.

In the stillness, I could sense every curve of Madison's body. I smelled her coconut shampoo and could practically hear her heart beating and the shallowness of her breath. In the silence, I wanted to grab her hand. I had an urge to pull her into the nearest room and tell her to forget about the book for an hour or two. We had time.

Suddenly, I wanted to confess my plan, to beg for her forgiveness and tell her I wanted to do this together —for real this time. But there were consequences to indulging weaknesses, and I couldn't keep repeating the same mistakes.

Talia returned before I could do anything rash. She came out of one of the rooms just as I'd predicted, her wide eyes lit by the moon. She paused by a bookcase in the hallway near us, giving it a quick glance.

The window closest to us lit the bookshelf, which was filled with colorful tomes but it wouldn't contain our book. No one would display a book as rare as the Verne in a bookshelf at the top of their stairs. Our book had to be in that climate-controlled addition Spider had found, along with the rest of Rutherford's valuable collection.

Talia finished her assessment of the bookshelf and said, gesturing to the room she'd come out of, "It's this way."

Madison followed her and I brought up the rear. Every step we took brought us closer to that book and I was second-guessing my decision to betray her. She'd been surprisingly generous with her resources this past week, and every time I came near her, I became intoxi-cated by her. Was I falling for this woman, or was she conning me the way I wanted to con her?

This is just a job, I reminded myself.

But somehow Madison had... *gulp*... become human to me. I was beginning to think of her as an equal rather than a target or a conquest. It was tempting to think like that—so tempting—but I had been here before. I'd trusted a woman and she'd betrayed my trust. My parents were the ones paying for that mistake, and I wasn't going to let anyone else take the consequences of my actions—not Talia, Spider, or Henry. Henry needed this money to save his restaurant. Spider and I needed to follow through on our plan.

Talia led us through the room, which made way to an inner hallway at the center of the house. Madison pulled out a flashlight and we walked along in silence until I heard something.

I put my hand on Madison's arm. She stopped and grabbed Talia, who did the same.

"What's that?" Madison whispered as she and Talia both caught the sound—a light scratching sound echoing through the hall.

"Probably only the dog, but let's be careful," I said.

"Dog?" Talia asked, her eyes going wide.

"It's just a poodle," I told her, shooting a sarcastic glance at Madison. She'd practically jumped out of her skin when we met that dog at the fence last week. She rolled her eyes, but then the scrabbling sound increased in speed and intensity, followed by a ferocious bark.

"Poodle?" Talia asked, a quavering quality to her voice. *Please don't start counting.*

"Turn your light off," I hissed at Madison.

The last thing the flashlight illuminated was a glint of fear on her face, and then the dog—no, *two* dogs—rounded the corner and came running down the hall toward us at full speed. My eyes weren't completely adjusted to the dark, but my ears never fooled me. Two distinct barks lashed through the darkness. The high-pitched poodle, and a lower-pitched, gruffer bark.

Talia froze, squeezing her eyes shut as she started counting. The poodle was coming at her, teeth bared, and without thinking, I shoved her out of the way. She stumbled through an open doorway and managed to pull the door closed behind her just as the poodle streaked past and collided with the wall.

Before it could get its bearings, I turned to Madison. I'd expected her to run, but she was frozen, too, and in the darkness I could just make out the whites of her terrified eyes.

"Get the steak out."

Madison didn't move. The big dog, a German Shepherd we hadn't seen on our only camera, was closing in on us and the poodle was shaking its stunned head, getting ready for round two. Madison made a weak attempt to grab for the backpack she wore, but she wasn't moving fast enough. I grabbed her hand and pulled her into the next open room, slamming the door behind us.

A thump followed, the German Shepherd colliding with the door. Then there was scratching and barking. My heart beat in my ears and it took me a moment to realize we were safe behind the thick oak door. Madison was breathing in shaky exhalations and as I went to her, I realized my breathing was shallow, too, as if we were braided together with fear.

Madison was shaking and I pulled her closer. "It's okay. Rutherford isn't home—we saw him leave, which means these dogs can bark all they want. We're okay in here."

She shook her head in response, unable to speak.

It was typical in our line of work to have an adrenaline response, but this was lasting longer than what I considered normal. It also didn't line up with what I knew of Madison so far. Wasn't *she* the one who pulled us out of the bank when the cops were closing in on us? This wasn't about getting caught—this was something else.

"What's wrong?" I asked, forcing my voice to be calmer than I felt. I put my hand on her shoulder. *She has to stop shaking.* "Maddie, talk to me."

"When I was a kid," she finally managed, her voice still uncertain, "we had a German Shepherd. It turned mean one day and bit me." Madison stared at the door as if it were made of paper rather than wood. "My dad put it down with a shotgun in the backyard."

She's scared of the dog.

This I could handle. This was like one of Talia's breakdowns. Hopefully she wasn't having one right now, because I could only deal with one at a time. I wasn't superwoman. Talia was in the next room over and Madison was in front of me, and I had to focus on her.

With both hands, I guided her away from the door, where the dogs were still snarling and clawing. "Just breathe, okay?"

"Where did that dog come from? We only saw the poodle on the feed," she said, her eyes still on the door behind me. "I knew we should have watched longer. Or come back to place more cameras."

"Look at me," I said sternly. I waited for her to do as I said, and when she finally did, even her eyelashes trembled. "We can't plan for everything."

"Why didn't he ever let the German Shepherd out?"

"I don't know. Maybe Rutherford let it out in a different part of the yard, where we didn't have cameras."

"I..." she swallowed.

"I know it's scary, but we were prepared for one dog. Now we just have to take care of two," I reasoned. "We need the steak in your backpack."

"The steak?"

"Remember, you packed it on top of every other gadget we could possibly need?"

If Madison had something to do, maybe it would distract her from her fear. She nodded, swallowed once more, then slid the backpack off her shoulders. She wasn't shaking as much now, and the noise outside was dying down, the scratching becoming a little less intense.

"I knew packing like you were going on a sleepover would help," I joked, trying to calm Madison even more.

"No you didn't," she said, keeping an eye on the door as she sank to the floor and slid her hand into a side pocket of her backpack. "And what kind of sleepover involves lock picking and night vision goggles?"

"The Hartley kind," I said, nudging her with my shoulder as I crouched beside her. She smiled, and my heart fluttered in response. She had a sweet smile that always surprised me with its gentleness. The feeling that I was doing something wrong tried to take control again. This was just like what happened with the cop—except this time *I* was the one doing the betraying.

Madison took out a steak wrapped in butcher paper, with a generous number of sleeping pills jammed into it. I held out my hand. "I'll offer the devil dog its treat. You stay behind me. As soon as he comes through, we'll slip out and trap them in here, okay?"

"Got it," Madison said, handing me the steak still in its paper. I paused to make sure she was ready. Her breathing had returned to normal and she no longer shook. If I concentrated, I could see the pulse in her neck illuminated by the moon and it was still elevated by my count, but no more than it would be if we were... *stop it, Cass. Back to work.*

Madison got behind me, clinging to my back like a late morning shadow, and I cracked open the door. I held out the steak and it didn't take much for the dogs to pick up the scent and start scratching and growling again. I opened the door just wide enough for the dogs to squeeze through, then tossed the steak to the far end of the room.

They both barreled past us, fighting each other for the steak, and I pushed Madison around me, following her into the hall and slamming the door shut.

Our momentum carried us into the opposite wall and we crashed into each other. I could feel her body acutely, her breasts pressed up against mine, and then her arms were around my neck, hugging me.

"We did it," she breathed, a tingle of desire working its way through me. "Thank you."

"Any time, Maddie," I said, my mouth moving involuntarily toward hers.

No. Shaking my head, I loosened her grip on my neck and backed away before I had the chance to follow through with that kiss. I needed space.

I needed clarity.

Talia.

I remembered her in the room next to ours and wondered if she was still counting. I pushed off the wall and opened the door, expecting to find her huddled in a ball in the corner. But she was just standing there, waiting for me to tell her the coast was clear. She stared at me, her eyes white in the moonlight. Still. Calm. My eyebrow raised. She was *fine*. Steadier than I was.

"We took care of the dogs," I said. "They'll be sleeping soon."

Talia nodded, then marched out of the room, resuming our course toward the book. Madison and I followed her and Madison whispered in my ear, "She's so weird."

"She was weirder before Tank," I said, wondering if those words were a compliment or a betrayal to my oldest friend. There was something about Madison that made me want to confide in her, be honest with her.

"He's good for her," she said.

Maybe he was. Maybe love was actually doing Talia good. In any case, I would be crazy to argue because Madison wasn't calling Talia a liability any longer. Nor was she touching me, which was the only reason I was still walking forward with my heart in my chest rather than flopping on the floor.

Talia guided us through the maze of the house, hallways branching off other hallways and winding deeper into the center of the house. She walked without hesitation or mistake until we reached the room where Spider thought the book would be.

The door had an old-fashioned skeleton key lock, probably to match the original hardware on the other doors of the house, as well as a more modern deadbolt. Madison took out her lock picking kit and knelt on the floor. The old lock was no match for her, but it took a few more minutes for her to pick the deadbolt. Ten minutes later, we were in.

The room was a library of what looked like rare books. Each of the four walls was covered with built-in shelving, less expensive volumes standing on every square inch of them. There were a couple of leather chairs to sit and enjoy the collection, and in the center of the room were a couple of podiums displaying Rutherford's most expensive treasures.

Our book stood on the closest podium to the door, his latest acquisition holding the place of honor. Its leather-bound spine was opened to a page in the center of the book where the illustrator had included a particularly beautiful rendering of Captain Nemo's ship, the Nautilus.

The three of us approached it carefully, as if it were a sacred text. I let Madison be the one to pick up the book. I lifted the glass dome it was protected under and Madison pulled a piece of felt out of her backpack, carefully wrapping the book and then sliding it into her bag.

All three of us let out a collective sigh of relief

before Madison said what we were all thinking. "Got it."

I replaced the glass dome, then we went back through the maze of the house and past the room where we'd left the dogs. They were no longer barking, no longer a threat, and we made our way back to the staircase, where Talia hesitated. She was staring at the bookcase.

"What is it?" I asked, sensing nothing.

"There's something different about one of these books." She scanned her finger along the spines without touching them.

"What are you talking about?" Madison asked.

"Talia remembers things," I whispered. "Is something missing?"

"No," Talia said, her brow furrowing. "But I could have sworn this one was an inch to the left. Now there's a space on the right."

Madison scoffed. "I don't know how you could know that. But it doesn't matter. We have the book—let's get out of here."

Talia nodded, then followed me and Madison down the staircase. Something irked me, though. Talia was never wrong about these things. If she said the book had moved, then it had indeed moved. But we were so close to the exit, I decided not to say anything. Maybe one of the dogs had knocked into the bookshelf on its way to us.

But that also bothered me. We hadn't known about that second dog. We really were flying blind here.

We got to the landing. The front door was ten steps away and Madison broke into a jog for the last few steps. I ran after her but behind me, there was an abrupt grating sound, like rock against rock. I turned just in time to see the wall at the base of the stairs swing out like it was on a hinge. It separated Talia from us, blocking her exit.

There was a buzzing, a cry, and then... silence. Nothing. The door swung shut and Talia was gone.

Panic squeezed my heart. "Talia!?"

I forgot all about being quiet—obviously, someone was home and they'd just pulled Talia into a secret passageway. I should have let her go first down the stairs. I should have listened to her, and to my gut. It had never been wrong before, but it was so clouded with Madison and with my own doubt, I had pushed the feeling away.

"We have to get her," I said, running back to the base of the stairs and searching the wall for a seam, but there was nothing—just a stone wall. "There must be a hidden button around here, or a lever somewhere. *Something.*"

I was frantic, and I barely noticed as Madison's arms circled around my waist, pulling me away from the wall. "We have to get out of here."

"I'm not leaving her," I said, fighting my way back

to the wall and running my fingers over every surface. "Give me some light."

The darkness remained. Then out of it, Madison's voice drafted over: "We already lost the book once."

"Are you kidding me?" I shouted. "Give me some damn *light!*"

Then the flashlight clicked on over my shoulder, and I studied the wall, my ears pricked for more sounds, but all I heard was silence.

12

MADISON

"We do *not* have time for this," I growled through my clenched jaw. I had the flashlight clutched under one arm and I was trying to tug Cass away from the wall, all the while my heart hammered in my chest and my mind reeled.

What just happened? Did Talia really disappear into a freaking *hidden passageway?* What kind of funhouse had we stumbled into?

"I know you don't care about your crew," Cass hissed at me as she looked for a seam in the wall, "but Talia's my friend and I'm not leaving without her."

"We're *all* going to get caught if we don't get out of here," I said, still trying to tug Cass toward the door. Right on cue, the tinny alarm on my wristwatch started to beep.

I'd given us thirty minutes to get in and get out, and that damn dog had eaten up at least ten. Picking the lock was another ten, and now this... I was beginning to think the whole job was cursed from the word *go*.

The front door banged open with force and I shrank away from it, but then I heard Tank's voice. "Everything okay?"

"Help me get Cass out of here," I said. Thank God for Tank, who never missed a step and had sprung into action the moment his synchronized watch beeped. No matter the job, no matter the circumstances, that alarm meant only one thing—time for an extraction.

He looped an arm around Cass's waist, lifting her off her feet with ease whereas I'd spent the last sixty seconds pulling and cajoling her to absolutely no effect.

"Where's Talia?" he asked.

"She's in there!" Cass pointed at the wall.

If my heart wasn't beating so hard and my adrenaline wasn't flowing so powerfully, I might have laughed at the visual—she was beating on Tank's arm and kicking her legs in the air like an angry badger while Tank just held her, immovable.

"What do you mean?" he asked.

"Somebody's in the house," Cass explained breathlessly. "Rutherford, maybe. He snatched her. There's a hidden door there!"

I saw a moment's hesitation in Tank's expression. *No, damn it, you're the extraction guy. EXTRACT US.*

Then he sprang into action and I felt a wave of relief—or at least a low tide of relief, given the fact that we were still standing in the foyer of a mansion belonging to a man we were burgling and who, apparently, had outfitted his house with secret passageways and guard dogs. Through the open front door, I heard sirens in the distance.

Shit.

Tank grabbed my hand, carrying Cass and dragging me along as we headed outside.

"No," Cass was screaming, loud enough to wake the whole damn neighborhood. "Let me go. We can't leave her!"

"I'm not," Tank barked as he put her down in the driveway. Spider and Bree were waiting in our getaway car and Tank looked into Cass's eyes. "I'm gonna get her back."

Then he ran back into the house and I was the one doing the screaming—or scream-whispering at least. "Tank, get back here. It's not safe!"

But he was gone, the front door closing behind him. Bree came around the car and put her hand on the small of my back, pointing me toward the back seat of the unassuming black sedan. Spider then got out of the driver's seat and put his hand on the back of Cass's head as he pushed her into the car like a cop on a police procedural show. Cass had gone quiet now that Tank had gone back for Talia, but her eyes were still wild.

"Come on," Spider said, getting back in the car. "Somebody called the cops."

He was right—the sirens were getting closer and it wouldn't be long before they were at Rutherford's house. How the hell had this happened? We watched Rutherford leave every single night, and between the six of us, there had been eyes on the house every hour for a week—no one else ever came in or out of the house.

A chill ran down my spine as a new thought occurred to me. *Did he know? Had Rutherford been watching us? Had he seen us place the camera? Was he waiting for us?*

As Bree slid into the passenger seat and Spider took the wheel, I took a risk. Cass had been nice to me when that dog came out of nowhere, after all. I put my hand on her knee, trying to comfort her. "Talia's going to be fine. Tank's great at what he does or I wouldn't keep him around."

Cass stared straight ahead, her eyes unblinking as the car started rolling. She didn't acknowledge me and her expression was blank as we passed under the streetlights.

"We did what we had to," I assured her. The car jolted as Spider hit a curb going about thirty miles an hour and I felt my butt lift off the seat a little. When gravity pulled me back down, it dragged my hand further up Cass's thigh.

I pulled it away quickly, feeling momentary warmth in my core. This was no time for thoughts like that, especially when Cass's mind was somewhere else.

As we turned the corner off of Carraway Lane, a couple of black and whites came up the street toward us, their lights flashing, and Spider slowed to a casual crawl. *Nothing to see here, officers. We're just out for a midnight drive.*

Then the street was dark again and I was acutely aware of Cass's shallow breaths.

"You don't have to worry," I said quietly, bowing my head so that my mouth was near her ear. "Tank will get Talia. He's never failed before and he won't now. This is exactly why we set a rendezvous point—they'll meet us at the motel and everything will be fine."

And we have the book, I thought. *Finally.*

Cass didn't say a word. It was as if she had left her voice back at the house. She seemed empty. Like a switch had turned off in her mind. And I had no idea how to turn it back on again.

S pider pulled into the gravel parking lot of the motel about thirty minutes later. It was two towns over from Mandy Lake, far enough to be outside the immediate search radius of the police and lax enough in their rental policy to take cash, but not so far that it would be hard for Tank and Talia to catch up to us.

The motel looked like it had been transported directly from the 1970s, two stories of pastel-colored stucco rooms arranged in a U-shape, with an indoor swimming pool that must have been the height of luxury several decades ago. I stayed in the car with Cass and Bree while Spider ran into the office to rent a room, and Bree turned around to look sympathetically at Cass.

"Is she okay?"

Cass sat upright and straightened the flyaway hairs that had come out of her ponytail. "I'm fine. In fact, if Tank doesn't get here with Talia in the next five minutes, I'm going back myself."

"No, you're not," I started to object, but then Spider was back with the room key and Cass shut down again.

Spider backed the car into a spot as close to our motel door as possible, around the back side of the motel where it wasn't visible from the road. Then he and Bree escorted us into the room, overplaying the bodyguard act as if they expected Cass to make a break for it. I slung my backpack over one shoulder and followed the three of them inside.

The room matched the exterior of the motel, a sunny yellow nightmare straight out of Mid-Century Modern magazine, but it was surprisingly large. Bree sat down at a round pedestal table in the corner and pulled her laptop out of her bag to check on our surveillance camera.

If the job had gone as planned, we would have grabbed that on the way out and no one would have known we were ever there, except for the empty pedestal in Rutherford's library. The chances of Tank having time to grab it after he extracted Talia... slim to none.

Spider walked around the perimeter of the room, checking everything out as if he suspected it had been bugged.

"I have to pee," Cass said, her voice even, almost monotone. I'd never seen her eyes so expressionless before.

I watched her go into the bathroom at the back of the motel room and sank down on the edge of the bed, ready to catch my breath for the first time since Talia disappeared. But Cass closed the bathroom door a little too hard and my ears pricked as I heard the lock click into place.

Shit. She's going to bolt.

I made a lunge for the door, knowing that it was already locked but trying anyway. I knew she was heading for the bathroom window because that's what *I* would have done if I were her and Donnie was in Talia's place.

"What?" Bree asked, alarmed.

"She's making a run for it," I said. "Spider, go around the outside and catch her if she comes out the window—it's not safe to go back to that house."

"I know," he said. "The cops'll be crawling all over it by now."

I heard the window sash creaking upward on the other side of the bathroom door and praised whoever made the decision to neglect renovations for the last four decades. The old building had probably shifted and settled over the years and it sounded like Cass was having trouble with the window.

I dropped to my knees and pulled the lock picking kit out of my bag. I made quick work of the cheap motel lock—much easier than the deadbolt in Rutherford's house, or the safe deposit locker in the vault. When I got the door open, Cass was standing on an avocado green toilet and attempting to squeeze through a ten-inch opening that she'd managed to make in the double-hung window. I kicked the door shut behind me and grabbed onto her hips, dragging her back into the room.

"What the hell?" she snapped, ready to go angry badger on me next.

I spun her around and put my hands on her shoulders, forcing her to look me in the eyes as I said, "I know you're worried about Talia and I admire your dedication to your friend." *More than a friend?* I wondered, narrowing my eyes as I studied her. But I pushed the thought from my mind. "However, you're going to have to trust *my* friend to extract her—going back now is only going to get everyone in more trouble. Take a deep breath." She looked at me with fire in those almond eyes. There was the Cass I knew. I repeated myself. "Do it—deep breath."

We breathed together, my hands rising with Cass's shoulders. Then she let out a long exhale and said, "I know you're right. It's just that I've been looking after Talia for so long. It feels like I failed her."

"It was out of your control," I reminded her. The eye contact was beginning to feel inappropriate—intimate—so I said, "Come on, sit down."

I pushed her shoulders and she sank to the bathroom floor without much prompting. I sat next to her, our backs against the matching avocado green bathtub, then I took her hand.

"I *do* care about my crew, by the way," I said.

"Huh?"

"In the house, you said I didn't care about them," I said. "Did you know that I've known Tank since I was ten years old?"

"No," Cass said, looking at me with curiosity. At least it wasn't anger anymore, or panic, or those dead eyes I'd seen in the motel room. At least it was *something*.

I took a deep breath of my own. Opening up didn't come naturally to me, but it seemed like she needed to hear this right now.

"It was the first time Child Protective Services took me and my brother out of the house. He was only six and we were both terrified when we got placed in a foster home that was already packed with kids. That was the first time I felt like I couldn't protect Donnie, and then I met Josh—err, Tank. He was a little older and he'd been in and out of the system a lot more than us. He made sure we were both okay. That's how I know he's going to make sure Talia's okay, too."

Cass put her head in her hands.

We sat in silence for a minute, and then she lifted her head and gave me a shadow of a wry smile. "Tank's real name is *Josh*?"

"You can't let him know I told you that—it just slipped out," I said. "He'd never forgive me."

Cass laughed and said, "I wonder if Talia knows."

"I'm serious, Cass," I said. "Forget I told you that."

"Your secret's safe with me," Cass said, and this time when she looked at me, there was softness in her eyes. I felt calm spreading across my chest and a warmth building in my right thigh, which happened to be pressed up against hers on the floor.

She started to lean toward me.

I wanted to lean toward her.

She just loved to tease me though. If I kissed her right now, she'd probably laugh and roll her eyes, then tell me how easy I was to manipulate. I looked away and said, "And don't think I didn't notice that you called me Maddie back there. I do *not* do nicknames."

"But Queen Madison is okay?" Cass teased.

"That's not a nickname," I said. "It's a title."

13

CASS

Madison sat with me on that bathroom floor for what felt like hours, but by her watch was only one hour. While normally I would be the one filling the space with stories or jokes, my mind could only focus on Talia and how I'd failed her. I imagined her in a dungeon being tortured by a sick fuck of a man—a man we'd obviously misjudged. I imagined Rutherford dismissing the police so he could do all sorts of things to get our identities out of Talia, and get his stolen book back. It involved sharp objects and severed fingers. Talia would try to resist, but she could only take so much.

Madison was the only thing that kept me from going out of my mind as we waited. She told me stories about her brother, about their relationship as kids.

"Things were actually pretty good when Donnie was a baby," she said. "Our mother got clean for a few years and she was actually a good parent. I remember her teaching me how to tie my shoes, and even at that age, I was surprised by her patience. Our dad was always the more unstable one, but he could be fun, too. One time when I was six and Donnie was two, Dad came home with a puppy—totally out of the blue."

Her expression darkened unexpectedly and it pulled me out of my own thoughts. I studied Madison's eyes and asked, "The German Shepherd?"

She swallowed hard. "Yeah. It grew up into a dog, and it was just one responsibility too many. Things got bad again after that."

I wanted to ask more, to locate the strength I could see running beneath those painful memories, but I could tell she was getting to the limits of her openness for the moment. So I said, "My childhood was a bit different. It was all about how to get past—"

A dull thump sounded outside. The motel door. I met Madison's gaze—she'd heard it, too. I didn't even finish my sentence. I jumped from the floor and ran into the room.

Talia was coming through the door, walking on her own two feet and holding Tank's hand... *and she had all her fingers*. In fact, she looked perfectly healthy, not a scratch on her. I crossed the distance to Talia and wrapped her in a hug so tight I thought I heard her ribs crack.

"You're all right!" I exclaimed.

"I'd be—better—if—you—let go," she choked out.

I loosened my grip reluctantly, releasing her.

"Thank you," she said, and gave me a smile. A *smile*. After what she'd been through.

I grabbed her free hand, not wanting to ever let it go again, and Tank released his hold as I pulled her toward the peach velvet couch and we sat on its springy cushions. "Tell me everything," I said, holding her hand in my lap. "What happened?"

Madison had followed me into the room and stood with her arms crossed over her chest at the end of the couch. She didn't look overjoyed or even particularly happy—she was back to poker-faced Madison.

But that didn't matter because Talia was back.

"I was afraid you were gone for good," I said, feeling pressure build behind my eyes.

Talia let out a long breath and slanted a look at Tank, who came and sat beside her, never taking his gaze off her. "Tank saved me," she said, her voice melting into breathy air.

"What did Rutherford do to you?" I asked.

Talia looked down, blinking twice. My eyes kept scanning her face for signs of trouble, signs of a melt-down brewing, but there was nothing. It was a miracle. "When the wall opened, I was about to scream and then my body tensed up, like a whole-body muscle cramp. It was awful."

"That was probably the buzzing I heard. He must have tased you," I said. "Do you remember what happened next?"

"By the time I opened my eyes again..." She swallowed hard. "I was pinned up against a rock wall in a narrow hallway and a man was looking into my eyes." She paused. I'd almost never heard her say so much, so I barely moved, hoping she would keep speaking. "It must have been Rutherford."

"How?" Madison asked. "We saw him leave."

"Maybe it was a setup," I said. "Go on, Talia. Finish your story."

She nodded. "I heard a banging sound behind him. Loud. Then Tank came in like a superhero and carried me out." The admiration in her voice was obvious.

"Rutherford tried to tase me, too, but he missed," Tank said. "I didn't stick around long enough for him to try again, but I saw him run down a flight of stairs at the end of the hallway. Must have been a secret entrance to the basement or something."

"He wants this book bad enough to challenge *Tank*?" Bree mused from her place at the table. Even as she said the words, her eyes didn't budge from her laptop. "I've been trying to figure out how he gave us the slip. He must have been watching us all along, but we *saw* him leave."

"Maybe he has an evil twin," Madison said.

Frankly, I didn't care if he had cloned himself and there were a dozen Michael Rutherfords scurrying through the walls of that creepy house. We were done with him. We had the book and we never had to see

141

him again. I squeezed Talia's hand once more. "That's it? You're okay?"

"I'm fine," she said.

I should have been overjoyed by this, but my initial excitement was settling into a different feeling. A dull ache in the center of my chest, dragging it down like a kettlebell attached to my sternum. Something was still off, still wrong. Ignoring my gut had led to Talia's capture, and I wasn't going to ignore it again. "You're sure?"

"How did you get here?" Madison asked, her question directed at Tank.

"We took side streets and walked out of the lake region to the main part of town. Picked up the last bus out of Mandy Lake and convinced the driver to drop us off a few blocks over."

Madison nodded. "And what about the police?"

"We got out just before they arrived. They didn't see us."

Madison nodded slowly again, her shoulders dropping.

That feeling was only getting worse as the conversation continued and I couldn't figure out why. We had the book. Talia was here, unharmed. And I was sliding headfirst into miserable. "What else?"

"Sounds like we should celebrate," Spider said. He bounced off the wall on which he'd been leaning silently and crouched at the minibar.

"They charge you through the nose for that stuff," Madison said.

"Who cares?" I let go of Talia's hand. She was staring into Tank's eyes. So much had changed in so little time. Maybe that's what I was feeling. The change in the air. Maybe I should just relax. "My treat," I said, standing up.

The alcohol would at least help me forget the feeling of dread hanging over me.

Spider pulled out a tiny bottle of clear liquid and a tiny bottle of amber liquid. "Wow, they sure go all out in this place. Who booked it?"

"It had good reviews on TripAdvisor," Bree said, still not looking up from her laptop. "I'll take a drink, if you're offering."

"You're going to have to fight me for it." Spider unscrewed the cap of the amber liquid. He took a swig and ran a hand through his dark, ragged hair. "Someone's going to have to make a liquor run."

"According to Maps, there's a store right down the street at the corner," Bree said.

"I'll go," I said, finding the room suddenly stifling. Small, even.

"It's too dangerous," Tank said. "We should be moving on."

Spider rolled his eyes. "The police will set up perimeters around Rutherford's house. It's best for us to stay here for a while. This place has no cameras and I used a fake name to rent the room. As long as Cass doesn't scream *I robbed Michael Rutherford* on her way to the liquor store, we should be fine."

"Then it's settled," I said. "I'm going. I'll be stealth."

"I'm going, too," Madison said. "In case you need backup."

"With the book?" Spider asked, gesturing to the backpack still slung over her shoulder. "No way."

Madison glanced at me, something searching in her eyes, and then she shrugged the backpack off her shoulders, laying it carefully on the edge of the bed. She fixed Spider with a warning glare and said, "Fine. I've got Tank and Bree to look after it in case you try anything."

"It'll be fine," I said, eager to get out of the room. I could feel my energy draining and I needed the fresh air.

"Here, take the room key," Spider said reluctantly, handing it to me.

"We'll keep an eye on the news," Bree offered, picking up the remote from the kidney-shaped coffee table and turning on a news channel. So far, nothing about any robbery appeared. It was safe to go to the liquor store and I high-tailed it out of there like a jackal was on my heels.

W hat the hell was this feeling? Regret?
Anxiety? My conscience coming into play for
the first time in twenty-two years? I walked fast down
the road with Madison jogging to catch up. *Oh, no.* In
all the mess with Talia, I suddenly realized I'd
forgotten to call off the double-cross with Spider.

But Tank had just pulled Talia out of Rutherford's
grasp. Everyone had been through enough—they didn't
deserve that now. And after all that sharing Madison
had done, I couldn't go through with it. I just couldn't.
It wasn't right.

I pulled out my phone and shot a quick text to
Spider before Madison caught up to me. *Hold off on
book for tonight.*

That should do it. Spider's phone was attached to
him like an appendage. He would see the text, and he
would listen. I hoped.

"Hey," Madison said as she put her hand on my
arm to slow my pace. "What's the rush?"

I put the phone away quickly and shrugged, trying
to be casual. "No rush—just eager to get the party
started."

We were alone on the road, an insignificant two-
lane highway with a few old buildings dotting it on
either side. As we walked, I barely noticed the night
sky, and as the liquor store with its bright neon sign
appeared in the distance, Madison surprised me.
"Thank you."

It was a genuine sentiment, with none of the biting sarcasm she was so fond of. I looked at her. "For what?"

"Helping me get the book," she said. "You were right—two crews were better than one for this particular job."

"You and your crew don't mind splitting the money?" I asked.

"It's not about the money for me," she said.

Her storm cloud eyes welled with emotion and all the walls that Madison worked so hard to keep up seemed to be crumbling away. She was being honest with me. Why?

"This is my last job," she said. "I'm going straight as soon as we give that book back to the museum it belongs in."

"You, going straight?" I asked. I shook my head. "That's a damn shame."

Madison smiled at my joke, and in any other moment, I might have felt the first tingle of desire building in my core at the way her eyes lingered over my lips. But there was that bad feeling again, a tightness in my chest.

Oh Christ... it was guilt.

It wasn't like me to go back on a plan. I should just take the book and run, let Spider carry out his plans, but something was stopping me this time. Before I had a chance to delve into that particular feeling, Madison pulled open the liquor store door and I stepped inside, squinting in the harsh fluorescents. I headed for the hard stuff, pushing our conversation out of my head.

"I hope you're not one of those cotton candy vodka-type people," I threw over my shoulder.

"No way." Madison lifted a bottle of Glenfiddich. "I'm more of a Scotch whiskey girl."

"Now you're speaking my language," I said. "Let's grab some tequila and a mixer while we're at it. Can't have a party without tequila."

I heard my words and their snarky tone, but it felt like they were coming out of someone else's mouth. It was like I'd been transported to an alien world that was shaped like ours and sounded like ours and smelled like ours, but it had a different, not-quite-right feeling to it.

I paid for the drinks, snatched the brown bag and started back, the silence overtaking us again when we hit the road. Half a block later, I pulled out the tequila. "Can you hold this?"

"Sure." Madison took the bag from me, watching me warily. She didn't trust me. She had a right not to trust me. I couldn't even trust *myself* in that moment. I felt shaky and a little unhinged.

Alcohol would make that better.

I took the bottle from her, unscrewed the top and swigged. It burned a path down my throat and I coughed, thumping my chest.

"You're going to get us arrested for drinking in public," Madison said quietly. "I've never been arrested."

"Seriously?" I asked, arching an eyebrow at her. "How is that possible?"

"Not once," Madison said. "Fifteen years in the business and don't get me wrong, I've had my fair share of close calls... but I've never been arrested. And I don't plan on starting now."

Then she snatched the bottle out of my hand, trading it for the bag she was carrying. I thought she was going to close it up and tell me to wait until we got back to the motel, but she tipped back her head, drinking an impressive amount, then wiped her mouth without gagging or coughing.

"You are... not what I expected," I said. No, in the moments where she let down her guard she was stunning. Surprising, in a good way. "I can't believe you want to give all this up."

"It will be worth it if it means I can get my brother back," she said. "He's the only family I have and you'll do a lot for the people you love." Then she narrowed her eyes at me and asked, "What about you? Are you in love with Talia?"

"What?" The question was so ridiculous I would have laughed except for the seriousness of those gray eyes and the slight pout of Madison's lips. "No, of course not. It's never been like that."

"You've been such a mess since she disappeared. I thought..." Madison trailed off, letting the bottle of tequila swing by her side. "I figured you'd be over the moon now that Talia's safe and we've got the book, too. What's going on with you?"

Something a whole lot more complicated than I could explain.

For one, Tank and Talia weren't the only ones who were hitting it off. Madison and I clearly weren't enemies any longer. We'd progressed through the teasing stage to friendship, and I found myself in that moment hoping... ridiculously... there would be something after all this. It was the biggest reason I had texted Spider to call off the double-cross. I wanted to explore what could be. To give us a chance.

I'd drawn a parallel between the time I'd been with the cop and this time, but this was different. Madison was a pro. I was older now, and everything in me told me she was genuine, unlike Laura. I had to start being honest with her. Honesty formed the bedrock of relationships, right? Or so I'd heard. I slid my hand over the top of hers and took the tequila.

"I'm the one who got my parents arrested." Shame burned in my cheeks. I couldn't look at her as I spoke, couldn't bear to see if judgment was in her eyes. But there it was... my big secret.

"I'm sure you didn't really—"

I didn't let her finish. "Yes, I did. I was dating... fell for... an undercover cop and didn't know it. I brought her right to them. Delivered Bill and Brenda Hartley— the most wanted jewel thieves in the country—on a diamond platter right into the hands of the law."

If Madison had laughed, I wouldn't have blamed her. I *had* made an awful joke. Not only that, but my foolishness was laughable. I deserved scorn at the very least. I took a swig of the tequila to calm my jittery nerves.

Madison didn't laugh. Instead, she snaked her arm around my waist and pulled me to her side. "Everyone makes mistakes," she said during our awkward, sideways hug.

"Not you, Your Majesty."

"Even me. All the time. You've heard some of mine. I never should have let Donnie walk out of my life for the last decade," she said. "Plus, that was five years ago, right? You were only seventeen. A kid."

"And my parents are still paying for it." I shook my head. Madison kept her arm around me and laid her head on my shoulder. Why was she doing this? Why was she being so nice to me even after what I'd just told her? She wouldn't if she knew my original plan was to double-cross her. She would hate every inch of me.

But each moment, my body melted further under her touch. We were approaching the motel again, but I didn't want to go back inside yet. I stopped just outside the door marked *Pool*.

"Do you think the water's warm?" I asked. I both wanted and didn't want her to answer. An image of her pulling off her shirt flashed through my mind and burned my cheeks.

Thank God for the warmth already there from the tequila.

"I don't know. Do you want to see?" Madison asked. Her lips parted. They looked so juicy I wanted nothing more than to find out if the tequila lingering on them would taste any sweeter when I kissed it away.

She took my hand and pulled me through the glass door to the pool. The smell of chlorine assaulted my nose. The water was still and quiet, and there was no one else around. I propped up the liquor store bag in the corner and turned to Madison. She looked so sweet, so vulnerable, pushing a tendril of her auburn hair behind her ear. Her eyes, her mouth, *everything* a question.

A question my body answered. No longer able to resist, I rushed to her and took her face in my hands, kissing her, tasting the tequila on her lips. It was better than I imagined. Warmth surrounded us as I gently pushed my tongue against her mouth. Her lips parted, her body melting into mine. All lingering questions drifting away.

My hands ran under her shirt, over the flat expanse of her stomach. I was chasing down a need I had barely acknowledged, running from something that was still on my heels. She kept up with me, her quickening breath paralleling mine.

I broke away only to tug her shirt over her head. She did the same and we came back together with a crash. Had it ever been this way with anyone else? Not that I remembered. Not even the cop. There had always been a space between me and my partner of the moment, a space where I was watching. But with Madison, there was nothing. No air, no third-person monologue, just skin warming to the touch and a rush of blood to all the right places.

My fingers skimmed over her thin silk bra, the hint of a raised nipple underneath. Madison moaned, then murmured against my skin, "I want you. *Now.*"

I pulled back. I had to look into her eyes to believe it, that perfect little Madison could want me as much as I wanted her. Madison held my gaze. Her cheekbones were flushed pink. Her eyes reflected the blue of the water next to us, like clouds parting to reveal a blue sky. A row of goose bumps rose on the flesh of her arm and part of me wanted to find a towel to wrap around her.

Another, stronger part of me wanted to find other ways to warm her up.

14

MADISON

The tequila was running through my veins and under more sober circumstances, the little voice in the back of my mind saying, *What? Why would you say that?!* might have screamed a bit louder when Cass pulled away from me.

But I could still feel the ghosts of her fingers on my breasts, my head was cloudy with desire, and all I wanted was to hear her answer.

"Well?" I challenged. "What are you going to do about it?"

I kept waiting for her to grab one of the liquor bottles, take a long drink, and show me that I was reading far too much into this whole situation. She was playing with me, teasing me as always.

But she didn't, nor did her smoldering eyes leave mine. My body moved of its own accord—while I was focused on the pounding of my heart and the unreadable expression on Cass's face, my hand took hers and put it back over my breast.

That was all it took to break the spell, and then we were groping frantically and clumsily at each other. I yanked her sports bra over her head and threw it on an ancient lounge chair along the wall, then bent to bury my face between the swell of her perfect, small breasts.

Cass let out a low moan that echoed across the ceiling of the pool room and over the water. It sent shock waves all the way through my body and into my core.

If she'd told me that first day we met in the bank that all our efforts would lead us here, I would have written it off as just one more instance of Cass Hartley bravado. But now that it was happening, I couldn't deny that it was all I wanted—even more than the Verne book in this moment.

"Come here," Cass said with a shiver as I swiped my tongue over her nipple.

She put her hands on either side of my face and pulled me back up to meet her gaze. There was something commanding about that look, like she and I both knew without a doubt that she'd turned me to putty and I was at her mercy.

She was still looking at me like that when her hand slipped beneath the waistband of my pants and ventured between my thighs. It was a look that said, *I own you,* and for once, I had no objections.

I unbuttoned my pants, clumsily shimmying out of

them in the singular desire to feel my body pressed against Cass's, naked and bare. She did the same, all of our clothes ending up in a heap on the lounge chair, and then she pulled me to her, our bodies entangling.

It was heavenly.

A new wave of warmth washed over me—this time it *wasn't* the tequila—and I relaxed into the moment. It was just me and Cass beside a slightly run-down pool, with no more excuses to pretend we hated each other. When I looked into her eyes, it felt like she actually saw me—the real me.

And then those honey-brown eyes went wide and she froze.

"What?" I asked.

"Shh!" Cass hissed, hugging me close as she looked beyond me to the door.

I turned and saw a man walking past it. My heart stopped for an instant, expecting the police to burst in while my arms were wrapped around Cass, much like I'd expected them to anticipate all my moves when I was a young thief, inexperienced and unconfident.

But the man was whistling casually, wearing a motel uniform and swinging a keyring around his finger. If that motel clerk turned his head just a little bit, he'd see two naked women in the midst of an indecent act—and then he might call the police. This was dangerous.

"Shit," I whispered as he disappeared, the alcohol making my brain feel like molasses.

"That was a close one," Cass said.

"If he caught us—" I started to object, a dozen different scenarios running through my head. All of them were bad and most of them ended with serious jail time when the police discovered the Verne book in my backpack. That whole door was nothing but a sheet of glass and it had been a tequila illusion to think that there was any privacy here. I opened my mouth to say we should go back to the motel room, but Cass silenced any protest by pressing her lips to mine.

She walked me backward until my back was pressed against the tile wall and we were out of sight of the glass door. And then her hand went between my thighs again. I was wet, eager for her, and my fears immediately melted beneath her touch.

I craved her, needed her, and I let my body take over for my mind.

Cass kept me pinned against the wall, her hand working between my thighs, until I saw stars and the whole world constricted until it was only the space between my legs. Her fingers played over me expertly, like she knew exactly what I needed and took great pleasure in giving it to me, then pulling back, then bringing me closer again in turn.

Her mouth came down to my shoulder, nibbling and then sucking and kissing her way back up my neck. Her fingers slid through my wetness and as she plunged into my depths, my whole body quivered around her. I'd been wanting her for so long—whether

I'd been willing to admit it or not—that I came fast and hard, clinging to her and letting her be the one to keep me on my feet as she pinned me to the wall.

I was panting, trying to catch my breath and not to make too much noise in case the clerk came back. When I finally recovered my senses, I looked up at Cass and there was a huge grin on her face, like she had me exactly where she wanted me.

My body swelled with desire again, this time hungry to return the favor. I wanted to touch every inch of Cass's body, explore her and make her mine.

I reached for her but she stepped back, so I followed her, reaching again. A coy smile played over her lips as she stepped back again, just out of my reach. I advanced again, and on her next step backward, her heel found the edge of the pool.

"Cass—" I started to warn her, but then in a whirlwind, I felt her arm snaking around my waist. She pulled me with her as she fell backward into the pool, water splashing all over the tile floor.

It crashed over my head and I held my breath as we went under the water. I opened my eyes and Cass was still holding me close to her, our bare bodies sliding deliciously against each other beneath the surface of the pool. Her hair was wild like a mermaid's, and when we came back to the surface, I pushed her up against the edge of the pool, determined to make her come just as hard as I had.

B y the time we got back to the motel room, I was feeling warm and happy. The combination of Cass and tequila had me relaxed and content, and I didn't think twice about slinging my arm around her waist as we left the pool room, our hair wet and the brown bag full of booze tucked under my other arm.

"They're going to think we got apprehended," Cass was saying. "We shouldn't have stayed at the pool so long."

"Do you regret it?" I asked, but I already knew the answer from the fawning way she was looking at me. "Anyway, I have a feeling they won't even notice how long we were gone," I said, thinking of Tank and Talia's surprisingly sudden bond. Spider clearly had a thing for Bree in the bank vault, too, and on any other night, the idea of walking back into the motel room to find a make-out party in progress would have annoyed the hell out of me.

Tonight, though, I couldn't think of anything that would spoil my mood.

Cass rapped on the door with one knuckle and when no one opened it, I noticed the voices inside weren't exactly congenial. It sounded like our crews were arguing, and then something thumped against the other side of the door. Not exactly the sounds of passion.

"What the hell's going on in there?" I asked while Cass fumbled for the room key in her pocket.

She unlocked it and shoved the door open, pushing my backpack out of the way—apparently, that was what had been hurled at the door. I picked it up protectively. I was about to yell at whoever had chucked a nearly priceless artifact across the room, but it was utter chaos—Spider and Tank were at each other's throats, yelling over each other so viciously I couldn't even make out their words. Talia was sitting at the table near the window, hunched over like she was trying to fend off another nervous attack, and Bree stood beside her with her arms folded across her chest.

"Hey!" Cass barked, raising her voice above the fray.

Everyone froze. It was pretty remarkable, actually, how commanding she could be when she needed to take charge.

"What's going on?" she demanded, kicking the door shut behind her.

"Why don't you tell us?" Tank asked, then pointed a finger at Spider. "I caught him trying to shove the book into his jacket and leave—Madison, they were going to double-cross us."

My heart dropped into my stomach. I fumbled the backpack open to find that the book wasn't in it—there were just a few tools left over from the Rutherford job. I looked at Cass, whose face didn't exactly exude inno-cence. She looked nervous, or guilty even.

I'm going to be sick, I thought. The tequila was churning in my stomach and my lower lip curled as a wave of nausea overtook me. "You were planning this the whole time, weren't you?"

"No—" Cass started to say, but her tone wasn't nearly so sure as it was just a minute ago.

I looked at our crews, and I felt cold all the way into my bones as my wet hair dripped onto my shoulders. All of it—the flirty looks, what just happened in the pool room, probably even the sob story about her parents and the undercover cop—lies.

Cass Hartley played me, and she played me good.

"It's not like that," Cass tried to explain, sending a withering look at Spider for my benefit. "This isn't how it was supposed to go down."

"How what was supposed to go down?" Talia asked from the table.

"It doesn't matter anymore," Cass said. "Madison, please. Let me tell you exactly what happened."

"Like I could ever believe a word out of your mouth," I snapped. The more I told myself, *Do not turn red,* the more my humiliation was written all over my face. I'd broken all my rules for Cass—she'd worn me down until I thought it was safe to trust her, and it was my own damn fault.

I couldn't even blame her for trying to put one over on me—I'd certainly made it easy for her by playing right into all her seductive looks and clever manipulations. Given Talia's reaction, Cass had even kept it from *her*.

"Where's the book?" I snapped, dropping the backpack along with our liquor store bounty carelessly on the bed. God, it was so stupid to let the book out of my sight!

"Talia has it," Bree said. "Don't worry, I'm watching her."

I noticed for the first time that Talia wasn't covering her ears and trying to shut out the arguments happening around her. She was flipping through the book.

"Don't touch it! Give it to me," I demanded, stomping over to the table. I reached over Talia's shoulder and she knocked my hand away.

"Wait!" she said, picking up the book. She spun around in her chair and held it up. "Look—there's a page missing at the front."

"What?" I asked, my blood running cold.

"The map is gone," Talia said and I looked at Bree, exchanging a silent question—*What do they know about the treasure map?*

"You want the map, too?" Tank asked. I could have throttled him if only I had the guts to step out of arm's length of the book, but I didn't trust anyone in this room except myself anymore.

"Of course," Cass said. "If it's missing that, it's just an old, dusty book. Let me see it, Talia."

She came over to the table and I put my hand on

her chest, holding her back. Half an hour ago, that act would have lit my whole body up with desire, but I was far too sober and far too angry to feel anything other than distrust pulsing through me.

"You can see it from there," I said.

Talia held the book up for Cass to see, pointing to a thin, almost imperceptible sliver of paper at the front binding. She was right—someone had cut out Verne's treasure map.

I had a sudden, nearly irresistible urge to crumble to the floor in a heap of defeat. Cass was right—without that map, the book was nothing but an antique, worth *maybe* a million dollars, and on top of that, I needed the map to repair my relationship with Donnie. Instead of going limp, though, a secondary emotion ran through me and I snatched the book out of Talia's hands, inspecting it.

"How do I know you didn't cut out the map while we were gone?" I asked. "Tank, search her."

"Madison—" he started to object. He wasn't going to do it—he probably thought he loved her, the idiot. How could he not see what was going on?

I gave the book to Bree and grabbed Talia's hand, intending to haul her to her feet and search her myself, but Cass stepped between us.

"That's enough," she said. "Talia would never destroy an artifact like that and I'm not going to let you humiliate her. For all I know, one of your crew has it."

"Fine," I snapped. I stepped into Cass's personal

space and did my best to make myself look intimidating as I said, "Bree, put the book on the table. Nobody touches it and nobody goes anywhere until I figure out who's trying to screw who."

Spider snorted behind me. "From the looks of you two, that part is obvious."

The cold water dripping on my shoulders did nothing to cool the heat in my cheeks and I heard him go over to the bed and open the paper bag from the liquor store. Bottles clinked together, and then he took a long drink.

15

CASS

I'd done a lot of stupid things in my life. Dropping out of college. Sleeping with the wrong women. Trusting that my parents were superhuman and could handle anything. But none of it was as stupid as what I had done to Madison.

From the moment we'd met, she crawled under my skin. She was nothing like the other girls I'd known. Whenever I thought I had her pegged, another facet of her personality would shine, like a gem turned in the light.

Now, her face was a mask of stone, her breathing almost imperceptible. I'd been able to read her body language from the beginning but now it was as if she'd slammed the book shut. Closed the door. Sunk underground. And that was story enough. *I* had no illusions about who was to blame. It was me. *I* had done that. I had turned her to stone.

Tank moved to Talia and they spoke together in hushed tones. Spider kept drinking and Bree gave Madison the book, which she clutched to her chest. The mood in the room was tense enough to snap.

And my tenuous bond with Madison was broken. We'd had so much between us only minutes ago, but now I'd destroyed her trust and for once, I was willing to own up to it. I deserved whatever came next. My wet hair hung heavy around my face, sending shivers down my shoulders and back. My fingers twitched at my side, wanting to do something, but the only thing that could possibly save me was my mouth, and that had gotten me into enough trouble as it was.

"Madison?"

She made no move to acknowledge me.

"Can we speak outside? Alone?"

Madison's eyelids flickered over her stony eyes. I went to her, words tumbling out of my mouth like the rushing of a stream after a spring swell. "I need to explain. I didn't mean to betray you, Maddie—"

"Don't," Madison said, her gaze moving to mine. A tiny hair in front of her face betrayed how she trembled. "Do you think I'm stupid? I know exactly what's happening here."

"I swear," I said, desperate for her to understand. "I swear I wasn't going to let it happen."

"But you intended to steal the book from me?"

Heat flushed my face and mingled with my cool,

dripping hair, creating a swirl of hot and cold that made me feel dizzy, like I was about to pass out.

"Tell me the truth." Madison's body faced the door, though her gaze was fully on me.

I considered myself a decent liar, and the urge to lie bubbled up in me. I could have gotten away with it... maybe. The excuses and explanations already had started to form in my mind. But I didn't want to. I'd started to show Madison some of the real me before, and I wanted her to see all of me now. I wanted her to accept me. As I was.

No one had ever done that before.

I shuffled my feet, wringing my hands. "Yes, I was going to steal the book from you."

Madison rolled her eyes, but I kept pushing through.

"But that was at the beginning. As soon as we got our hands on the book, I decided to call it all off. But then with Talia... I tried to text Spider to let him know... and..."

Madison's mouth curled up in a half-smile that, for the first time, looked almost cruel. "I can't believe this— oh no, wait. Yes, I can." She stepped closer, so close I could smell the chlorine mixed with her coconut scent. "You're the daughter of the most notorious criminals around. Of course you never learned common decency."

"I deserve that," I said, lifting my chin.

"Or truth."

"You're right. My relationship with the truth is somewhat questionable."

"Your relationship with everything and everyone is questionable. The only person you care about is yourself. Didn't you prove that when you chose a woman over your parents?" This comment hissed through Madison's teeth, bitter and poisonous. It seemed to take form and lash against my skin.

The cold overtook the rest of my body, my eyes welling with tears. Her challenges made me want to fight back. Was it true? It *wasn't* true. My parents were one thing, but there were other people in my life. Henry—I cared about him. And Talia, too. My relationship with the undercover cop was just a mistake... Madison had said so herself.

She's only saying this because you hurt her.

"Maddie." I reached out a hand and she flinched. "What can I do to help you trust me again?"

Her nostrils flared as if they couldn't possibly contain her anger. I expected her to lash out, but she didn't. "Nothing," she said. Then, wrapping her arms around the book, she turned toward her crew. "Tank, Bree, pack up your stuff. It's time to go."

"No," I said, though the word caught in my throat. "No, we made a deal."

Madison turned her back to me. "You broke that deal when you decided to betray me. You forfeited your right to the book."

"How do you figure that?" I asked, trying to edge

around her to get her to look at me. Her eyes remained steadfastly pointed at any other object in the room except me.

"That's just how it works," Madison said.

"Says who? The criminal handbook?"

"Always so clever, Cass. I hope that keeps you warm at night. Come on, Bree. Hurry up."

It was all slipping away. The book, and more importantly, Madison. I had to stop them somehow. I touched Madison's arm. "You can't leave. We work better together."

Madison raised a slender eyebrow, but she still didn't look at me.

"We do and you know it," I insisted. "We would never have gotten this far alone. We've been going about this all backward. We should... do some trust exercises or something."

Madison barked a laugh. "We're way beyond that."

She let out an impatient sigh, marched over to where Tank was giving Talia one last lingering kiss and tugged on his arm. The effort was like an ant trying to move a deer. Tank didn't even budge. "Tank, please," she whispered, and I could tell she was barely keeping herself together.

"Fine," Tank said. "I'll get us a car."

He went outside and Madison sighed, then snatched the backpack off the floor where she'd dropped it. As she was wrapping the book carefully back inside its felt covering, she sneered at me and said, "I would say it was nice knowing you, but—"

Suddenly, Spider slid out of the shadows and pressed his gun to Madison's temple. "You're not leaving with that book."

My shock was soon replaced with anger. This was the last thing we needed. "Put. The gun. Down."

My heart thumped in my chest and Madison's face went deathly pale. She clung to the book, like it had magical powers that would protect her. She opened her mouth and closed it again, but no words came out.

Spider's pupils had taken on a look I had never seen. Hard. Pinpointed. And small. He didn't sweat. He seemed calm. Too calm for what he was doing. "Not until she gives up the book."

I, on the other hand, trembled like a scared rabbit. I snatched a glance at Madison, whose face was ashen. Her eyes were as wide as saucers and I could only imagine how she was feeling. "We don't have to resolve this with guns," I said. "Guns have never been our thing."

"Neither was working with another crew, but things change, don't they, Cass?"

It wasn't a question.

My trust in Spider, built brick by brick over years of working together, crumbled in an instant, turning to sand. It threatened to pull me under. He was supposed to be my number two, my dependable man. What was he doing?

Maybe Madison had been right about me and relationships. I'd misjudged Spider, misjudged the
authority I had over him. Why had I thought a text was
enough to call all this off?

I couldn't breathe. Holy shit. This, too, was all *my*
fault. Mine. I had created this mess. And I had to fix it.

Forcing breath into my protesting lungs, I closed
the distance to Madison and Spider, careful not to
move too quickly. When I put up my arm to take the
gun, Spider's eyes jerked to mine. "I swear to God,
Cass, I'll blow her head off if you put one finger
on me."

My hand froze an inch away from his arm. How
had I misjudged him so thoroughly? How had he
changed so much? The Spider I knew would never
have done this... would he? It struck me then, I didn't
really know. I'd never exactly had a heart-to-heart
conversation about his beliefs, or how far he'd go to get
a job done. And we had been drifting apart lately. He'd
been frustrated about Madison and I hadn't listened.

I glanced toward the door, praying for Tank's swift
return. Then I moved my hands slowly and carefully
and placed them on Madison's forearm. If I couldn't
convince Spider to stop, I had to help Madison. Her
skin was as cold as mine, but I kept hold and squeezed.
"I'm so sorry. I never meant for this to happen."

Her eyes drifted to mine, but they were empty. It
didn't matter. I had to show her how I really felt.

I leaned close, my lips nearly brushing her ear.

"None of this would have happened if I'd just let you take the lead."

Madison flinched, and when I pulled back, something had changed in her eyes. She didn't move, but the light in those storm clouds was somehow different. Her gaze softened.

Spider's grip on the gun was firm, but he hadn't shot her yet. That was a good sign. Maybe it meant that he wouldn't shoot her at all, that he didn't have it in him. But I couldn't afford to be totally confident of that. And what was my next step? Only two options presented themselves to me. I could ask her for the book, which would further destroy her trust in me, though perhaps it would save her life. *Give me the book so I can prove to you that I was betraying you all along. Trust me, even though you have no reason to.*

My second option was to wait for Tank. That was the more dangerous option, obviously, since I didn't know how long it would take him to procure a car. In the middle of the night at a remote motel, it could be a while.

I opened my mouth to do the first, but I just couldn't. Nothing I could say would help. Then a third option presented itself to me. I had to take Madison's place.

I wrapped my arms around her shoulders in a hug and twisted us slowly.

"What are you doing?" Spider and Madison asked together, Spider's voice finally betraying a tremor.

"You said not to touch you. I'm not. I'm touching her." I continued to twist, and Spider didn't move until I was the one with the gun to my head. Madison and I were face to face, the book sandwiched between us, and her eyes flicked back and forth between mine. I told Spider, "If you want to shoot her, if you want to get the book, you're going to have to go through me first."

I could feel the gun at the back of my head, hard and cold against my wet hair. His breath was ragged now. Mine had practically stopped. Madison's eyes filled with tears and she was trembling in my arms but I kept my hold tight, trying to tell her with just my touch that it was going to be alright. It was. It *had* to be. It couldn't end here.

I released one hand and wiped a stray tear falling down Madison's cheek, then tucked a strand of hair behind her ear. "It's only us. Don't be scared," I whispered.

Please don't shoot us, I mentally begged Spider. *I have so much more I want to say.*

Just then, I heard the click of the door and I took the opportunity to kick backward. My foot landed in flesh. *Oomph.* The gun disappeared from my head. Adrenaline pumped in my veins and I dragged Madison behind the couch.

"I'm okay," Madison said. I didn't let her go, but I peeked over the top of the cushions, witnessing what I'd hoped would happen. Spider was no match for

Tank, being about half his size. He squeezed off one round, missed, and then Tank had him in some kind of wrestling hold where Spider's shoulder looked like it was about to detach from his body. Tank squeezed Spider's wrist until his hand opened and the gun dropped out. Without letting him go, Tank picked up the gun.

Spider might have been neutralized, but I wasn't. I let go of Madison and charged out from behind the couch. "You son of a bitch! I can't believe you did that."

Spider's face was red. "You betrayed us."

All of my pent-up anger poured out of me. "I did not. You went rogue."

"That book belonged to *us*."

"No, it didn't. Madison has as much a right to it as we do."

"What do you want me to do with him, boss?" Tank asked, barely any sign of strain on his face as Spider fought underneath him. He was talking to Madison, looking over my shoulder at the couch, but I wasn't done.

"Take him somewhere he won't get away until we're done with all this," I said.

"What? Cass. Seriously? I did it for us," Spider said.

"You did it for *you*," I said, coldly. "Tank, you can take him back to my command center—"

"Hell no," Madison said, finally emerging from behind the couch. She looked more like herself now, confident, and it was a relief to see that Spider hadn't shaken her totally off her game, even if she was mad at me. She growled, "Nobody goes anywhere until we figure this out. Tie him to the chair if you have to."

"You're putting me in time out?" Spider spat sarcastically.

"We're done, Spider," I said. "You're no longer welcome in my crew."

Spider blanched at this. "Good. I don't want to be in your crew." I ignored him and he apparently didn't like that. "Cass, you're over-reacting. Just because you fucked—"

"Shut up," Tank growled, jerking Spider quiet. He dragged Spider over to the table and Bree gave up the chair so Tank could throw Spider into it.

Madison stared at me, the book still clutched tight in a hug. I wanted to get on my knees and beg her forgiveness, but instead I stood there, quiet for once. Then Bree cut the tension. "I have some good news."

When neither of us said anything, she showed us her laptop, flipping it around in her arms. "I might have found the missing map. Look."

Madison glared at Spider, then said, "Bathroom— we need privacy."

Bree followed her inside and I grabbed Talia. I half expected Madison to close the door in my face, but she let us in—perhaps a thank you for getting the gun off her head earlier. Madison closed the door and bent toward the computer screen. There was a picture of the Verne book flipped to one of the first pages, with a sliver of paper running down the middle.

"The map was already gone when the book was sold to Rutherford," Bree said softly.

I didn't say a thing. Maybe Madison had recovered, but I needed a moment here.

Bree continued, keeping her voice low so it wouldn't carry beyond the bathroom. "The book had been in the same hands for decades. My bet—the original thief has it in his possession."

I stared at Madison, willing her to look at me. If I saw any accusation remaining in her eyes I would leave. I would walk out of there and forget about the book, and try to forget about her. I deserved that. But I didn't want to do that. I *really* didn't want to do that.

Madison blinked at the screen, then straightened, narrowing her eyes at me.

16

MADISON

She wanted to go after the map. I could see it in her eyes, when all *I* wanted to do was get out of that damn motel as fast as humanly possible. We'd been there too long already.

I was still shivering from my cold, wet hair and yet the bathroom had become tiny, claustrophobic and sauna-like in the last couple of minutes. I could finally catch my breath after Spider had taken that damn gun away from my head, but that didn't make it any easier to stand there and argue with Cass.

How could I ever trust her again? She *had* to have given Spider the gun back, after all, even though she agreed there wouldn't be any guns on this job. I'd seen her lock it in that desk.

I hugged the book closer to my chest, wondering who would stop me if I just made a run for it, wondering if it was even worth it without the map.

176

"We need the map," Cass said as if she could read my mind.

"Forgive me if I'm not eager to go on another adventure with you," I said. "I'm still recovering from the sensation of having the barrel of a gun pressed to my head." *Along with other terribly confusing sensations...* "We'll find a buyer for the book as-is, call this whole thing a loss, and then we won't have to deal with each other anymore."

"We'll only get a fraction of what it's worth without the map," Cass objected, and I didn't like the way Bree was looking at me, either.

"She's right," Bree said softly. She'd turned the laptop back around again and was tapping away with it balanced in the crook of her arm. "We're looking at around a million dollars if we sell what we have. Add the map and we're easily over five million—maybe up to nine."

"A million isn't much split seven ways," Talia pointed out.

"Six ways," Cass corrected. "Spider's out after what he did."

She looked at me hopefully, as if that gesture would make me trust her again. I did a quick tally in my head and said, "Seven ways—I still have to pay my demo guy for his help at the bank."

"That's less than $150,000 a piece," Bree said, disappointment written all over her face. "Hardly seems worth all this trouble."

177

I had to agree with her. It would barely cover the mortgage on my penthouse for the next year. The money from this job was supposed to set me up for a while, give me time to figure out what I wanted to do with my life in the straight-edge world. Maybe I could get my GED and go to college... but not without some capital.

$150,000 was a tenth of what I pulled in last year. A pittance.

Even more importantly, if there was no map, I had nothing to bring to Donnie. Nothing to use as leverage when I made my big plea—*I'm done with the life of crime. I'm sorry I let that stand between us all these years but I used my final criminal act to restore something that you love. Now maybe you can love me again?*

It made my stomach hurt to think about it. I set my jaw and asked Bree, "Where do you think the map is?"

It did not escape my attention that Cass's eyes lit up and my body responded with butterflies taking flight in my stomach. These reactions were not going to fly if we kept working together—I was pretty good at repressing things and the sooner I could forget everything that happened at the pool, the better.

"Pennsylvania," Bree said. "That's where the transaction with Rutherford was processed, and I did some digging in the internet archive. It looks like the police questioned a man named Oscar Duncan back in the 90s when the book originally went missing. He was their primary suspect but they could never establish any hard evidence so they had to let him go."

She turned her computer around again to show us all a mug shot of a man with a salt-and-pepper beard and crow's feet around his eyes.

"He's got quite a rap sheet," she added. "I think he might be one of us."

"A con artist?" Cass asked, examining the photo. I leaned in to do the same—not too close—and Bree nodded.

"He worked at the museum the book was stolen from," she said. "He was only there about six months—a night janitor—and he disappeared as soon as the police gave up their investigation."

"Sounds like our man," I said. Then I frowned. "He looks like he's about fifty in this photo—that would make him around seventy now."

"Yep," Bree said. "Seventy-two. His residence is listed as an assisted living facility in Philadelphia—looks like he got Alzheimer's and his kids put him there a couple years ago."

"Oh, great," I said. "So he's probably a dead end. For all we know, he used the map to wrap a Christmas present years ago."

"Well, we can't leave that stone unturned," Cass said. "Wanna go to Philadelphia with me?"

Her expression was far too optimistic. I scowled at her just to let her know that I was by no means over the whole gun-to-the-head incident, then said, "Yeah. If you think I'm letting you out of my sight for a second before this is over, you really don't know me at all."

"What if I have to pee?" Cass asked, throwing me a flirtatious smile.

How dare she.

"I'll be there to hand you the toilet paper," I said. I marched out of the bathroom and scooped my backpack up, then tucked the book under my arm while I unzipped it.

"What are you doing?" Talia asked as everyone followed me out of the bathroom.

"I'm keeping this until it's all over," I said, my words cutting a little more harshly than they probably needed to. Ordinarily, Talia was easy to intimidate—it seemed like all you had to do was make a loud noise and she'd fall down like a fainting goat—but this time, she didn't back down.

"No way," she said, hands on her hips. She seemed to be drawing her energy from Tank, who had Spider pinned in the chair. Talia said, "If you don't trust us, then we can't trust you. The book has to stay in a neutral location."

Wow, somebody grew a backbone. Tank must have been good for more than just making googly eyes at her during inopportune moments. But she had a point. I sighed and pulled the book back out of my bag. "You're right. What should we do with it?"

We all thought for a minute, then Cass said, "Put it in a safe deposit locker?" I snorted and she said, "No, really. Just look at how much work we had to do to get into the one Rutherford rented. If it makes you feel any better, I'll even let you carry the key."

I looked for holes in her logic, sneaky little ways that she could use a safe deposit locker to screw me over, but she was right—it had taken a pound of dynamite, an oxy-acetylene torch and a lot of conveniently timed circumstances to get into Rutherford's locker.

"Fine," I said. "But Tank stays here and watches Spider like a hawk, and you and I are the only two going to the bank. I don't even want the rest of our crews to know which bank we choose."

"Deal," Cass said, coming over and extending her hand to me. Against my better judgment, I shook it, then spent the next few minutes actively pushing away intrusive memories of how her hands had felt against my body in the pool room.

We moved quickly. I didn't want to spend any more time sitting still and letting Cass spin invisible webs around me than I had to, and the faster we got the map, the less time she'd have to come up with a new way to double-cross me, if that was her game.

The two of us chose a bank at random in a town neither of us had been to before. We waited until business hours and went together to drop off the book, then

I tied the key to a string around my neck. Cass went along with all of this without argument, possibly as some form of penance for what she'd done. I still didn't trust her. The cold metal of the key brought up goose bumps on my skin as I got used to it and every couple of minutes, I put my hand over my chest to make sure the key was still there. I already knew Cass was a good manipulator and a world-class liar. Who knew if her skills extended to pickpocketing?

Bree bought us a couple bus tickets to Philadelphia the next day—two hours that felt an awful lot more like an eon—and before we left, I pulled her into the bathroom of the motel.

"Don't let Talia out of your sight and call me immediately if Spider tries anything with Tank." I paused, shaking my head, and said, "I can't believe I didn't see that betrayal coming."

"You like her," Bree pointed out, as if it was a compliment rather than an insult to my instincts. "And you weren't thinking right with that gun to your head. I was paying attention to Cass and Spider's interaction, and I think she's telling the truth—"

"Just keep an eye on everybody," I growled.

I didn't want to hear it, and it wouldn't matter even if it was true. What was done was done and all I wanted was a quick, productive trip to Philadelphia and back.

Unfortunately for me, Cass had other ideas.

From the moment our butts hit the brightly colored

bus seats, she seemed bent on not allowing a moment's silence to pass between us.

"You haven't really let me apologize to you," she said as the driver lifted the parking break with a hiss and the bus began to roll out of the depot. "Or explain my side of things."

"That's because I don't want to hear it," I said, digging through my backpack for a pair of headphones. I put them in, then put my head back and closed my eyes. Before I'd even had time to identify the song I was listening to, Cass yanked the headphones out of my ears. "What the hell?"

"We've got two hours and you know from the pool that I've got excellent lung capacity," she said with a wink. "The sooner you let me say my peace, the sooner you'll get your headphones back."

"Fine," I said, crossing my arms over my chest to let her know that I was participating in this conversation under duress. It wasn't like she was *really* giving me a choice anyway.

"You were right," Cass said, her tone surprisingly sincere—or at least she was good at faking it. No matter how angry I was, I had to admire her talents. "I *was* planning to let your crew do all the work and then take the book. Can you blame me for working smarter, not harder?"

She was being cheeky now, and I rolled my eyes at her, pressing my lips together to avoid giving her the satisfaction of a smirk. *Do not laugh at her jokes, Madison.*

She went on.

"All of that was before I got to know you, before I knew how important the book was to you," she said, and then she slipped her hand into mine and my cheeks instantly began to burn. She locked eyes with me and added, "And before I started to like you."

What the hell did that mean? If this was another one of her manipulations, then I needed to get a grip because God help me, it was working. Those deep, sparkling eyes... that careless attitude that scared the hell out of me just as much as it thrilled me. *Damn it, Cass.*

"Why didn't you call it off, then?" I asked, making my tone as bitter as possible as I took my hand away from hers. "If you changed your mind, why didn't you make sure Spider understood?"

"This is going to sound so stupid," Cass said, "but I didn't expect things to go like they did between us. I sort of got caught up in the moment. I'm not sure when I went from flirting with you because it was fun to push your buttons, to flirting with you because it was just plain fun. Everything happened so fast, I was worried about Talia on top of it all, and I was struggling to catch up. I've never felt this way about anyone before and I didn't know what to do with that."

She was right about that—my head hadn't stopped spinning since I met her.

"How did he get the gun?" I asked. That was the last piece of information keeping me from giving in to Cass's charisma and those pretty almond eyes. *You better have a good answer.*

"I didn't give it to him," she said. "That was never part of the plan. When I said we don't use guns, I meant it—the lock on the desk drawer was broken, but I didn't think Spider knew that. If I had, I would have moved it somewhere more secure."

"Well, thanks for not letting him blow my brains out," I said. I could feel myself forgiving her, and with those words, my willpower to stay angry melted away.

"Any time," Cass said with a laugh. Then she took my hand again, I let her, and she said, "So, do you want to place bets on just how senile old Oscar is going to be?"

The nursing home where Oscar Duncan spent his days turned out to be much swankier than Cass and I were expecting. I arched an eyebrow at her as we got out of our cab at the marbled entrance to a very large, ornately decorated building on a dozen acres of lush, neatly manicured lawn.

"So he's got money," I said as Cass tipped the driver and then put her hand in mine. "No janitor could afford a place like this. Bree must have been right —he's one of us."

"Good," Cass said. "That means we're on the right track to get the map back, as long as he remembers where he put it and we can convince him to give it up."

"You're just going to have to turn on the charm," I said as I let go of her hand and opened the door to the lobby. "Remember our cover story?"

"I've got this on lock, *big sis*," Cass said with a wink. We'd come up with our plan on the bus.

I nodded, holding the door for her, and then we walked across the finely appointed lobby with all the confidence of a pair of grandkids coming to visit their favorite Grandpa Oscar. I put one elbow casually on the expensive granite counter as I told the woman behind the desk, "I'm Abigail Duncan. My sister, Olga, and I are here to see our grandfather, Oscar Duncan. I called about an hour ago."

Cass raised her eyebrows. *Olga?* she mouthed, a smile dancing all around her lips. I shrugged. Might as well have a little fun while I was pretending.

"Oh, yes," the receptionist said, smiling warmly at us and missing our quick exchange. She looked completely trusting as she picked up her phone and said, "Dana? Oscar's grandkids are here. Is he ready for them?"

I couldn't blame her for her lack of suspicion—how often did people make up lies so they could hang out with the residents of a nursing home? What *had* been lucky was the fact that Oscar himself hadn't sent up any alarm bells when I called from the bus to request a visit. If he had, we would have needed to think of a plan B, and quick. But he hadn't, which meant he might be as senile as Bree described.

A nurse came through a door behind the reception desk a minute or two later, giving Cass and I the same warm, trusting smile as she led us through the wide hallways of the facility to a large day room with activity tables, games, expensive-looking recliners, and a television nearly the size of one wall.

There were about two dozen residents scattered throughout the room, and it was lucky that the nurse walked us right up to Oscar, sitting patiently in a rocking chair near a bank of windows. I'm not sure I could have recognized him twenty years after his mugshot. He was hunched over in his chair, feeble-looking, and his beard had gone from salt and pepper to full gray.

"Oscar, look who's here!" the nurse said, talking to him in an insulting baby voice. "It's your granddaughters, Abigail and Olga."

Moment of truth, I thought as he met my eyes, then Cass's. My heart stopped beating momentarily—maybe I shouldn't have given such a ridiculous name for Cass —and then it started again as Oscar smiled benignly and gestured to a pair of overstuffed arm chairs across from his rocker.

"Have a seat, dears," he said, his voice a little shaky. "Wow—it's been so long, I don't even recognize you."

I shot a cautious glance at Cass, who just smiled

broadly and said, "We're sorry, Grandpa—you know if we didn't live so far away, we'd be here every week."

The nurse smiled, happy to play her part in this family reunion, then wandered away. Cass sat down in one of the arm chairs, leaning back as casual as ever, and it was only when she tugged on my shirt sleeve that I realized I was still standing, displaying my nerves.

I sat, my posture arrow-straight, and Oscar leaned forward as well. He narrowed his eyes at the two of us and the shakiness was now gone from his voice as he asked, "What brings you to see old Grandpa Oscar, my dears?"

17

CASS

I f the old man wasn't faking it, I would go directly from the nursing home and break my parents out of jail. In fact, I would break them out, apologize to them for being a neglectful daughter, and then I would introduce them to Madison over homemade lasagna. *That's* how sure I was that old man Oscar wasn't as senile as he was making himself out to be.

But even as the thought was forming in my mind, his face clouded over, a shade coming down over his obvious intellect.

"We're looking for something, Grandpa," Madison said. "And we're hoping you can help us find it."

I leaned my chin on my hand, faking boredom. The best option at the moment seemed to be to sit back and watch to make sure I was right. It was possible what I had seen was just a *moment* of clarity, after all. That happened sometimes with Alzheimer's patients, though not as often with ones who were supposedly as far along as Oscar.

This waiting had a secondary effect of letting Madison feel like she was in charge again. After what we'd been through, she deserved a bit of deference. She deserved to get what she wanted. I'd already let her keep the safe deposit locker key, though I wouldn't be letting her out of my sight any time soon with it. She may have forgiven me, but that didn't mean she trusted me.

Having her so close, I was aware of her every movement, every shift, every breath. I knew what *I* wanted —to touch her, but I resisted. Madison looked toward me and nodded. Right. We were here for a reason, and it was time for me to start pulling my weight.

"We're looking for Aunt Carol's antique map. Our mother said that you would know where it is. Can you remember, Grandpa?" I said, my voice sweet as honey.

Was that a flicker of a smile at the corner of his lips?

"Carol?" he asked, his voice scratchy and empty of meaning.

"Yes. Your sister, Carol," Madison said. She elevated her voice, enunciating each word carefully and slowly.

"Where is Carol these days?" he asked. Was that a test?

I leaned forward, clasping my hands. "Maine. On the coast. Do you remember coming to visit and swim-

ming in the ocean on New Year's Day with all of us?
The polar plunge?"

Oscar's eyes narrowed to slits before he shuddered
and his neck vanished into his shoulders. His lips
parted, as if to emphasize the point that no one
was home.

Yeah, right, old man.

We weren't just making up random information. In
preparation for the trip, Bree had dug up as much as
she could find. Family tree information, real estate
records, social media accounts, marriages, births,
deaths. It was amazing what you could find online, the
picture of a life you could create when you knew
where to look.

If I was right, and he was of sound mind and recognizing this information, then he must be wondering
who the heck we were and why we were there. He had
every reason to remain vacant and unresponsive. We
were strangers, and strangers who *knew things*. That,
in my experience, never boded well. He probably felt
the same.

"I think he remembers, Olga," Madison said,
breaking me out of my reverie with a hand on my knee.
A warm hand. "Did you see him shiver?"

So Madison picked up on it, too. I decided to stay
in character. "Yes, I did. Mama thought that he
wouldn't be able to tell us where the map is, but I think
he remembers."

"Alright, who are you?" Oscar asked, keeping his voice low but vicious. "What do you want?"

Madison looked to me nervously, then glanced toward a nurse standing at the other end of the room, fidgeting with the remote control for the large flat screen television a couple of the other residents were watching. She leaned toward me and asked, "Do you think we should move this along?"

I smiled, playing into her nerves. "You think it's time to bring out the pliers? You know, I bet Grandpa Oscar *could* use a little dentistry."

I swallowed a laugh at the old man's horrified reaction. He was *not* a con man after all—he had no control over his face. He was probably just a thief who got lucky—maybe more than once by the looks of this facility.

I watched Oscar squirm a little, then I sat back in the chair. "No, I don't think that's necessary." I had another idea. "These are some lovely digs, aren't they, Abigail?" I asked Madison, keeping my voice conversational.

She frowned, but went along with what I was saying. "The nicest nursing home I've ever been in."

"The only problem is that it's so far away from Maine." I never took my eyes away from Oscar, watching for any sense that we were hitting on a topic that meant something to him. "I was thinking we should move him closer to us. They don't have anything nearly as nice where we are—and in any place we could afford, you'd be lucky if you got your clothes changed and a hot meal once a day. But wouldn't it be nice to be closer to family?"

That statement produced no change in him. Madison nodded heartily. "Then we could visit all the time," she said, her voice artificially chipper. "Do you think Grandpa would like that?"

"It doesn't look like he's really taking in his surroundings," I said. "And it would save us a lot of money. I had no idea how much of our inheritance Mama was spending on Grandpa's care until I got here and looked around. Wow."

"We could really use that money, too," Madison said, catching on. "Maybe if she got an anonymous tip that the nurses here were abusive..."

"She'd have no choice but to move Grandpa closer to keep an eye on him," I said.

Oscar's eyes had narrowed on us. Even if he wasn't senile, he had grown soft in his old age, not much more than skin and bones. In the time it would take him to rise from his chair and charge me, I would be out the front door of the facility. His scowling didn't scare me.

The nurse came back to check in on him and as soon as Oscar caught sight of her, he went back to his turtle shell posture. She gave him a cup filled with water, and another with a small amount of cherry red liquid and asked, "Are you tired, Oscar?"

Nothing.

"Just drink that, honey. There you go. That's a good boy."

I swallowed my laugh as the tips of his ears turned pink. Some men wouldn't mind being coddled, but evidently Oscar wasn't one of them. The nurse didn't seem to notice. She watched him take his medicine, then smiled at us before she left.

Now I knew for *certain* he was faking it.

Maybe it was the two days we'd had with little rest and too much excitement, or maybe it was that I just wanted to be alone with Madison again, to hold her hand and work on regaining her trust. She *had* forgiven me on the bus, after all, so maybe there was a *something next* for us after this job ended. Maybe it was all of that making me want to end this conversation.

"Cut the crap, old man," I whispered, leaning close so no one could hear.

He blinked, startled.

"I know you're not sick. Tell us where Verne's treasure map is."

It was a bold move, coming right out and asking for what we wanted. It meant I had shown him my hand—and that was a no-no in the con world. I even felt Madison flinch next to me, as if I had launched a grenade in the room and we were all waiting for it to explode.

The old man's mind was ticking, the gears working, and I let them. We'd given him a lot of information, some of it veiled, and if he needed a moment to put that all together. That was fine.

He straightened in his seat, eyeing us suspiciously. "You're not cops?"

"No." I burst out with a laugh. "Do we look like cops?"

"Cops don't often look like cops, trust me."

"Are they after you?" Madison asked.

Oscar shrugged. "Ever since I lifted that book, they've been sniffing my trail. There was a period of time when I was free, but then the snooping picked back up about seven years ago. I sold everything, put the money in an account my daughter controls, and pretended to go senile so they'd leave me alone. I was foolish to think my daughter could hold on to all that money without getting greedy. She thinks just because she put me in the nicest nursing home she could find, it absolves her of the guilt."

Oscar's eyes kept moving from us to the door. It must have been difficult for him keeping up that act all the time, getting next to no mental stimulation all day. I actually felt bad for him. Even as we spoke, I could see some of the life coming back into his face, a little color in his cheeks, a sparkle in his eyes.

"But you kept the map," I said, pressing him.

"I always wanted to go after the treasure," he said. "I had a... friend... who was going to go with me. But the timing was never right. Somebody was always looking for me."

"What is it going to take for you to give it to us?"

Oscar let his gaze drift off above our heads and for a moment his eyes really did look vacant. Then he looked back at me. "I'm an old man, but not *that* old. I want to be free. Really free. Do you know what I mean?"

I did, in a way. I was born with the weight of the Hartley name on my head. Everyone in the business knew my parents. I had *never* been free, not really, and my parents had never even given me the choice to do anything else. Still, I was freer than them, and freer than Oscar was here.

"I really like the sun," he added.

"What does this have to do with the map?" I asked, getting impatient.

"I'm getting to that. Hold your horses." Oscar took a long swig of water from the plastic cup the nurse had brought him. "I need two new identities—one for me, and one for my *friend*. And a place for us to stay. And some money to get out of here—a million should do it."

"Oh, is that all?" Madison quipped.

"Try again," I said.

We had a staring contest, but this was where I had the upper hand. Madison was the one who wanted the map. She needed it for her brother, and now I wanted it for her, too. What did Oscar *really* want? What did he need? Was he willing to give up his chance at freedom for a stupid map?

"We'll get you the IDs," I said. "And we'll even cut

you in on the reward, but the rest you're going to have to find on your own. Do you want your freedom or not, old man?"

"Yes," Oscar said, faster than even my assessment of him suggested he might agree. "I've been foolish long enough. I'm ready to be done with all this. Give me two days and I'll put you in touch with someone who can do the transfer for us."

We waited while Oscar went to his room and retrieved a picture of his friend, an old man about his age, and he handed it over wistfully. Then we stood to go, and as we did, Madison's hand touched mine and I shivered involuntarily. We'd done it. We were a step closer to finding the map. And better yet, we'd done it together. As soon as we left the building, I took her hand and kissed it, not daring to look and see how she would react to the gesture. Not daring to say a thing. Not daring to even think beyond the next step.

Getting the map and returning the book were the last things we had to do, but I didn't want any of this to end.

18

MADISON

I t was hard to walk out of that assisted living facility feeling anything other than victorious. Our little *good granddaughter, bad granddaughter* act had come across flawlessly, and if Oscar Duncan thought the cops were after him, so much the better for our deal. But I could never totally relax—not while I was in the middle of a job, and especially not during one that had been as disastrous as this one.

We got busted at the bank. My ski mask was in police evidence. I'd had the barrel of a gun pressed to the back of my head. And now I was falling hard for someone who'd planned to double-cross me and all I had to reassure me that she really had changed her mind was my stupid, irrational heart. I touched the key at my chest to make sure it was still there, and when it was, let out a breath.

"We need to be careful," I said as Cass and I waited at the bus depot for our ride back to the motel.

Cass sat close to me and every time she shifted on the bench, I could feel her thigh against mine. The effect was like a short circuit in my brain—it made me forget everything I ever learned about keeping a professional distance and remaining detached.

"What are you talking about?" Cass asked. "That went great."

"The old man thinks the cops are after him," I said. "What if he's right? We just went into that nursing home without disguises, and what if Rutherford had cameras in his house—"

"You need to relax," Cass said, putting one hand on my thigh. There it was again, the jolt of electricity that scrambled my brain and made me want to believe her. "He might be faking the extent of his senility, but Bree did the research on that guy—he's a small-time thief, and clearly, he's paranoid. That's totally in our favor because all we have to do is get him the fake IDs he wants, cut the reward eight ways, and the map is ours. You and I both know he could have insisted on a lot more."

"That's the other thing," I said. I was looking at Cass's hand on my leg—I wanted to touch her, to take her hand, to chase the feeling that I'd gotten at the pool. Instead, I said, "This job is already far riskier than the ones I usually pull. It was supposed to be a simple bank robbery, and now we're chasing artifacts all over the Mid-Atlantic region."

"It's fun, though, isn't it?" Cass asked. She was grinning at me with that trademark Cass Hartley charm and it seemed like everything in her life was just another interesting game. "Are you sure you want to give all this up?"

Must be nice to be so carefree, I thought, and for once, there was no bitterness in the thought—just longing. *Teach me how to be that way, Cass.*

But the job wasn't done yet and we needed to focus. "I have to give it up, for Donnie. Now, the next problem—I don't want to bring any more people into this job. The crew's too big as it is, and none of my people can forge documents."

Cass nodded. She understood where I was going, and I was relieved when she answered with reassurance. "Spider's one of the best forgers I've ever known—and thanks to my parents, I've met a few. He'll do the job fast and well."

"But can I—can *we*—trust him?" In all my years pulling heists and con jobs, I'd had a few guns pointed at me, but having that cold metal pressed against the back of my skull was a new sensation entirely.

Cass picked up my hand and folded it into hers, saying, "We need him to help us get the map. Honestly, I've never seen Spider fly off the handle during a job like that and I don't know what got into him, but between me and Tank, we'll make sure what happened in the motel doesn't happen again. Do you trust me?"

She was looking me in the eyes, searching my face for signs of deflection. There was no lying to Cass Hartley. It was better to just tell her the truth. Despite it all, as stupid as it may seem, I *did* trust her. I took a deep breath and said, "Yes."

"Good," Cass said. Then she leaned in and planted a kiss on my lips before I even saw it coming. I allowed myself to sink into the kiss, then the loudspeaker announced the arrival of our bus and Cass pulled me to my feet. As we walked outside, she said, "Tank is already keeping an eye on Spider—we'll get him to supervise the work, too, just in case."

"Thank you," I said, squeezing her hand in mine.

It was late in the evening by the time we got back to the motel room. Spider was tied to the chair while Tank sat on the edge of the mustard-yellow bedspread and stared at him. Talia sat by Tank's side, his beefy arm circled protectively around her waist, and Bree was sitting cross-legged at the head of the bed, alternately observing the room and tapping away on her laptop.

The tension was palpable and I let go of Cass's hand as we walked through the door.

"Well?" Bree asked.

"The old man definitely has the map," Cass said. "And he's willing to sell it to us—but he needs something first."

"Of course," Spider grumbled. "They always do."

He strained against his bonds—bungee cords Tank had rustled up from the trunk of the getaway car. Cass said, "We need your forging skills—he wants a couple of fake IDs."

Spider rolled his eyes at Cass and that lit a fire in me. Was he really going to sit there and give her attitude when he was the reason we'd all been at each other's throats?

"She said you're good," I growled at him. "You better be."

Spider's lips lifted in a sneer, and I tried not to flinch. Tank was sitting between us and there was nothing that *he* could do to lose my trust, but Spider was a wildcard. He snarled, "Why should I help you? I've been a prisoner in this room for the last 36 hours with that goon staring me down the whole time."

"We're going to untie you," Cass offered. When I gave her a challenging look, she added, "So you can work. When you hand the IDs over to Tank, that'll be the end—we'll be all squared up."

"What about the money?" Spider asked. "My share—"

"You'll get what you deserve and not a penny more," I said.

Tank stood up, careful not to disturb Talia as he

came and towered over Spider. Spider took one look between me and Cass, decided it wasn't worth the fight while Tank was looming over him and his hands were bound, and nodded. "Fine."

"Take him to the command center," Cass said, sliding a glance toward me. "He has all the forging supplies he needs there."

Tank untied Spider and the two of them moved toward the door. Tank, holding Spider with one hand, held out his other hand for Talia. She hopped down from the bed and took it, and then Bree stood up.

"What about me?"

"Go with them," I said. "Help them get whatever information they need to make the IDs."

I watched our melded crew walk out the door, and it was only after the cool night air stirred through the room and made me shiver that I realized Cass and I were the only ones left. We were alone again.

I turned to her and she seemed to have come to the same conclusion. She asked, "Now what?"

"I guess we go home," I said reluctantly. "Get some sleep maybe. There's nothing to do until Spider finishes the IDs."

Cass considered that for a minute, frowned, and said, "I'm hungry. What about you?"

"Starving," I said.

I'd bought us a couple of candy bars and some chips out of a vending machine in Philadelphia, but I couldn't remember the last time any of us had slowed down enough to eat a real meal. Tequila at midnight certainly didn't count.

"There's a restaurant not far from my place," Cass said. "I know the owner and he makes the best Denver omelet this side of Colorado."

My stomach growled audibly at the mere mention of food, but the idea of going to a restaurant... it was just so impersonal. After the day we'd had, and the way Cass kept looking at me and finding reasons to touch me, hold my hand, brush up against me, I had something a little different in mind.

"I'm not really in the mood for eggs," I said. "But I'd be willing to go toe-to-toe with your restaurant owner friend on the subject of grilled cheese sandwiches."

Cass laughed. It was a ridiculous offer and despite the chef's kitchen with the marble island and profes-sional-grade appliances that she'd seen when she let herself into my penthouse, I rarely expended more effort than it took to order takeout. Grilled cheese sand-wiches were one food that Donnie always liked when we were kids, though, and I got pretty good at making them.

"Okay," Cass said.

I smiled. I figured it wouldn't take much convincing to get her over to my place again.

Those grilled cheeses turned out to be the two most sensual sandwiches I'd ever cooked. Cass stayed beside me at the stove the whole time they were sizzling in the pan and I nearly dropped my spatula when she trailed her finger down my spine.

I felt her breath hot against my neck and if I wasn't so damn hungry, I would have let the sandwiches burn while I pushed her against the marble island and undressed her. The thought crossed my mind a time or two—or a dozen.

As it was, we were both ready to scarf down our food, willing to burn our tongues just to get through the meal faster, and Cass's lips tasted like butter when I finally circled my arms around her and pulled her down to the floor of the kitchen.

It was different this time.

The pool room had been all about satisfying animal urges. Every time I so much as looked at Cass before that, I'd felt warmth growing between my thighs until the desire finally overtook me at the pool.

This time, we undressed each other urgently and our mouths came together ravenously, but as soon as our bodies connected, naked and entwined on my kitchen floor, the mood changed and we started to take our time. We weren't fucking—suddenly, unexpectedly, we were making love. Cass's mouth found my nipples, her tongue moving in slow circles over every inch of me as I closed my eyes and ran my hands along the gentle curves of her breasts and her hips.

I lost track of everything but the sensation of her hands, her mouth, her body against mine.

I lost time. I lost space.

I lost myself completely to Cass.

It was a long time before I became aware of my surroundings again. It was at least an hour later and Cass was lying on her back. I was tucked into the curve of her shoulder. The tile floor was warm with our body heat and I wrapped my arms and legs around Cass to hold her as tight as I could.

The moment was perfect and I superstitiously pushed away every thought that could possibly break us out of it.

What if Spider—No. *What happens if Oscar*—No. *Does Cass really care about*—NO. I touched the key, still at my neck. If Cass had wanted to steal it from me, the best time to do it would have been a few seconds ago. But she didn't. She was just as consumed in the moment as I was.

Cass bent and kissed my forehead, silencing my thoughts with a question. "Will you tell me about your brother?"

"Huh?"

"You're doing all of this to get Verne's treasure map for him," Cass said. "I want to know why he's worth all that trouble."

I twisted in Cass's embrace to stare up at the ceiling, and the thousand-dollar pendant lights hanging over the island. Why did any of this *stuff* matter? It was hard to come up with an answer while I was lying in her arms.

After a minute, I said, "You wouldn't know it to look around this place, but we were really poor growing up. I told you Donnie and I were in and out of the foster system a lot."

"Yeah," Cass said, hugging me a little tighter.

"It was awful," I went on. "As soon as I got old enough to start fending for myself, I promised Donnie that I'd be the one who kept him safe and fed and loved. And that's exactly what I did. When I was fourteen, I met some guys who needed an innocent-looking kid to run a diversion on a robbery and they offered to cut me in. It was better money than I could ever hope to make babysitting, or shoveling sidewalks, or whatever else a fourteen-year-old kid could do on the bad side of town."

"I hear you. It *was* kind of fun at that age. Like a game."

I smiled. *Fun.* It was, I supposed. Until the fun ran out. "I never wanted Donnie to know so the cops couldn't use it against him, and it worked for a couple of years. But when he was twelve, he found out all our money was coming from con jobs and he didn't want anything to do with me *or* the money. He said he'd rather take his chances in the foster system."

"That's awful," Cass said. "You were just doing what you thought was best."

"I tried to go legit for a while," I said. "I got emancipated. I got a cashiering job. It wasn't even enough money to pay the rent on a studio apartment, and Donnie was still so mad he wouldn't talk to me. So I went back to conning just to pay the bills, and then because why not? My brother didn't care about me anymore, my parents *never* cared, and it was interesting work. And look at me now."

I gestured at the huge, expensive and meaningless apartment, then let my hand drop to the floor. I barely ever spent any time there, and when I did, the open floor plan and spacious living areas felt cavernous and hollow.

"So what changed? It's been... what? Ten years since you left? More?" Cass asked with a frown.

"More. I saw him at Trader Joe's about six months ago," I said. "He was in the produce department and I wasn't even sure it was him at first—I hadn't seen him in over a decade. He didn't see me and I didn't have the guts to talk to him. I had Bree track down his phone number, but I haven't had the nerve to call him. If he didn't like what I was doing when I was a teenager, he couldn't possibly understand my current lifestyle."

I looked around the apartment again. Those hand-blown pendant lights had been ugly since the day I bought them, but everyone knew Barovier & Toso lighting was the height of luxury so I'd picked them and watched the saleswoman's eyes light up with dollar signs.

"The stolen Verne book meant a lot to him when we were kids," I explained. "He followed the whole robbery drama on television for weeks. I thought if I could return the book to the museum and get him a copy of the map, there would be no way he could turn me away. He was always convinced Verne's treasure was real."

"Don't worry," Cass said. "We're going to get the map."

I kissed her again, long and hard until desire began to build in me again, and then I stood up and pulled her off the floor, saying, "I'm a terrible host. I haven't even offered you a tour. Let's start with the bedroom."

19
———

CASS

I woke in a dreamland, awareness dawning slowly. My head was nestled in pillowed softness, my skin caressed by the most luxurious sheets I'd ever felt. A warm, heavy object lay on my stomach, trapping me in place, but for some reason, I didn't care.

The reason became apparent a moment later as the woman beside me sighed contentedly and rolled toward me. Right. *Madison*. I turned just my head to look at her, trying to memorize every bit of her in the morning light. The way her hair glinted like copper in the sun. The slight upturn of her nose. Her naturally rosy cheeks. The way she smiled in her sleep, something she rarely did even in her unguarded waking moments.

For a moment, I let myself hope.

With the sun streaming through the window,

shining off the white of the pillows and the duvet and the walls, it seemed possible. It seemed possible that we could get the map and mend Madison's relationship with her brother. It seemed possible we could save Henry's restaurant. We could return the book to its rightful home at the museum, distribute the money... but, then what?

Then what?

Madison would leave and there would be no place for me. She couldn't have one foot in the business by being with me and the other foot out the door. I could see how it would unravel now. She would say it was okay at first, but then she would worry and something would happen, and she would demand I go legit, too. Or I would worry too much about our association getting her in trouble and I'd go legit for her and wind up unhappy.

The deposit locker key hung on a string between her breasts. I could easily just take it and go. Leave the penthouse and forget all this happened. Cut to the part where someone breaks someone else's heart before that someone has to see pain written all over the other's face.

But I didn't want to. For once, I wanted to stay. Even if that meant misery. Even if it meant heartbreak. For once, I wasn't going to be the one inflicting the pain before it could be inflicted on me.

My mood didn't change much during breakfast. Though I tried to relax and enjoy the bacon and eggs Madison had made us, I couldn't. I wanted to *move*. To do something.

Madison sipped on her coffee, lifting her gaze to mine periodically, and my heart thudded louder in my chest. *Not that thing. Down, girl*, I thought, as I stood to grab my phone from my coat pocket. "I'm going to call Spider and Tank to see how it's going."

We couldn't get *too* distracted here. We were on a timeline. We needed the map. In fact, it was odd that I hadn't heard from Spider yet. He was usually much faster than this with his forgeries.

I dialed Tank and put the phone on speaker, setting it on the island counter between us. As the phone rang, Madison put down her coffee and leaned in. After a greeting from Tank, I jumped right to the point. "How are the IDs moving?"

"Not so fast," Tank said.

Madison folded her arms, the hinted curve of her breasts against her thin T-shirt shooting right through me. My mind flashed to the night before. To my hands on her aroused nipples, to her hands on my body. My cheeks started to heat with the memory of it. *Damn it, Hartley*.

Madison's gaze was somewhere off in the middle distance, her mind far away. Where was she? Not in the place I had just been. There was no pleasure on her face.

I edged the speaker of the phone toward me. "May I speak with Spider?"

Tank grunted. I heard his low voice, muffled, on the other end of the line. He returned a moment later. "He doesn't want to talk."

The heat of anger replaced that other kind of heat. *Son of a...* "Can't you make him?"

"Can't make a man talk if he doesn't want to," Tank said.

"But you can make him listen. Put the phone to his ear, please."

Tank grunted again and I waited a few seconds for him to do as I asked. In the meantime I reached out and squeezed Madison's hand. She gave me a smile in response, but it didn't quite make it to her eyes. I kept hold of her hand.

"Spider?" I asked.

No answer.

I shifted in my chair. *Okay, then.* "I know you can work faster than you are. Are you blue balling us?"

I thought I'd at least get a laugh out of this from someone—Madison or Tank, or Spider, even—but still nothing came over the line.

"If you're delaying, I swear to God, I will tie your balls in a knot—" Madison let out a sound like air hissing from a balloon. A chuckle followed. *There it*

CARA MALONE & ANNA COVE

was. Her laugh was contagious, and I soon found my own mouth pulling up in a grin as well. "-and slice them up like boiled eggs."

Well, at least I got someone to laugh. Spider didn't even emit a soft chuckle. He should have. He should have done whatever I told him after the stunt he'd pulled.

When guns were involved, shit happened. People got shot. Sometimes accidentally. And you couldn't take that back. Spider knew that, yet he had decided it was a good idea to go into my desk and retrieve the gun, and bring it on the job. Unilaterally. And I couldn't help but hate him a little for that.

"I need twenty-four hours," he said.

"Twelve. That's all you get." I hung up the phone. There was no need for a response from him. He had twelve more hours, which was far longer than he should have needed, and I meant to use every one of them to further prove to Madison that I was more than just a criminal.

Until a few days ago, I'd been hiding a lot of my personal life from Madison—from everyone. But I'd told her the story of my parents and now it was time to tell her about another important person in my life. "There's someone I'd like you to meet—he's *my* reason for going after the book."

I t was a little early for dinner; but we had time to kill before going to the command center, and we'd only eaten breakfast before falling back into bed again for most of the day. I, for one, was *starving*. Yet I found myself hesitating outside The Wooden Spoon. My palms slickened and I let go of Madison's hands to surreptitiously wipe them on my pants before opening the door.

Madison gave me a sweet smile as we waited near the door and my heart hammered in my chest as I tried to answer her smile. The place was dim, lit by candle-light for the evening meal. A few couples dined at the windows. A group clustered at the table in the middle.

Why was I so nervous? This was *Henry*. He was the closest I had to parents, to family, nowadays. And he had sounded so excited to meet Madison on the phone when I explained what I'd wanted and what this meant to me. He hadn't even teased me about falling for her once I told him about how our crews had joined.

He opened the door and appeared, rubbing his hands together.

"Welcome to The Wooden Spoon," he said, smiling and gesturing us inside like we were a whole crowd of new visitors rather than two non-paying customers. That's how he was. And that's why, I reminded myself, he was getting my share of the proceeds from the Verne book. Every penny.

A single light illuminated a table dressed finer than all the others with a tablecloth, flowers and candles. He'd understood my mumblings about *someone special*. "You didn't have to do all this, Henry. I'm sure you have enough on your plate."

"For my girl?" He hugged me close and kissed my head. "I wouldn't do anything less."

I ducked to hide the flare of heat in my cheeks and gestured toward Madison. "This is... Madison," I said, not totally sure how to introduce her. Not sure how she'd *want* me to introduce her.

Henry took Madison's outstretched hand and kissed her knuckles. "It's lovely to meet you, Madison. I've heard so much about you."

"You have a wonderful place here. I love it," Madison said. Thanks to the bare-bulb chandeliers above, or maybe the candlelight, she had an extra sparkle in her eyes. She looked more beautiful than I'd ever seen her, hair curled and wearing a simple dress, the key at her neck somehow complementing the whole look like it was a fine diamond. And I found myself swelling with pride.

Henry smiled, though I noticed he had deep circles under his eyes. He was still in trouble, yet he'd agreed to make special arrangements for us. "You two better be hungry. I've got an incredible meal prepared. Go ahead and sit down, get settled, and I'll be right over with the first course."

We settled at the table and Madison's eyes

widened as she took in the place from that new angle. "How do you know Henry? Are you a regular here?"

I paused. How had I not told her yet how important he was to me? Man, I had a lot of truth-telling to do. "He's a friend of my parents."

Madison's eyes widened. "One of us?"

"Retired. This restaurant was his baby after he went straight. He—oh, Henry, that looks beautiful."

Henry interrupted us with a tray full of sliders. Madison rubbed her hands together at the sight in the most adorable way. "Oh my God, I want to put all of this in my mouth right now."

"Patience. Food is best when savored." Henry chuckled and poured a glass of wine for each of us. Then he pulled a chair from a neighboring table and sat. Each appetizer was in mini form, crafted like its own little piece of art. The alcohol flowed easily, the food tasted scrumptious, and before I knew it, I was totally relaxed in my chair, laughing at Madison's near orgasmic reaction to the sliders.

"So, how do you two know each other?" Henry asked us as we finished off the appetizer tray.

"I picked her up on the corner." I smiled broadly, the warmth of the wine and the food releasing me from whatever tension I had felt earlier.

Madison pursed her lips and sipped her glass of wine before speaking. Then, she turned to Henry. "Has she always been like this?"

"Like what? Charming? Gorgeous? Hilarious?" I

supplied.

Madison raised an eyebrow. "More like..."

"You mean the using humor as avoidance thing?" Henry said.

"Yes, that." Madison turned to Henry. "Every time something serious happens, she's there with a joke."

"I'm just trying to lighten the mood," I said, though no one was listening to me. They had turned toward each other, faces close, eyes sparkling with wine and good humor as they talked about me.

I didn't like that so much.

"I don't know about *always*, but at a very young age, yes," Henry said. "She once interrupted a fight between her parents with a performance of *Annie*, complete with a wig and a dance she choreographed herself."

"I wish I could have seen that," Madison said, laughing.

"I might have pictures upstairs. And there was this one time..."

"This wine is lovely. Where did you get it, Henry?" I asked, trying to change the subject.

"...when she replaced her mother's tools with rubber replicas. *That* her parents didn't find so funny."

No, they hadn't. I had been eight, and I had already gone on my first con jobs. They were planning a larger one at a jewelry store and I hadn't wanted to participate. I wanted to go to the roller rink with my friends. I swallowed down the feelings of eight-year-old Cass and tried to put on a smile.

"Don't you think that's enough digging into my past?" I asked.

"But she can be serious sometimes, too. When her parents were arrested," Henry said, his laugh dying on his lips. "She was more worried about *me* than about herself. She's the one who suggested I follow my dreams and open this restaurant."

"That's really sweet," Madison said, shooting me an admiring glance across the candlelight.

I swallowed as the emotions of the current day crashed with those of my seventeen-year-old self. I hadn't done it for Henry. I'd done it for me. Encouraging him to open The Wooden Spoon was my way of apologizing for screwing up his entire livelihood. "It's not as sweet as it sounds."

"Yes, it was," Henry supplied quickly.

I'd never told him the real reason my parents got arrested. He didn't know. And now... there was a chance he would lose all this. The thought of telling him the truth, of him losing that smile in his eyes... My throat and eyes burned and my breath locked in my chest. "I need the bathroom," I said.

"What did I say? Oh, Cass, wait," Henry called after me. "I'm sorry."

My eyes clouded as I made my way to the

restroom. I wanted to cry. I wanted to scream, really, which was ridiculous because Henry was just telling stories. They were just stories, so why did they make me feel like this?

With some effort, I pushed those feelings away, massaged the worry lines from my forehead and breathed deep. *This is no big deal, Cass. No. Big. Deal. You've done this before.* But I hadn't. I hadn't ever brought anyone to meet Henry. I hadn't let anyone see me cry, or even gotten this close to tears. I had never, ever felt so wrapped up in someone else.

Except I had. With Laura. For once I allowed myself to think of her name rather than calling her *the cop.*

Was this any different? Was Spider right? Was I jumping headlong into a selfish relationship and jeopardizing the lives of my friends and coworkers?

The restroom door opened, blowing a strand of hair across my mouth. Madison popped her head inside, her lips parted and her eyes full of worry. "Are you okay?"

"Yeah, I'm fine." I shrugged and the mirror version of me looked more uncertain than ever.

Madison slipped into the room and let the door close behind her. She wrapped me in a hug, pulling me close to her body. "I'm sorry if we upset you. I just wanted to know more about you."

"Yeah, well, here's the short version: I had a shitty childhood."

"Me too," Madison said, pulling away, her face artificially bright. "We're both part of the shitty childhood club. Go us!"

I smiled at her attempt at a joke, though at the same time the tears spilled over. She was *everything*. My shoulders shook as my eyes finally released the burden of so many tears unshed. Madison frowned and pulled me back into a hug, and right away, I knew my doubts were silly. This *was* different. Being with Madison made me better, but Laura had *never* made me better. I sniffed, clearing the tears away from my cheeks.

"Why don't we leave the avoidance humor to me, huh, babe?" I said.

Madison laughed, pulled away, and let her hands trail down my arms to my fingers. "You got it... *babe*."

It hadn't struck me until she repeated the word that it had come out of my mouth, but it had. And, for once, I didn't care or try to joke it away. Madison tucked the stray hair behind my ear and kissed me on the cheek, transferring my salty tears to her lips. "Let's go back out there so we don't give Henry a heart attack worrying about you."

She clutched my hand, threading her fingers through mine, and pulled me out the door.

"I haven't cried since I was twelve, you know," I whispered into her ear. "I feel so... ridiculous."

"You'll get better with practice." She squeezed my

hand and smiled. "Welcome to confronting reality. Your maturity level just grew ten sizes today."

"Yay," I said, with no enthusiasm in my voice. I *did* feel better, though. Lighter. Like I had shed some of the burden I'd been carrying for years. I'd been carrying it alone, and now I didn't have to anymore.

When we returned to our table, Henry had set out a full meal. Food and wine and safe topics of conversation occupied the next forty-five minutes. As the night went on, I could now see that my reaction to topics about the past seemed overblown. Wasn't that why I had brought Madison here? To show her a bit of my past as she had done with me? So what if it was hard? Her history wasn't easy, either. We shared that commonality.

When it was time to go meet Spider, Henry gave Madison a hug and she walked out the door. I offered him a hug and he wrapped his arms around me, lifting me up until my feet didn't touch the floor. "Keep her around. She's a good one," he said.

I didn't feel the need to break the moment with a joke, though a few sprang to mind.

Instead, I nodded and smiled. "I'll do my very best. Hey, Henry, about that trouble you were in the other night. Are you still...?"

"I'll be fine, Cass. You concentrate on your new girl and I'll concentrate on finding the money to keep this place going. That's all that matters."

Henry was parenting me like he always had. But

this time, I was going to make him see that I could help him, too. That there were two people in this relationship and both of us could benefit. And now, with the strength of Madison behind me, I was in a better position than ever to get it done.

20

MADISON

I could hear shouting inside the old textile factory all the way from the crumbling parking lot.

"What the hell's happening in there?" I asked Cass as we broke into a run toward her command center.

"I don't know," she said, keeping pace with me.

What a way to top off a perfectly peaceful, delicious meal—by sloshing it around in my stomach like I was on a Tilt-a-Whirl. I had a slight stomach ache by the time we made it inside and found Tank with his meaty hands pinning Spider to the desk on the foreman's platform.

This is what you get when you play house while your crew is working. I scolded myself, then jogged up the rusty metal stairs that led to them.

Tank had Spider so thoroughly pinned that he was

turning a little blue in the lips, and he was swinging his feet wildly, kicking Tank in the shins to absolutely no effect. Bree had managed to reserve a portion of the desktop for herself and was tapping frantically at her laptop while Talia stood a few feet away with her hands over her mouth, a horrified look in her eyes.

"What's going on?" I barked, commanding everyone's attention.

Spider stopped squirming. Bree stopped typing. Even Talia lowered her hands from her mouth.

"He was trying something," Tank snarled. "Said he needed to use the computer to pull up reference photos, and then Bree caught him on some chat website."

"Let him go," Cass said, coming up behind me.

"But—" Tank began to object.

"In that chair," Cass went on, motioning to an empty one on the other side of the platform.

"Thank you," Spider started to say.

Then Cass added, "Pin him down if you have to. He's not going anywhere."

Tank hauled Spider across the platform by the nape of his neck and threw Spider into the chair. Then Cass was on him, her hands on the arms of the chair and her whole body leaning forward in an intimidating stance.

It would have been a little bit funny if it weren't for the fact that Spider had pulled a gun on me just a few days ago. Cass was tiny but fierce, snarling at him like a honey badger about to do her worst.

"What the hell were you up to?" she demanded.

"I was just making the IDs that you asked for so sweetly," Spider said, petulance dripping from his voice.

"Bullshit," Cass said.

"He was talking to someone with the handle *Honeybee86*," Bree said. "All he said before we caught him was 'Layer mask not working, need some help'."

"Yeah, genius," Spider said with a roll of his eyes, "and what was the name of the website?"

"PhotoshopGeek.com," Bree said.

Spider looked at Cass with a roll of his eyes, as if to say, *Can you believe these idiots?* "You want quality fake IDs, you have to give me the tools I need to get the job done."

"And did you get the job done?" I asked, crossing my arms over my chest.

"Almost." Spider nodded to a folding card table that someone had set up at one end of the platform. There was a special printer sitting on top of it, as well as several bright task lights and a few different tools spread across it. "Just gotta hit print. I figured out the layer mask, no thanks to these two."

I nodded at Bree, who did the final task of printing the IDs. I waited impatiently until they dropped out of the printer, still warm in my hand.

Oscar Duncan had been transformed into William

Brice, age sixty-seven, a resident of Sarasota, Florida. And his *friend,* as Oscar had described him, was a handsome older man with a square jaw and a full head of salt-and-pepper hair whose new name was Anthony Thompson.

From what I'd gathered, in between the lines of what Oscar told us, this man was more than just a friend, and they must have been separated, either by circumstance or necessity. It was actually sort of sweet —these IDs would give them another shot at love after who knew how many years apart, and given the time period when Oscar and his lover would have been together, it was certainly not *only* a life of crime that had forced them apart.

They might actually be happier now.

Damn it, Cass, I thought as I caught myself being sappy. If she wasn't so close, I probably wouldn't even be thinking like this. *Like a hopeless romantic.*

I bent over the table and inspected both of the IDs carefully under the task lighting, and after a minute or two, I stood up. "They're good. I guess we can let Spider go now."

"Just like that?" Tank asked. "After he pulled a gun on you?"

"Well, we're not in the business of taking hostages," I said. "So I guess so."

Cass stood upright and the moment she let go of the chair arms, Spider jumped out of it and brushed himself off irritably, puffing out his chest. "I wish you'd just trust me. I do excellent work and Cass knew that until you came along and made her lose her mind." He turned to Cass, the pitch of his voice rising in anger as he said, "You know, some of us do this for a *living* and not just because it's fun to follow in mommy and daddy's footsteps. But I guess it never would have occurred to you to ask before you cut everyone's take in half just because you were chasing tail, *again—*"

"Hey," Tank barked. "Your business is done here— I think you better be on your way."

"Wait," Cass said as Tank grabbed Spider by the arm. "You're right—we should have discussed it together first. But we never would have gotten through this job without Madison and her crew."

"Whatever," Spider said, ripping his arm away from Tank's grasp. He headed for the staircase, calling sardonically over his shoulder, "Wire my cut to my bank account."

"You better keep your mouth shut until then," I called. I didn't trust that man... not one bit.

"I can't believe today is finally the day," I said the following afternoon as Cass and I got off yet another bus, this time in a seedy neighborhood in North Philadelphia.

Talia had come with us this time—we needed her brilliant memory, and I spent the bus ride praying that she was a real savant and the thing with the bookcase in Rutherford's house hadn't been just a fluke.

"Do you think Oscar's lawyer is just going to hand over the map?" she asked, doing a better job than I wanted to admit of mirroring my own reservations.

We'd been working this job for what felt like forever—especially compared to most of the in-and-out burglaries and heists I'd pulled in my career. It was hard to believe that this was the last step before we could hand the book over to the museum and claim our reward.

I was so close to being done, to getting my brother back.

"Oscar promised he would," Cass said, looping her arm around mine as we walked away from the bus stop. "And we know how much he wants these IDs. It's not just about money for him."

I put my hand on top of hers, allowing myself to lean into the feeling. A week ago—hell, just a few days ago—I would have recoiled at a show of affection like that, especially in front of another crew member.

But I loved the way Cass rested her head on my shoulder when she got tired of traveling. I loved how the sensation of our lips locking together was beginning to feel like it belonged to me. I loved the look in her eyes when she brought me to meet her friend, Henry, the other night, like she was showing me off.

There was more on the line with this heist than there ever had been before, but with Cass by my side, I was getting used to working through every challenge with a sense of calm and security.

It would be okay.

Everything would be okay.

Our destination was a low-traffic strip mall a few blocks from the bus stop. Oscar had told us he'd entrusted the map with a lawyer just before his family put him in the assisted living facility, and he'd made arrangements to handle the trade. I was putting up a deposit of good faith money from my own bank account, with the agreement to pay out the remainder after we turned the book in to the museum. Cass had the fake IDs in her wallet and the safe deposit locker key still hung on a string around my neck, ready to use as soon as we got the map.

"This place seems shady," Talia said as we turned into the parking lot of the strip mall.

There were only about five operating businesses in the whole, long chain, and the parking lot was pocked with broken asphalt. Everything seemed yellow, like it could use a good pressure washing, but I spied our target in the middle of the sprawling building.

Angelo Diamanti, Attorney at Law.

It was hand-painted on the windows at the front of the store, and Talia was right—it looked shady as hell.

"What is this guy, a mob boss?" Cass asked.

"No, but I bet some of his clients are," I said. I was trying to lighten the mood, which only served to make

Talia more anxious. She walked a little closer to Cass and Cass put her arm around Talia's shoulders.

"The guy makes his living as a middle-man between criminals," Cass said. "It's not like he's going to bother with a high-rent building downtown."

"Yeah, this is standard operating procedure for guys like Diamanti. I've been to offices like this for jobs I've pulled before," I said, trying to reassure Talia—and myself. The possibility that Oscar Duncan still had some tricks up his sleeve even at his age had crossed my mind, and I was on the lookout for clues that we were about to get ripped off.

The inside of Diamanti's office was a lot nicer than the outside. He had a personal assistant who led us through a small waiting room to a well-appointed office at the back of the small space. It was decorated with mahogany furniture and expensive-looking vases flanked both sides of the desk. Diamanti himself was a middle-aged man in a finely tailored suit, and when he smiled and extended his hand across the table to us, I saw a glint of gold in his mouth.

"You must be Mr. Duncan's associates," he said, shaking each of our hands in turn. "He didn't tell me he was sending Charlie's Angels to pick up his parcel."

"Just call me Farrah Fawcett," Cass said, giving him a sharp *don't mess with us* look.

"Calm down, toots," Diamanti said. "Sit." We did— in three identical leather chairs arranged along the front of Diamanti's long desk—and he said, "I'm to understand that you have a package for Mr. Duncan?"

"Yes," I said. "We'd like to examine the map before we hand it over, if you don't mind."

"Why, worried it's a forgery?" he asked with a hearty chuckle. It was obvious this man found himself amusing pretty often, and to facilitate the trade, I forced a polite laugh.

"You can never be too careful," I said.

Cass set the IDs on the corner of the desk, where Diamanti could see them but where she'd be able to snatch them if anything funny happened. Then he used the intercom system to call his assistant back into the room.

"A pair of fake IDs in exchange for a real-deal treasure map," he said as the woman lay a thick manila envelope on the desk in front of them. "You must be real slick talkers to negotiate a deal like that. Though I wouldn't expect it was too hard with the man in the state he's in."

"The Alzheimer's? You do know he's faking that, right?" Cass said.

"Oh no. The Alzheimer's is real. Right after he was diagnosed, he made me promise to keep the map for him until he called for it."

Madison frowned. "How were you supposed to know if he was of sound mind? What if he was being forced?"

"I shouldn't be telling you this." He leaned across

the desk, glancing conspiratorially between us. I had a feeling he wasn't exactly full of scruples and did stuff like this often. Maybe he even enjoyed it. "Oscar pretended he had dementia early on to elude the cops, but then he actually *got* the disease. When his family realized he was getting worse, they took power of attorney over his money and put him in the assisted living facility. Dropping off the map here was the last thing he did before they locked him away with the old folks. A fate worse than prison, I say."

"Wow," Cass said.

"Go ahead, check it out." He pushed the map toward us.

Talia carefully pulled the map from the envelope. It was small—it had been printed on a single page folded double in the original *Twenty Thousand Leagues Under the Sea,* and its colors had faded after so many decades of storage. For all we knew, this careless lawyer had kept a multi-million dollar artifact crammed in a file cabinet in North Philadelphia for the last twenty years, but it was still beautiful.

I had a hard time not picking it up to admire it myself. All that hard work, all the planning, and the rollercoaster ride that Cass had taken me on over the last two weeks... it all culminated in this little piece of paper.

For the next couple of minutes, Talia carefully examined the map and I barely breathed. I took Cass's hand beneath the edge of the desk where Diamanti wouldn't notice our connection. When he reached for the IDs to verify the quality, I let him pick them up.

"This is it," Talia finally confirmed, sliding the map carefully back into the envelope. "It's real."

I let out a long-held sigh of relief, then Diamanti put the pair of fake IDs in his desk drawer. "Your forger does good work. Mr. Duncan will be pleased. And the money?"

"Transferred his cut this morning," I said. "You can check the account."

Diamanti did so—he wouldn't be a good shady lawyer if he didn't—and while we waited, I frowned at the thought of what would happen to Oscar next. If he was really ill, then maybe he should stay where he was. "Will he be okay out in the world?"

"Oh, yes. I have it on good authority that, uhh," he glanced down at the IDs, reading the name of Oscar's companion, "Mr. Thompson here will take good care of him." He turned back to his computer, nodded, and said, "Money's all there—we will, of course, wait for the remainder upon return of the book."

He stood, shaking hands with each of us again, and then Cass took the envelope from Talia and tucked it into my backpack. We walked out of his office and into the late morning sun, and as soon as we got to the parking lot, Cass let out a whoop and threw her arms around both of us.

"We did it!" she shouted. "We freaking did it!"

A tiny part of me—the old Madison—wanted to

say, *Be quiet, you don't know who's listening! Be professional!*

But I told that Madison to shut the hell up, and then I planted a long, celebratory kiss on Cass's lips.

Yes, we freaking did it.

"Are you ready?" I asked.

Madison took a shaky breath, let it out, and nodded. "Ready as ever."

There was only one thing to do before this was all over—return the book to the museum. We'd been over a number of possibilities for how to do that, including using Oscar's skeezy lawyer as a go-between, but ultimately, Madison had volunteered.

"I'll do it. I need my brother to see that I'm serious about getting out of the business," she'd explained.

My heart had sunk when she'd said those words. After associating her face with the book, she would never be able to work a con again. If she did and she got caught, they would nail her to the wall on this and who knows what else. Cops were always looking for connections.

But the more we talked about it, the more she'd dug

in her heels. "It has to happen this way," she'd said, "so Donnie knows I'm really out." That's what had done it for me.

Now, we sat four blocks from the used bookstore where we would start our final mission. We'd borrowed Talia's car and were holding hands, waiting for the right moment. The sun peeked through the bank of clouds for the first time that day, but just as quickly disappeared.

She might be ready, but I'm not. "Let's go over the story one more time."

Madison groaned. "We've been over it fifty times already."

"Please, for me. I think we're missing something."

Madison sighed and tapped her finger on the dashboard of the car. "Fine, but it can only take five minutes. If we wait much longer we won't make the evening news cutoff."

She closed her eyes and took her hand away from mine, as if she was gathering all her strength to herself, as if she was pulling herself away from me. Would this ever work? If she was getting out of the business, then would she risk fraternizing with a criminal like me afterward? It certainly wasn't the safest option for her, and I knew it, and it made me want to cuff her to the door of the car and beg her never to leave me.

But I couldn't do it. She loved Donnie, and if I had any feelings for her I had to let her do this. She would never forgive herself or me for distracting her from that mission.

"I'm a graduate student. I'm studying great adventures in classic fiction and I stumbled on this book. I'd been on a research trip to the museum last semester, read about the theft, and noticed that they were offering a reward. It was serendipity that I happened to be in this bookstore and found a copy that looked a lot like what was stolen. Now, ask me questions."

"Okay," I said, pushing away that unfamiliar tug of desperation and settling back into myself. "Want to make out with me?"

Madison punched my shoulder, then in the next second leaned over and kissed the spot where she had punched me. "This is serious."

"Yes, it is." *I should ask her to stay*, I thought, as a shiver ran down my shoulder from the spot where she had kissed me. My eyes held her gaze until a fine line appeared between her brows and I remembered what I was supposed to be doing. My throat felt like I had swallowed sandpaper. I cleared it, and by the time I was done with that, I'd lost my nerve to beg. "Okay, for real this time. Where did you find the Verne book exactly?"

"It was in the back of the bookstore under a pile of dusty books," she said, the worried line remaining between her brows, making her look exactly as I thought her student researcher alter ego might. Serious. Studious. All she needed now were some glasses, though that was a little cliché. "I love to search for buried treasures in bookstores."

"Nerd."

Madison continued without acknowledging my interruption. "It obviously hadn't been touched for years."

"And what did you do when you found it?"

"I decided to buy it and bring it to the museum, just in case. Turns out, it was the real thing."

"And what are we going to do about the bookstore? What if they want a cut?" I asked.

Madison chewed her lip. "We already know they have a copy of *Twenty Thousand Leagues* in their inventory—it was on the bookstore website. I'm going to buy that copy, then switch it for the real one. They'll be sorry they didn't realize what they had, but if they didn't catch it, why should they get a cut?"

"You're right. That makes sense."

"Maybe we'll throw them a few thousand," she added after a moment of thought. "For the optics."

I nodded, but didn't move. We sat in silence for a moment, staring at the city outside. At the parents walking their kids down the street. At the college students with their heads down, hands clutched around the straps of their bags. It was all so *normal*. Would Madison and I ever get close to something normal like that?

Just as I was about to kick her out of the car to avoid making a blubbering fool of myself, Madison took my hand again. "We have to stay away from each other until all the media attention dies down. It could be a few weeks."

"Yeah," I said, the word barely a whisper. *Or forever.* "That makes sense."

"But I don't want it to be the end. Okay? Promise me it won't be the end." It was as if she'd plucked the words out of my mind. All I could do to avoid a cascade of tears was nod and squeeze her hand. "I'll call you in three weeks if the coast is clear," she said. "Don't try to reach me before that—it'll be too dangerous."

She leaned forward, placed a kiss on my lips, and before either of us could say anything more, she opened the door and stepped out. All that was left in her wake was a breath of cold air. I could only hope it wasn't the last thing Madison would leave me.

I'd promised Talia I'd return her car after I left Madison at the bookstore, but I didn't—not right away. I drove it to a Walmart parking lot and sat. The car, even though it wasn't Madison's, still smelled like her coconut shampoo. I could still sense her sitting on the passenger seat next to me, could picture her and hear her as if she were there.

Ugh, what am I doing? She's not dead. She would call me in three weeks. She had said it herself. She wanted to be with me, and if I was going to deserve her,

I needed to start trusting her. I needed to trust her words. Starting here. Now. Meanwhile, I needed to do my job, which was to make sure this all went off without a hitch.

I pulled out my phone and started scrolling through the news.

Only an hour or so had passed. It would take maybe a half hour for Madison to do her thing in the bookstore, then an hour to catch a bus into the city to go to the museum, and who knows how long it would take before she finished talking to the right people and the museum notified the media. I refreshed the museum's Twitter feed over and over, then leaned back in my seat and stared up at the roof.

I must have fallen asleep, because the next thing I knew, it was dark. I wrenched the seat into an upright position and refreshed the feed on my phone again. A new tweet came up at last, and it was about the Verne book. There was a hashtag and I followed it. The story caught on quickly—everyone loved a good treasure hunt—and the news media on Twitter were already bursting with activity.

Missing Verne book found! Had it been right under our noses all along?

Museum offers $9 million reward, book found by local grad student.

Missing classic discovered after twenty years.

I clicked on one of the links in a tweet from a local news organization and stumbled on a live feed. The headline flashed on the screen. *Grad Student Discovers Missing Jules Verne Novel.*

And right there, right on the five o'clock news, right where she wanted to be, was Madison.

The light from the cameras caught the gold in her red hair and she practically sparkled through the lens. Her eyes looked wide and innocent, though her mouth quirked with smiles as the reporters spoke to her.

In the privacy of the car, I let out a *whoop* and smacked the roof. She had *done* it. Of course she had, but seeing it, seeing her there, made pride swell in my chest. I forced myself to settle down to listen to the interview.

"And what made you suspect it was *the* stolen edition?"

"Well," Madison said, "it was just a hunch, really. I got lucky."

The reporter, a blonde woman in her fifties, smiled. "You sure did. Well, there you have it folks. An amazing story from an amazing young woman."

She had done it. She fooled them all. Madison clearly deserved this. She deserved the life she wanted. She was good. Good in a way I never could be.

I decided then and there never to hold her back, no matter what that meant for me.

The money came a few weeks later, but it didn't bring with it the usual burst of adrenaline. I was waiting for Madison's call.

Since I'd left her at the bookstore, I hadn't ventured out of my hotel room once. Talia had tried to call, and had even brought Tank for an impromptu visit, but I couldn't bring myself to let them in. Even showering was a challenge. What if Madison called while I was otherwise occupied and I missed it?

But when the funds dropped into my account, I realized I wasn't the one who needed the money. Henry needed it. And if I didn't get out of that hotel room soon, he could lose the restaurant for good.

So I risked a shower and stepped out of the hotel for the first time in weeks. The weather had warmed since I'd last been out, the trees turning greener by the day, but I scarcely noticed it, I was so preoccupied. It was a walk I'd done hundreds of times, anyway, so I didn't have to pay attention.

When I got close to the restaurant, though, something new pricked my senses. At first, I couldn't tell what it was. The outer walls of The Wooden Spoon looked the same as always, but there was no one around. And *that* was odd.

The restaurant was in a newly trendy portion of town which, at this time in the afternoon, should have been busy. Other than a single stringy, beanie-capped dude at an outdoor cafe across the street, there was no one around. I remained where I was for a moment, listening, but couldn't hear anything out of the ordinary.

You're imagining things, Hartley.

Still, my senses were on full alert as I rang the door-bell for Henry's apartment above the restaurant. I hoped things hadn't progressed further during the time I'd gone AWOL. Why hadn't I texted him? What the heck had happened to me in the last few weeks? Could I really not function without Madison? Was I that far gone?

I rang the bell again and, just as I was about to leave, Henry pulled open the door. His face was pale and drawn. He had circles under his eyes and there was something about his nose—it looked... fearful. But noses couldn't look fearful, could they?

"Henry, I'm so glad you're here. I—"

"This isn't a good time," he said, barely moving his lips, the words no more than a whisper.

My heart hammered in my chest. I watched his face for clues, but it was completely blank. And I mean *completely.* Gone was the warmth and the affection I *always* saw in his eyes. Gone was the fear I'd seen a moment earlier. Gone was the sadness I'd seen when he told me he might lose the restaurant.

"You need to go. Quickly." He shooed me, and I jumped back to avoid his flapping hand.

"Is something wrong?" I asked.

"No. Leave." He tried to close the door on me, but I

wasn't having any of that. I stuck my foot in the crack and forced my way in. As soon as I cleared the opening, Henry slammed the door shut.

"You said everything was fine, but it's obviously not. I'm not leaving until you tell me what's going on. Is someone after you?" I clenched my fists, but the fear —his fear—washed over me in waves, and I vaguely wished I had Spider's gun with me. It felt *that* dire.

"It's none of your concern."

"It is, Henry. You're important to me. That's why I'm here. If you're in trouble, I can help you."

Not a moment later, the doorbell rang again. Henry's eyes closed. Then he nodded once and grabbed my shoulders. "You can still get away. Go out the back door and go far. Stay away, okay?"

"Not until you tell me what's going on."

"I need to answer the door quickly."

"But—"

"Go. Before they see you here." He pointed, his eyes searing into me. The bell rang again, followed by a series of loud bangs.

I followed his finger, slinking in the direction he wanted me to go, but only because I didn't know what else to do. Henry was in trouble. I thought back to those trench coated men—had he taken loans from some bad people? Maybe he'd had a falling out with some of his old friends. Maybe the cops were after him for some old charge.

Whatever the case, I held back, hiding just around

the corner, close enough to hear... and help, if necessary. Henry took a breath and opened the door.

"Henry Almansa?"

"Yes," Henry said, calmly.

"I'm Detective Thomas Wilson."

So it *was* the cops catching up with him. *No no no no no no.* Henry had been out of the business for years. He had been clean, well, as far as I knew. Surely the failure of his business confirmed this? If only I had done the Verne job faster, we could have done something about his money troubles. It had to be related to money. Didn't it?

I had to do something. I had to tell them it was a mistake. They had the wrong guy.

Henry was trying to negotiate with the detective. How many cops were there? Probably at least two. They would never send just one man. Maybe I could do something about this after all.

The detective was still talking but my heart was pounding in my ears. "We wanted to ask you a few questions about—"

I stepped into the entryway, and everyone froze. "Hello, gentlemen."

The detective's words trailed off in his mouth and Henry looked horrified. Suddenly, I was second-guessing myself. What was I doing, putting myself under a microscope like this when I really needed to lie low? Madison could be calling me right now for all I knew...

"That's her," the other cop, who looked like a frat boy straight out of school, muttered. Henry looked defeated, and that's when I realized they weren't here for him. They'd laid a trap for me.

"Cass Hartley, you're under arrest," Detective Thomas Wilson said, pushing his way through the door. "You have the right to remain silent."

Henry was being clumsy on purpose, doing an awkward dance as the cops tried to pass him in the narrow hall, but my feet froze to the ground. I couldn't run. I threw a desperate look to Henry, but his face only showed apology and guilt. Had he planned this somehow? It couldn't be. He would never do that to me. This was something else altogether.

Looked like the Hartley luck—no, the Hartley fate —had finally caught up with me.

22

MADISON

Cass and I predicted the media circus that came after I handed the Verne book over to the museum, and we'd planned accordingly. I knew my cover story front and back, we'd accounted for every possible question the museum, the police and the media might throw at me. Then we set everything up so that when the museum paid me the reward, I could funnel it to my lawyer right away and have him start cleaning the money to pay our crews, and Oscar.

What I never could have predicted was how soul-crushingly much I missed Cass.

Of course we couldn't talk to each other while there were reporters gathering outside the little studio apartment I'd rented by the month—or rather, the studio Madison the grad student had rented—near the university. We didn't even want to risk talking on burner phones. I was willing to torch my criminal career so I could win back my brother's affections, but Cass still loved that life and I couldn't take her out with me.

This way, everyone got what they wanted... only with every passing day that I had to pretend to be the world's luckiest grad student, I missed her more.

How could she matter so much to me in such a short amount of time? It was illogical, impossible, and yet a growing part of me kept insisting that it was probably what love felt like.

Soon, I would tell myself every time I thought of her, counting down the days until it felt safe to reach out to her.

I took every opportunity I had to deflect attention away from myself. When reporters met me outside my temporary living quarters—with the scratchy sheets and mysterious carpet stains that would only be worth it when I had Cass back in my arms—they always wanted to know what I was going to do with the money. And camera-shy Madison the grad student would always squeak out a response like, "Well, I gave some of it to the bookstore where I bought the book—it didn't seem right to pay only $20 for something that was worth millions."

"And the rest?" they always pushed.

"I don't know," I'd say, making myself as uninteresting as possible for the cameras. "I'll probably save it for a rainy day."

It worked—slowly.

At first I was worried that somebody might recognize me and start asking questions. I lost more than a couple nights of sleep because of that damn ski mask in police custody. What if they saw me on the news, figured out the book was actually at the bank when I was telling the world it was in that old bookstore, and connected the robbery to me?

But nobody ever came knocking on my door and the media cycle never slept. It was only about a week before the reporters stopped camping out on my doorstep. A week later, they were talking about some fourteen-year-old who had written a New York Times bestseller, and the week after that, I finally had the privacy I needed to call my brother.

He didn't seem surprised to hear from me, didn't even question how I got his number. I felt an enormous weight lift off my chest when he agreed to meet me at his old favorite restaurant in the neighborhood where we grew up.

I took a lukewarm shower in my crummy studio apartment and changed into my most conservative, big-sisterly outfit—a cozy sweater and a pair of jeans. I tucked my hair into a baseball cap to lower the risk of being recognized by anyone who'd seen me on the news and wanted to congratulate the lucky grad student. Then I put on a pair of Converse sneakers that I bought because they reminded me of life back when Donnie and I were a team.

Granted, these were limited edition Chuck Taylors

and the best I ever had as a kid had been a beat-up pair that my mom brought home from the thrift store on my eleventh birthday. The shoes were different, but the sentiment was the same—I wondered if the sight of them would take Donnie back to that time, too.

He'd been so damn jealous of those threadbare sneakers, I had to go out and steal him a pair of his own. He never did figure out why his shiny new Converse were so much better than mine.

When I found him in the restaurant, he was sitting with his back to me. He was in the same booth we always liked when we were kids. I used to bring him there just to get out of the house for a few hours. My heart started to climb into my throat the closer I got to him—his carroty hair was cut short and neat, and he was nearly fifteen years older than the boy I last knew, but I would have recognized that hair anywhere.

"Donnie," I said softly as I approached the table.

He turned, our eyes locked, and his mouth twitched. He wouldn't let himself smile and he ignored me when I opened my arms for a hug. He just motioned me into the booth to sit across from him.

"I ordered us coffee already," he said, his voice much deeper than I was expecting. I was struggling to reconcile this grown version of him with the boy I remembered—seeing him all those months ago in Trader Joe's had not prepared me to actually talk to him. When he added, "I can't stay long enough to eat," I just nodded.

"Okay," I said. "How have you been?"

"Good," he said. "You look well."

It seemed like a great effort for him to dole out that compliment. My heart stopped its climb, constricting as I realized he was still looking at me with the same contempt he'd worn all over his face on the day he told me he'd rather live in foster care than with a criminal sister.

"Thanks," I said. "So do you."

He didn't say anything else. He just sat patiently, his hands folded on top of the table while he studied me. The waitress came by with a couple small porcelain mugs and a coffee carafe, and Donnie busied himself adding cream to his coffee.

"I have something for you," I offered, pulling a carefully folded piece of paper out of my back pocket. I glanced around the restaurant—there were about twenty tables there and most of them were full, but no one was paying us any attention and the waitress didn't seem to be in a hurry to come back around. I unfolded the paper and laid it on the table between us, then whispered, "It's Verne's treasure map."

I studied Donnie's eyes, looking for some spark of excitement in them—evidence of the little kid who had been completely obsessed with the *Twenty Thousand Leagues Under the Sea* robbery and the promise of real treasure.

He didn't react except to glance at the paper, so I added quietly, "Well, not the real one, of course. I had to give that back to the museum, but I had a high-quality photocopy made first. I asked a friend to look over the original to make sure there were no details—hidden messages, stuff like that—that wouldn't be transferred to a photograph. We could go after Verne's treasure together if you want."

Donnie looked at me, his eyes devoid of emotion. "You think there's really treasure to be found? Wow, you haven't grown up a bit, have you?"

"Come on, it might be fun. You never know," I said, trying to keep my tone chipper as my heart plummeted to the floor.

"This is ridiculous. It's all a lie." As he spoke, a fire started burning behind his steely eyes. It was nice to see *something* in them, even if it had to be anger.

"What's a lie?" I asked.

"Well, for one thing, I'd love to know when you started studying classic literature," he said, folding his arms across his chest and leaning back like he'd made up his mind about me once and for all.

"You saw the news segments," I said.

"Of course," he answered. "They were all over the place—I couldn't miss them. That's what you wanted, wasn't it?"

"Yes," I said. "Yes, exactly. I wanted you back in my life because you're my brother, Donnie."

"I go by Don now," he said, his lips pressing into a thin line.

"Don," I corrected. I was working hard to keep my

composure now as a lump formed in the back of my throat. It wasn't supposed to go this way—I'd spent so many months dreaming about our reunion, and in those daydreams, he'd always welcomed me back with open arms. "You're right. I put myself on TV because I wanted you to see me. I wanted you to know I've changed, that I'm done with crime and I couldn't go back if I wanted to—you saw my face, you heard my name, and so did every cop in the country. I'm out of that life."

He narrowed his eyes at me.

I held my breath.

Please believe me.

"So you're studying adventures in classic literature," he said sardonically. "Is that for your master's or your Ph.D?"

I looked down at the map still spread across the table. "Well, that's just my cover story."

"A lie," he said pointedly. "Like everything else. You haven't changed—you'll never change."

"Look, I didn't just go out and become a thief because it was fun," I spat, reaching the limits of my shame. "Everything I did was for you, to take care of you in the only way I could because our parents were unreliable pieces of shit."

"I *never* asked you to be a criminal for me," Donnie shot back, then he stood to go.

That was when I noticed four broad-shouldered men in police uniforms walking through the door of the restaurant. An icicle shot through my chest and I froze. If I was a betting woman, I would have laid down every last penny of my cut from the Verne book that they were coming for *me*.

"Shit," I muttered under my breath.

"What?" Donnie asked.

His eyes went wide when he saw the men and there was no questioning it now—they were making a beeline for our table. I could have died when I saw the look in my brother's face as he turned back to me, and maybe a little part of me did. It was an unmistakable *I knew it* look—not angry, just disappointed.

It was too late to run—too late by at least five minutes—so I quickly folded the map and tried to slide it across the table to Donnie. He shook his head and took a few steps away from me. I had just enough time to shove the paper into the crease of my seat before the four police officers surrounded the booth. Every head in the restaurant turned to take in the spectacle and I had no choice but to sit there and meet my fate.

"Madison Blackstone?" one of them asked. I nodded and he showed me his badge, then announced, nice and loud so the whole damn restaurant could hear, "You're wanted for breaking and entering in Mandy Lake. Why don't you come downtown with us?"

"Do I have a choice?" I asked, arching one eyebrow. Over the man's shoulder, I could see Donnie's face. This was it—the very last bridge I would ever get to burn in my relationship with my brother. He would never believe another word I said.

"If you want to put up a fight, we'll do this the hard way. Madison Blackstone, you're under arrest," the officer said, and then as if it was personal, he added with a smirk, "Girl like you, I'm sure you know exactly how this is gonna go down."

"I can guess," I said, sneering at him as I slid out of the booth with my wrists extended. The only surprise as he grabbed me roughly by the arm and slapped a set of handcuffs on me was that they wanted me for breaking and entering and not theft. Did they know about the Verne book?

I didn't look at my brother as they walked me outside and stuffed me into the back of an unmarked black car. I didn't want to see the look on his face, and I definitely didn't want him to see mine.

As I sat in the back seat and tried to practice deep breathing to calm my racing thoughts, the only fear I could not tamp down was about Cass's safety. If Rutherford knew I'd been involved in the break-in, was it just because of the news reports, or was he onto Cass and Talia, too?

23

CASS

I knew I was in trouble when they didn't speak to me right away.

The police put me overnight in a cell with no soft surfaces, some unidentifiable mush they called food, and no company except the frat boy cop, sitting at a desk nearby and keeping watch. With only water and the gray walls to distract me, my brain went wild with questions.

Why were they holding me like this—alone? Had Henry betrayed me? Or had the police been following me? I would have thought the latter, perhaps, but I couldn't shake the look on Henry's face.

What if they had Madison, too? I pictured her in another holding area in the station, alone. We had been careful, for the most part, but we had made mistakes along the way. Too many mistakes, now that I was tallying them in my head. There was the ski mask I'd carelessly thrown on the floor of the vault, Madison's poodle-phobia that kept us from placing more cameras at Rutherford's, and the trip to the liquor store. Even Madison's appearance on TV, in light of all that, seemed like a foolish decision.

I'd been blinded. Again. I should have known better.

"Get up," a voice said, making me flinch from my perch on the bench. I hadn't even realized anyone new had come in... that's how distracted I was.

My arresting officer was standing outside my cell. The frat boy cop, looking smug as a cat with a mouse's tail sticking out its mouth, stood near his desk while Detective Thomas Wilson, dressed in a shirt and tie and a dark blue jacket, adjusted his utility belt. They were ready for me.

"Cass Hartley," Detective Wilson said. "You're to come with me."

My heart fluttered.

I always considered myself an actress of sorts. A woman who could read other people and situations transform into who I wanted to be. Now, I would have to put on the biggest performance of my life, especially if they asked me about Madison... and all on an empty stomach.

He sat me in a metal folding chair in a windowless room not much bigger than the table and three chairs it held. I was facing a lady detective on the same side of the table as me—Detective Linda Maynard, bad cop counterpart to my now good friend Detective Wilson. I could see right through what they were doing. They offered me no water, no food, and no breaks. They drilled me, barely allowing me to speak.

"Where were you the evening of April 21?" *More than a month ago? I honestly have no idea. Probably at home.* "Was anyone with you?" *I generally hate people so no, probably not.* "Were you at the First United Bank of New Vernon on April 21?" *For an interview, yes.* "After hours?" *Why would I be at a bank after hours?*

The lady detective had a vein over her left eye that bulged in response to some of my answers. Though her voice was laced with honey, her eyes started to narrow on me like a laser on a target.

"We have a credible witness placing you at the scene," she said.

The vein was fully illuminated now, stark against the woman's pale face. Her yellow hair was slicked back so tight that I could see it pulling at the skin. I focused on this to remain calm, leaning against my chair, arms folded. I was past the point of exhaustion now, but felt my gaze and my mind sharpen. "Scene of what?"

"Don't act stupid. The crime," she said. "And we know you were casing the joint beforehand."

"I already told you I had an interview."

"An interview where an employee's keycard was stolen. We know what you did."

"Then why bother questioning me?"

"Because we believe others were involved," she said.

My heart gave one strong pound of denial. *Answer quickly, Hartley.* "Who?"

"I don't know, you tell me."

"*I* don't know."

"Don't mess with me, Ms. Hartley. We know who you are, and we know—"

Detective Wilson, who had been silent throughout most of the questioning, leaned forward, putting out a hand to Linda, stopping her mid-question. "Are you certain you don't want a lawyer present, Ms. Hartley?"

Nice cop. And an interesting tactic. I knew my rights. The moment I invoked my right to a lawyer, this meeting would end. But I didn't want it to stop. Linda had said they knew about others. Who? Talia? Spider? Madison? I needed to find out what they knew before I saved myself. I needed to find out if they knew about Madison.

Plus, a lawyer would try to convince me to turn Madison over, and that I would absolutely never do. I had the upper hand at the moment. These cops wanted something from me and I knew it.

I sat back and waited for someone else to speak. Detective Wilson stood, pacing the small space between the chair and the wall. Two steps forward, turn, two steps back. He stopped, bracing his hands on the table. "We can help you, you know—if you tell us who was there with you."

Who did he think I was, Susie McCriminal Virgin? Sure, I'd been stupid enough to out myself at Henry's, but that had been because I thought he was in trouble. But this wasn't my first rodeo. I kept my lips pinned shut. So far, they had told me nothing. For all I knew, they were trying to trick me into talking about my crew, and I wasn't going to fall for it. Hell, they hadn't even told me what they had on me yet.

"I told you, I wasn't there after hours. I'd been there earlier in the day," I said.

Linda scoffed. "The apple doesn't fall far from the tree, huh, Tom? Liars, them Hartleys, every one."

"Now, now. That's a little presumptive, huh, Linda?" I said, getting sick of this whole charade. "We don't even know each other yet. We haven't even been on one date."

Linda's eyes widened slightly at my forwardness, but she recovered quickly enough, clasping her hands on the table and somehow managing to keep her composure. "We have a ski mask with female DNA on it. We know you've robbed banks in other states. You could go away longer than your parents."

The ski mask. Madison's ski mask. My hands went

cold and clammy at the thought. Panic sprung under my arms. Madison wanted to get out of the business. She could get out. She didn't have the same history I had. The moment people looked at me, they saw my parents. Even if I wanted to go straight, my legacy would follow me.

But they had the mask. Which meant they were only one step away from Madison. And if they caught Madison, it would not only mean jail time, but losing her brother all over again. I knew what it was like to lose family. I knew that all too well, and I wasn't going to let her go through that.

She was too good.

I was not.

Not to mention, they would find a way to pin me to the bank robbery, too. Even if they got Madison, they were coming after me, too, and there was no sense in us both going down.

All of this whipped through my mind in quick succession. I placed my sweaty hands on the table and looked Detective Linda Maynard in the eye, letting out a shaky sigh. What could I do? How could I get out of this? I needed time to think. "I'm tired. Can we take a break?"

"Tell us who was with you and you can rest."

"I *wasn't* there. I wasn't anywhere near the—"

"Mildred Fillingham has a different story to tell," she said. "She's got a very interesting story about how you stole her keycard and replaced it with a non-functioning fake. Hers is the card that opened the deposit room vault around midnight, and yet her husband says she was sleeping in her recliner by nine o'clock."

Just like that, they had won. The authorities had been dogging me for years, and they'd had nothing until now. I wished more than anything I'd spent last night sleeping and eating and nourishing myself for this moment. Maybe then I would have been able to think of something, some way to get myself out of this. But my sharpness was slipping away and I couldn't see how to get out of this. If they tested the DNA on the ski mask, they'd know it wasn't mine and they'd have another suspect to search for. Eventually, it would lead them to Madison. But there was a chance...

This was it. This was *the* moment. The moment that would decide the rest of my life. I could still choose to save myself, but that didn't seem like an option any longer. It was a long shot, but one I had to take. For Madison. "The mask is mine. I robbed the bank. I was the mastermind."

"Who else was with you?" Linda said, barely missing a beat.

Like a den of bed bugs, this woman. Couldn't get her off my back.

I expected to doubt my decision the moment the words came out of my mouth, but that wasn't what happened. My brain was quiet, relief and determination filling me. "No one," I said.

"Ms. Hartley, we know there were others—"

"Do you want to put the last remaining Hartley behind bars? It was me. All me. If you know anything about me, you know I never work with other criminals."

"There's no way you broke into that bank alone. There were multiple entry points," Linda insisted.

Tenacious woman. I had to give her something that would distract her. "You don't think I'm capable of it? Memphis, Tennessee. Sacramento, California. Albany, New York." I ticked the cities off on my fingers. "And, oh yeah. New York City, too."

"What are all those locations?"

"They're all the places I robbed without anyone finding out. I'm capable, *Detective Linda Maynard*. I'm capable of this and so, so much more."

Twenty-five years to life. But the alternative—turning Madison in and ruining her life as well as my own—would be a guaranteed life sentence of guilt, on top of the one I was already serving for my parents.

"You're confessing," Linda Maynard said, her nearly invisible white-blonde eyebrows as flat as her tone. "To a bank robbery. That you committed alone. You took down the guard, swiped Mildred Fillingham's keycard to enter through the vault door, then cut a hole in the wall just for the fun of it."

"Yes, that's about the size of it," I said. "I'm confessing, and there was no one else there."

"Why are you doing this?" she asked.

"Why does it matter to you?"

"I think it's time we take a break. Get you some food and some water, Ms. Hartley." Detective Wilson rose from his seat and offered me an elbow. I didn't take it. Still, he patted my arm like I was a little girl as he opened the door for me. "You did good today. Next up, we're going to have to turn this over to the Feds."

I'd done *good*. For once. It wasn't over yet. It would take some finagling to keep Madison out of the investigation, but she'd never been caught before. She was clean. They didn't have her DNA in the system to match with whatever they'd found in that mask—if they found anything in the mask at all. And as long as she stayed out of the system, she would be fine.

We walked down a narrow hallway. All I wanted was to sleep. None of the rest mattered. I let Detective Wilson guide me and barely saw where I walked. A couple of people hurried past. Someone took in a quick breath, a gasp. I lifted my heavy head and swiveled my neck around to see who it was... and caught the fluorescent lights glinting off the unforgettable auburn strands of Madison Blackstone's hair.

G etting booked was a blur.

I'd had my fair share of meetings with the cops—anyone in this line of work would —but I prided myself on never actually getting arrested. If I'd just been sensible like Cass wanted me to be, if I'd kept my face and my *name* out of the news, I'd be safe right now.

I could be with *her* right now.

But I had to try to win my brother back, didn't I? A fool's errand, it turned out.

A surly police officer ushered me through my mugshot, then mushed my fingers into black ink and rolled them across a piece of cardstock. Not only had I just lost all hope of ever winning back Donnie's affections... no, he went by *Don* now... I was officially in the system. Madison Blackstone, criminal.

"Surprised we haven't nailed you before," the

officer said as he tossed a tissue box at me so I could clean my fingers.

"Surprised you're so underfunded you're still doing ink and paper fingerprinting," I shot back.

He didn't like that. He narrowed his eyes and grabbed me a little too hard by the arm, hauling me out of the booking area and leading me through a doorway, then turning down a narrow hallway.

"We're going to have a little chat about that house and what you were doing inside it," he said, sneering at me. "I saw you all over the news. What's a pretty grad student like you doing in other people's houses? And then you found that rare missing book—what an unbelievable coincidence!"

Shit. They knew it all. Did Rutherford tell them or had they put it together themselves? All I could hope for was that Rutherford didn't have the guts—or the skill—to hunt down Cass and Talia. Because if he did, then I'd put both our crews in danger for a relationship with my brother that was never going to be saved. The police could be out there looking for Cass right now for all I knew.

Oh, Cass... why didn't we take any one of the half-dozen signs the universe was giving us that this whole damn job was one massive bad idea? *Because then we never would have fallen for each other,* a voice in my head answered loud and clear. It was a little startling, as if someone else was speaking for me, but I knew it was true.

Now all I could do was keep my mouth shut and try to protect everyone else on our crews. I'd give myself up, take the full rap for the book heist if it came to it. With any luck, I could convince the police that most of the money had vanished into thin air. My lawyer was good and there would be no paper trail for the funds. Then Cass could make herself disappear along with it. *Goodbye, Cass...*

The officer practically dragged me down the hall-way. If he told me his name, I didn't catch it, and it didn't matter. I was pretty sure he wasn't about to go all *good cop* on me in the interrogation room. My wrists were cuffed together in front of me and when another officer came up the hallway from the other direction, leading a woman with her head bowed, we made an awkward shuffle to move past each other.

And then her dark hair fell out of her face and I let out a gasp.

Cass!

She looked like hell, like she'd given up on life, and all I wanted to do was throw my arms around her in a protective cocoon. But then Officer Surly hitched his knee into the back of my thigh, surprisingly sharp, and grumbled, "Keep moving."

I averted my eyes quickly, turning my head so they wouldn't notice our connection. I thought it worked for a minute—we kept walking in opposite directions—but then the officer's hand closed tightly around my arm again, making me wince.

"Stop," he demanded, turning to look back up the hallway.

Shit, shit, shit.

"You know her?"

"No," I said, trying to keep my voice slow and steady. He didn't buy it. I guess you don't get to be a police officer, even in a small branch like this, by being born yesterday.

"Come on," he said, yanking me around by the arm to follow Cass. "Change of plans."

Officer Surly threw me—and I do mean *threw* me—into a holding cell that was a few hallway branches off of the one where I first saw Cass. I had to put my hands out to catch myself against the wall before I got a face full of gray cinder block, and then I heard the heavy steel clang of the door closing behind me.

It took me a second to regain my footing and when I turned around, Cass was sitting on the only bench in the small cell, which was bolted to the side wall.

Our eyes locked and I was relieved to see a little more life in Cass's honey-colored eyes than there had been in the hallway. But there was something else there, too—dread. *What do they have on you?* I wondered, my heart pounding.

I opened my mouth to ask—it was all I could do to

keep myself from running across the room and pulling her into my arms. But she interrupted me, giving me a hard look and saying, "I'm Cass. You?"

She glanced through the bars to a guard's desk about fifteen feet away. There was yet another officer sitting there, his arms folded in front of his chest and a curious look on his young face. He was definitely listening in. My spirits fell as I realized this was exactly what Officer Surly had put me here for—he'd noticed my connection to Cass in the hallway and he wanted us to spill our guts and save him the trouble of an interrogation.

"I'm Madison," I said, sinking down to sit on the filthy floor in the corner of the room, opposite Cass. The jeans I was wearing would have to be trashed when we got out of there, but at least I was out of the guard's visibility, shielded by the cinder block wall.

I mouthed the word *break-in* to Cass. Then I mouthed *Rutherford*.

She knit her brows, then shook her head subtly so the guard wouldn't notice. She had no idea what I was trying to say and I realized that, of all her incredible talents, lip-reading had apparently never been necessary before.

Well, shit. I didn't mouth that part, but from the expression on Cass's face, I didn't have to.

I kept trying for another ten minutes or so, thinking of all the different words I could mouth to convey our situation as I understood it. *News. Cameras. I'm sorry.*

Cass couldn't respond the same way because the guard was watching her like a hawk, so she put her hands on her thighs and started twitching her fingers. I figured out, after a couple rounds, that a right hand twitch meant *yes* and a left hand twitch was *no,* and just when we were starting to get somewhere, another officer appeared and yanked open the door.

"Dinner time," he said, dropping a plastic tray on the bench beside Cass and then swinging the door shut again.

"What about her?" Cass asked.

"Boss didn't say anything about her," he answered with a shrug, then slammed the door. "Eat up, Hartley —they're gonna want your written confession soon."

My blood went cold and my eyes were wide as saucers when Cass looked at me. As soon as the officer disappeared beyond the cell wall, I mouthed, *Written confession?!*

There was that look of dread again. What did she do? She regained her composure impressively fast for the guard's sake, then said dispassionately to me, "You want some of this?"

She tilted the plastic tray up so I could see it—a squished sandwich in plastic wrap, a pudding cup, a plastic spoon and a cardboard carton of milk. My stomach rumbled involuntarily but I shook my head.

"Come on," Cass said. "You gotta eat."

She stood and carried the tray over to me. All I was thinking was that it looked like a minefield of DNA collection traps—if I put my mouth on that spoon or my backwash went into that straw, they could put me at both the Rutherford house *and* the bank. They'd be able to put me away for decades.

I shook my head again, but Cass just rolled her eyes and nodded toward the cell wall. Her back was blocking the guard's view and suddenly I understood what she was doing. He wouldn't stand for it long, but it was enough.

"I confessed to save you and the others," she whispered as I took the sandwich from her. "They don't know about the book."

"Yes, they do," I said, frantic. "They saw me on the news."

"Shit," she said.

"Confessed to *what*, Cass?"

"Hey," the guard barked before she could answer, his chair scraping along the concrete floor as he stood. "Whatcha up to in there, ladies?"

Cass took a step backward, ready to retreat to her bench, but I grabbed her wrist in a flash and whispered, "I love you."

My heart was pounding harder than it ever had when I was running from law enforcement, or when I was in the middle of a particularly adrenaline-fueled heist. The words came out of me like they had a will of their own and I didn't have time to add the second half of that sentiment—*and I'm going to take the fall for you. Don't say anything else!*

I didn't have time because the guard was resting one arm on the bars of the cell, scrutinizing us.

Cass smiled sweetly at him and said, "I was just sharing my dinner. I don't like PB&J."

"Who the hell doesn't like PB&J?" the guard scoffed, but I held up the sandwich to corroborate her story and he rolled his eyes. Then a buzzer sounded and the door next to the guard's desk opened.

Officer Surly was back and he marched right up to the cell door. "Blackstone—it's time to sing."

He had me put my hands through a slot in the door so he could cuff me again, then he unlocked the door and ushered me out. The whole time, I was dying to sneak a glance at Cass—it felt like my heart was going to burst in my chest. Did she hear me? Did she love me, too? Did she think I was crazy?

I might well be.

But I couldn't look at her because any interaction could be used against us, and I couldn't risk that now that I knew she'd confessed to something. We both might be facing quite a few years in prison. I might have burned my last familial bridge this afternoon... but I had to save her, whether she loved me back or not.

Surly took me back up that narrow hallway to the interrogation room.

It was small and windowless, just like on television, and he brought another detective into the room to sit beside me at the steel table. Surly at least did me the service of not cuffing me to the table like a dangerous

CARA MALONE & ANNA COVE

animal, and when his friend came into the room, this one was all smiles.

"Hi, I'm Detective Thomas Wilson," he said. "You can call me Tom."

Oh, brother. This guy was really making the *good cop* concept into an award-worthy performance. He did uncuff me, though, and for that I was grateful. I was starting to develop raw, red marks around my wrists and I massaged them as I sat and waited for them to start their little routine.

"We'd like to talk about the break-in at Michael Rutherford's home in Mandy Lake," good-guy Detective Tom said. "He just so happened to be watching the news a few weeks ago and says he saw a familiar face in a segment about a rare book. Would you happen to know anything about that?"

My heart was pounding hard in my chest. I was completely out of my element and I had to find a way to save Cass before she said anything else to incriminate herself. There was no reason for both of us to go down.

Think, Maddie, think!

"Are you implying that Rutherford is accusing me of breaking into his house to steal a book that itself is a high-profile stolen artifact?" I asked, my mind going a mile a minute. Could I find a way to pin it all on Rutherford?

"We're not *implying* anything," Surly said. "We certainly wouldn't want to *imply* that it seemed like you were getting familiar with that spark plug of a cell mate you had this afternoon."

"Familiar?" I asked. *Make him spell it out.*

"You know her, don't you?" Surly asked.

"We could always work out a deal of some sort," Tom said, lightening the mood and offering me a way out right on cue. "If she were connected to the book in some way."

"Actually," Surly said, sneering at me, "between you, me, and Tom, we've got that girl here on an unrelated crime, but you know what? There's one piece of evidence that's just not lining up."

Uh oh.

"Will you excuse me?" he asked, uncharacteristically sweet. I just sat there, staring him and his rhetorical question down until he left the interrogation room.

With just Tom and me in the small room, I wondered if he was going to turn into a bad cop. Instead, he stuck with his act, leaning forward confidentially and saying, "You've never been arrested before. It's obvious that if you *were* working with Hartley, it's because you fell in with a bad crowd. Her whole family is bad news, but she does have certain charms, doesn't she? A jury would understand that—they would take pity on you."

My stomach knotted at the idea of rolling over on Cass. Never—not on Cass, not on anyone... I wouldn't even rat on that creep, Spider.

I narrowed my eyes at Tom, fixing him with a withering glare, and he shrugged, sitting back in his seat. "Just think about it."

Then Surly came back into the room, a plastic evidence bag in one hand. He slammed it down on the table right in front of me, staring me down as I looked at my black ski mask inside the bag.

"Recognize that?" he asked.

"It's a ski mask," I said, amazed at how stone-faced I could be. "Some people call them balaclavas if you want to get etiological."

"You'll never guess what color hairs we found inside it," Surly barked.

"Purple?"

I had no idea what was making me suddenly so cheeky with these guys. Some of the Hartley charm must have rubbed off on me after all our time together. Maybe it was purely survival, or maybe I was just riding a particularly cheeky high of exhaustion, fear and a little bit of elation at having just told Cass that I loved her.

Whatever the case, Officer Surly didn't like my attitude.

"Red," he snapped. "Just like yours."

"Yeah, well, like Detective Tom said, my DNA isn't in the system," I said. "That could be anyone's hair."

Surly rolled his eyes and reached across the table, yanking a clump of at least five or ten hairs out of my head. My mouth dropped open and tears sprang involuntarily to my eyes with the pain, then Surly held the hairs up in front of my eyes. "We have the legal right to obtain DNA samples from any suspect who walks through our doors. You should know your criminal code if you're gonna be a thief."

I glanced at Detective Tom, not so much because I wanted the good guy in my corner but simply because there was nowhere else to look. He took it as encouragement and chastised his partner. "Gee, Frank, you could have asked her nicely. I bet Madison would like to cooperate with us if we give her a good reason."

Officer Surly ignored him, pulling an empty evidence bag out of his back pocket. He stuffed my hairs into it and sealed it up, then put the bag on the table next to the ski mask and sat down across from me.

He folded his arms on the table. He stared me down. He waited, maybe assuming I would crack if he stared at me long enough.

Then after a minute or so of silence, he said with a grin, "You're in the system now—DNA and all, as soon as we get that hair processed. If you're connected with the Hartley bank robbery, we'll know soon enough." He glanced at Detective Tom, then back at me, smiling even wider like a wolf about to devour a wounded prey animal. "We're going to figure out everything you did and exactly who helped you. I suggest you start thinking about the story you want to tell, and just how long you want to rot in jail."

25

CASS

One of the true pleasures of being an adult was that I could say basically anything I wanted without serious repercussion. Anyone could, though they usually didn't for fear of social retribution. But I had. For so many years, I'd said most of what was on my mind. I'd made jokes and laughed things off and conned my way into places where I had no business. Looking back, barely anything I'd said was true. I'd used words as weapons just like I'd used people as tools.

But when Madison had said those words to me—*I love you*—I saw what words truly could be. How they could be bare and pure and soft all at the same time. How they could serve as a caress, soft and warm as a chenille blanket.

And what had I said in return? Nothing. My throat had become as dry as the Sahara. Then they'd taken her away. My eyes, on the other hand, hadn't stopped leaking from their corners since she'd left.

Madison loves me.

And I love her, too.

I'd never been so sure of anything in my life. Hadn't my actions proven it? Hell, I'd given myself up for her. Offered my freedom for her. If that wasn't love, what was? I was done hiding from the truth. The hiding had been exhausting all my life and now I could see it had never been worth it.

Would we ever see each other again? Would I get to tell her the full extent of my truth?

I sniffed, wiping the leaking trail on my face, the hard bench digging into my thighs. I slept a little, and when I woke, reality pressed into my gut.

My confession was pointless.

Madison had been arrested for the Rutherford breaking and entering, and it was only a matter of time before the cops put all of it together. We would both go to prison. Madison could take care of herself—she had proven that to me—but she would never be the same again.

But all was not lost—not yet. We still had one option, though it would put more people at risk. I thought I'd been protecting everyone by confessing and giving in easily. Talia, Madison, Henry. I'd done things *for* them. But what if, for once, I trusted these people?

Novel idea, eh?

I stood and went to the cell door. I wrapped my

hands around the bars and rattled them. The frat boy officer at the desk looked up, his baby face turning crimson like I'd surprised him in the middle of a porn video. I bit back a snide comment.

"I'd like my phone call now. Please," I said.

The man glanced at his watch and nodded once. There was one word I hadn't used yet. One word that would set into motion a series of events that might fail, but if they succeeded, they would bring freedom to me and Madison, and everyone else involved in this whole mess.

Clementine.

Okay, now that I was about to use it, I recognized it lacked a certain *oomph*. No one was going to be threatened or driven into action by the word *clementine*. It was just a sweet little fruit that preschoolers ate at snack time. It also sounded kind of dumb saying, "I'm *dying* for a clementine," when calling a friend from a police station. But it was something Talia and I had joked about years ago—a code word we'd never changed.

The phone call was short, less than a minute.

"Hey, I got arrested. Can you find me a lawyer? And tell him to bring a clementine. I'm in need of some vitamin C."

Talia's voice cracked when she asked, "Are you sure? A clementine?"

I wanted to yell, *"That's our code word, remember?"* but that would have given me away. They might have transferred me, or tried to lock me up more securely, and neither of those things would be conducive to a clementine.

We should have come up with something more obvious, but at the time it had only been a joke. At the time, I never thought I would find myself so close to incarceration. So I hung up the phone and prayed she'd understood.

One, two, three, four. I tried to count the minutes passing, then what felt like hours passing, once I returned to my cell, but my digs didn't have a clock. Nor did they have any natural light I could estimate by. The frat boy at the desk wasn't responsive to my inquiries.

Too busy with the porning.

Every few minutes I stood to stretch my legs, not wanting to be stiff as I waited for something to happen. I should have caught some shut-eye early on, right after the phone call, but as time marched forward I couldn't risk the grogginess.

My mind started to swirl with potential outcomes so I tried to settle it by focusing on Madison. On our time together. Each moment flashed through my mind like a movie. The look of surprise on her face after I'd kissed her that first time in the doorway of the bar. How equally adorable and frustrating I'd found her when she'd waltzed into my command center. The time of bliss at the motel and all the moments that followed.

That soft blanket Madison had woven with her words settled over me, tugging my lips upward in a smile. What a strange time to smile, to feel peace.

My peace was shattered a moment later when a strobe light started flashing and a piercing alarm shot through my head. The officer at the desk picked up his radio, said something I couldn't make out, then put it up to his ear. Someone appeared at the doorway, a someone who seemed to be wrapped in smoke. The smoke billowed in and frat boy gave me one look—with a flicker of fear—before he ran into the hall.

Leave it to the New Vernon Police Department to trap a prisoner in a burning building.

I could only hope this was Talia's version of a clementine. Otherwise, this smoke did not bode well for my ongoing survival.

"That was almost too easy," Talia said as she tested the keys the frat guy officer had left on the desk, looking for the one that would unlock my cell. "You'd think a bunch of cops would be able to handle a little smoke."

I chided myself for having doubted her. She was a memory genius—*of course* she remembered what clementine meant. Yet I stared at her now with a measure of skepticism. I was looking at Talia, but the voice coming out of her and the certainty of her movements were decidedly *not* the Talia I knew. "Is the building actually burning?"

Talia shrugged, a shadow of her former self in that movement, but even this was dwarfed by her confidence as she spoke. "Nope. I started the alarms with a lighter in the women's room, then Bree took control of the central system and spread the alarm throughout the building. The smoke bomb was a little something I added to conceal our departure."

I jumped a little on my toes, priming my legs for a run. Talia slid a key into the lock. "Is Tank with you?"

"He's in the car."

"He's not in here with you? How did you manage that?"

"I convinced him that the cops wouldn't suspect little me of creating such chaos." Talia looked up at me with her wide, dark eyes, then fluttered her eyelashes. "He agreed, and *voila.*"

The door to my cell opened. I stood for a moment, staring. "What has that man done to you?"

"What? Nothing."

"You're... different."

"If I'm different, it's because of me, not him."

She was right. Still, I didn't move. In that moment, sprinklers descended from the ceiling and shot a fine spray of water in all directions. Talia grabbed my hand. "We have to get you out of here. The smoke bombs won't last long and the fire department will be here any moment."

I swallowed down my disbelief, forcing myself to think clearly. The drenching from the sprinklers helped. As we reached the hall, I stopped short, causing Talia to rebound against me. I could only see our hands clasped in the thick, misty smoke. "We can't go yet. Madison is here."

"Where?" Talia asked, shouting over the hissing water and screaming alarms, not missing a beat.

I couldn't remember where the interrogation room had been. I really could have used Talia's memory earlier when Detective Tom was taking me there. "I don't know, but we have to find her."

Talia's face materialized out of the smoke, her delicate features set in determination, her hair plastered to her temples. The last time we'd been in a situation like this—in the bank—she'd been so scared she hadn't moved. Even in the collector's house, she had been timid and hesitant. But something had changed in the meantime. I'd seen it happening, but hadn't fully realized the extent of it until now.

"Let's start trying doors and see if we can find her," she said. "We can spare a couple minutes to search, but then we have to leave."

The alarms were still going off and a loudspeaker was screaming about a lockdown. It would be risky to just open doors, but I couldn't think of anything better to do in that moment. So we started testing the keys from the ring. It was slower than I would have liked, but Talia moved with sure hands, no sign of a shake anywhere. It was impressive, especially given that I wouldn't have been able to do the same. I couldn't get my mind to calm.

What if we couldn't find Madison? What if we found her but she was hurt or locked up? We'd only been through two doors before someone ran straight into me.

We're done, I thought, my body going cold. *We're caught.*

But then there were hands on my shoulders, and a familiar face squinting through the smoke. Her mascara was running and her hair darkened by the sprinkler system, but she was still the most beautiful woman I had ever seen. *Madison.*

I was so happy to see her, I cupped her chin in my hands and planted a kiss on her lips. I could feel them pulling up in a smirk, then giving in as the rest of her body melted into mine.

"Let's go, lovebirds," Talia said, tugging at my sleeve.

Reluctantly, I released Madison's lips. "How did you get into the hall?"

"I'll tell you later," Madison said, pulling her hands from around my shoulders. "Let's get out of here."

"Are there any officers that way?" Talia asked, nodding in the direction Madison had come.

"They were walking me back to the holding cell when the alarms and the sprinklers went off," Madison said. "I fought them off and ran. Is the building actually on fire?"

"Nope. Just smoke bombs and some computer tweaking by Bree. Come on." Talia took my sleeve and forcefully dragged me through the smoke. Madison had my hand. *Madison*. She was here. We were together. We were going to get out of this.

"Where are we going?" I asked.

"I'm hoping we can slip out the front door," Talia said.

"Just... walk out?"

"Did you have a better plan?" Talia asked, securing us behind a doorway panel. The blaring siren, the flashing light, the water and the smoke were so disorienting I couldn't tell where we were any longer.

Truthfully, I didn't have a better plan. I had to trust Talia—what other choice did I have? And how much *more* trouble could I be in if we got caught? Madison squeezed my hand. I glanced back at her and caught her actually *smiling* at me. I smiled back. "It's all you, Talia. Just tell us what we need to do."

"Most of the cops are outside, evacuated, but there will be a few in the lobby. Darn. Those are sirens. The firefighters are here, too." I waited for her to think of something. "I'm going to set off another smoke bomb. We'll have to slip out the door in the confusion. Tank is parked around back. Ready?"

"Ready," I said.

"As ever," Madison said.

"Count to thirty and then follow me." Without checking to see whether we heard her, Talia slipped through the door and disappeared.

I had counted to eleven when Madison gasped and I felt her freeze beside me. "Shit," she whispered.

"What?" I asked. I could feel her terror in the thick smoke of the hallway.

Then I heard something else - voices and footsteps coming toward us. We were cornered, trapped. They hadn't seen us yet through the smoke, by the sound of their voices, but it was only a matter of time.

Luckily for us, there was an open door right next to where we stood. I pulled Madison inside and pinned us to the wall beside the door.

A brief memory flashed of us doing this once before, when the Rutherford's dogs were after us. Madison had been afraid then, and I'd consoled her. Now, it was the opposite situation. My hands shook in Madison's, and I realized for the first time in a long time, I had something to lose. I had many things to lose.

"This must have been what it felt like on the Titanic when it was going down," I murmured.

"Shh," Madison said. She pressed her body up against mine, trying to quiet me. In here, the smoke wasn't as thick. I could see her face. But it soon began to blur with the water running down my face and into my eyes. *What if they separate us when they bring us to prison? What if this is the last moment?*

"Maddie—"

"Just be quiet. We're going to get out of here. It's going to be fine," she said.

I shook my head hard, sure she was wrong. This was it. This was the end. And if it was the end, I wanted to go out on a strong note. On a truthful note. I wanted to leave Madison something she could wrap herself in as well, like she had left me with her blanket of love.

I kissed her, my very breath shaking, and I let her feel all of it. All my vulnerability. Everything I'd worked so hard to hide over the years. To keep myself upright, I held her shoulders. "I love you Madison Blackstone. I love you and I want to be with you for the rest of my—"

26

MADISON

"Oh, Cass," I said, a storm of emotions brewing in my chest. "Don't say that right now. I love you, too, more than I knew I could love anyone, but we're going to get out of here."

Disappointment started to cut into her expression and I wanted to reassure her—it wasn't that I didn't want to hear her say those words. I'd been dying to hear them ever since Officer Surly dragged me out of the holding cell. But the adrenaline pumping through my veins had hit critical mass and the smoke in my lungs was nearing the same. I couldn't focus properly on Cass's words, and I wasn't convinced she could, either.

"How?" she asked.

That was a question I *didn't* know the answer to. I turned around, squinting into the smoke. It was thicker near the door, where it had seeped into the room from the hallway. Beyond the edge of the smoke, I could see tall forms on the wall opposite us. Lockers.

And one of them was hanging open.

"Cass, you saved us when you picked this room," I said, pulling her through the smoke. With every step, I prayed that locker wouldn't be empty.

Please, God or universe or flying spaghetti monster —whoever's out there—let there be a uniform in that locker... something we can use!

It didn't seem logical, but the universe was smiling on the criminal lovers desperately trying to bust out of a police station. When we looked into the locker, we found a uniform jacket and pants hanging from the hook. Whoever it belonged to must have been changing when the bomb went off, and now he was running around the building in his undershirt looking for us.

"There's only one jacket," Cass said, pulling it off the hook and holding it up. It was enormous, but it had the letters *NVPD—New Vernon Police Department* —printed on the back in giant yellow letters, and that was the important part.

"Doesn't matter," I said, snatching the jacket out of her hands and holding it up for her to slide into. "Hurry up, before someone comes in here."

"Me?" Cass asked. "No, I think you should—"

I held up my hand, an open set of handcuffs dangling from one wrist. "It has to be you. I'm your prisoner and you're escorting me through the chaos."

"Oh yeah?" she said, a seductive smile forming in the corner of her mouth, and God help me, I wanted to lay her down on the locker room bench and make love to her right then and there. She could make any situation worth experiencing—even being hunted through a police precinct with alarms blaring.

"We'll roleplay it later," I said, matching her smile as I shoved her arms into the jacket. Then I held out my hands and she clicked the handcuff shut over my wrist.

"How *did* you get away from the cops?" she asked.

"I used my feminine wiles," I said, and as Cass closed one hand around my wrist to perp-walk me out of the locker room, I added, "and I may have kicked an officer or two in the jewels."

Cass laughed, then yanked on my hand to bring me to a quick stop right beside the door. She gave me a kiss, then said, "Let's get out of here."

"Yeah," I said. "Quickly."

We kissed one more time—for good luck or simply because it felt right, I'm not sure. Then Cass took a deep breath and opened the door, her hand firmly latched over my handcuffs.

The hallway was still impressively smoky. My hat was off to Talia for this bag of tricks, but by my count we were going on at least fifteen minutes since this all started and we were well into the danger zone. The initial panic was wearing off and the smoke was slowly dissipating. The officers in the hallway would be closing in, to say nothing of the fire department.

"Get moving," Cass barked at me, playing her role as the heroic cop who captured one of the escapees.

She nudged me in the direction of the door and it was a good thing she remembered because I'd gotten pretty turned around in the smoke. We walked as fast as we could without drawing attention to ourselves— there would be no good excuse if someone spotted an officer sprinting down the hall with a suspect. And we got lucky again, because we heard voices behind us in the smoke, but we didn't meet anyone between the locker room and our point of escape.

When we got back to the lobby, I stopped and glanced over my shoulder. "You're with me, right?"

My heart was pounding and all I could think of was a pair of *real* police officer hands separating us at the last minute, dragging Cass back into the smoky building. *Maybe I should let her go first...*

"I'm gonna be on your ass like white on rice," Cass said with a snort. "Go, Maddie."

So I did.

I walked straight into the lion's den of the lobby. The police had all evacuated and there were a few fire-fighters making their way inside. They barely even gave us a second look. *Nothing to see here. Just an officer escorting a criminal.*

Somehow, we made it outside. In the exposed air, I began to shake. It was so bright and the breeze drew goosebumps from my soaking wet body. Cass ran her thumbs over my wrist and I relaxed. In the chaos outside, no one noticed us edge our way around the side of the building.

Cass leaned forward and placed a kiss on my neck as soon as we spotted Tank crammed into Talia's car, Talia in the passenger seat beside him. "We did it. Good job."

"Maybe we should try this at home some time," I said, motioning to the handcuffs, but my voice was shaking, the adrenaline catching up to me.

"It's about time. Let's go," Talia hissed from the car. She got out and grabbed both of us by the hands, hauling us over to the car like a scolding teacher. "We thought you got caught!"

"Sorry," I said. "I thought we could go back for my evidence bags, but we didn't get them."

As we approached the car parked in the little alley that ran along the back of the precinct, I noticed Bree was in the back seat. Talia shoved Cass and I into the back with her like we were luggage and Bree held up her laptop protectively. Then Talia ran around the car and jumped into the passenger seat. "Drive, Josh!"

Tank revved the engine and flew up the narrow alley, emerging on a street that was miraculously free of traffic... or maybe that had something to do with the fire trucks blocking the roads around the precinct. I saw flashing lights at the other end of the block—a police barricade—but we were going in the other direction and I breathed a sigh of relief, relaxing against the seat.

"Thanks everyone," I said. "That was one hell of a jailbreak."

"I can't believe you pulled that off, Talia," Cass said, beaming as she leaned forward and patted her friend on the shoulder. "I couldn't have come up with a better clementine myself."

"Clementine?" I asked.

"Code for *get me the fuck outta here,*" Cass said with a laugh. She whooped and clapped her hands, then grabbed me and kissed me hard. "That was incredible!"

"It really was," I said.

When she let go of my face, I looped my cuffed hands over her head and pulled her into a tight embrace to kiss her again. She slipped me a little tongue and for once in my life, I simply enjoyed it instead of wondering what her angle was, or feeling embarrassed about the fact that we were in a car full of people.

I fucking love this woman.

"Excuse me," Bree said, putting her hands on my back to try to preserve her personal space in the cramped back seat. "Do you think you can wait until we get out of here before the make-out session begins? You're not the only ones back here."

"Sorry," Cass said, but she was looking at me as she said it and the glimmer in her eyes said she wasn't sorry at all. I grinned—was this what teenagers felt like when they fell head over heels for each other? I'd never had the chance to find out.

I disentangled my arms from Cass and she pulled a bobby pin out of Talia's neatly pulled back hair. Cass took my hands into her lap as she worked on picking the locks on the handcuffs.

Beside me, Bree asked, "Where *are* we going?"

"Boss?" Tank asked, looking at me through the rearview mirror.

I looked at Cass. "Just drive a while?"

She nodded. "We need to get out of the city—I think we burned all the bridges we could here, so I hope you're all okay with taking a bit of an extended vacation and lying low for a while. The good news is we have a hell of a lot of money to fund that vacation."

"Bermuda, here I come," Bree said, beaming.

"Let's go at least three hours outside the city," I told Tank. "I've got some friends in Virginia who owe me a favor from an old job. We can hole up at their safe house for a day or two while this blows over. Then we can decide what's next."

I said this last bit directly to Cass. I'd be lying if I told myself that what she'd begun to say in the smoky police locker room hadn't been running through my mind on repeat ever since the worst of the danger passed. *I want to be with you for the rest of my...* What was the rest of that sentence? *Life?* She couldn't be serious. We'd known each other all of a month and a half, and it was crazy.

What was even crazier was that I loved the idea.

———

I t was night by the time Tank pulled into the dirt driveway of a farmhouse in rural West Virginia.

Cass had made short work of freeing my hands from the cuffs and had settled into my side, wrapping her arms around my waist. Bree had fallen asleep on my other side and I was pretty sure she was drooling on my shoulder, but I didn't mind. I smiled every time I glanced into the front seat and saw Tank and Talia's hands linked over the center console.

When the car came to a stop, Tank turned around and said softly, "Wake up, sleepyheads."

"Huh?" Bree asked, sitting abruptly upright.

Cass woke more sluggishly, snuggling closer against me and fighting the necessity of opening her eyes. I kissed the top of her head and said, "We're at the house."

"I'll go inside and make sure it's all clear," Tank said.

While he was gone, Cass sat up and stretched, her arms extending all the way across the narrow back seat and putting a cross look on Bree's face. Then she poked Talia in the shoulder and asked, "So what's going on with you two?"

"I don't know," Talia said. "I can't explain it—I've never connected with anyone the way I do with Josh."

"I don't understand it either," Cass said with a shake of her head. I noticed Tank coming back outside after a minute or two and Cass had just enough time for one more question directed at Talia. "So, you're happy?"

Talia smiled, the most unreserved expression I'd ever seen on her. "Yeah. Are you?"

Cass put her arm around me and said, "Hell yes, I am. And you did *amazing* back there, Talia. Thank you."

Then Tank opened the driver door and said, "Looks like there are three bedrooms. Cass and Madison, I assume you don't mind sharing?"

Cass gave him a smirk and that was all the answer he needed. He got back in the car and said, "I'm going to park the car in the garage to be safe."

He moved the car around the back of the house and got out to open the manual garage door, then we all piled out and he pulled inside. We waited for Tank to come back before entering the house. He pointed us upstairs to the bedrooms, then we all parted ways. Bree disappeared into her single room and Tank put his arm around Talia to lead her down the hall to their room.

I put my hand out for Cass. "Shall we?"

"We shall," Cass said, and my heart was beating fast again.

We went into the room—small and quite a bit more

modern than the motel room we'd shared after our job at Rutherford's house, and surprisingly clean for a safe house maintained by a bunch of criminals. I locked the door and Cass went over to sit on the edge of the bed, bouncing on the mattress.

"Beats the hell out of a jail cell," she said as I crossed the room toward her.

"It sure does," I agreed.

It felt like all the air was sucked out of the room and I wondered if she was feeling the same thing I was. It was hard to imagine—happy-go-lucky Cass Hartley feeling nervous? It wasn't in her nature.

I sat down beside her, then put one hand on her cheek, guiding our mouths together. I closed my eyes and felt Cass's hand on my thigh, inching upward in a teasingly slow manner. We had a room all to ourselves and all night to enjoy it—really, we had the rest of our lives if we wanted it.

My breath caught in my throat.

I pulled back. "Cass?"

"Hmm?" her eyes were still closed, her head still tilted forward, seeking my lips, and in that moment I'd never seen her look more beautiful.

"Did you mean what you said?"

I was expecting her to ask for clarification, to play coy or be genuinely confused. Instead, she opened her eyes and locked her gaze on mine as she said, "Every word of it. I love you, Madison. And I want to be with you. I know it's crazy to talk about forever so soon, but—"

"I want that, too," I blurted before I lost my nerve. Cass stopped talking and I grinned.

"What?" she asked.

"You're speechless," I teased. "I don't think that's ever happened before."

"What about your brother?" she asked.

"It's a long story," I said, letting out a sigh and releasing every last thread of hope for that life, which was obviously never meant for me. "I met with him and I did my best, but he didn't understand what I'd done for him. I'm starting to realize that nothing I did would have changed how he felt. It doesn't matter, though, because I have you. I *love* you."

A smile began to form at the corners of Cass's mouth.

"I love you, too," she said. "I'm really sorry about your brother, but if he's too much of an idiot to appreciate everything you did for him, then he doesn't deserve you. Me, on the other hand..."

She pounced on me, throwing me onto my back on the bed and climbing on top of me. Her eyes were full of light and a powerful urge to tear her clothes off surged through me. I had to have her.

I locked onto her gaze, narrowing my eyes challengingly at her, then took her by surprise and flipped her over, changing our positions. Straddling her and looking down into her gorgeous, honey-brown eyes, I said, "Cass Hartley, I choose you. I choose this crazy life we're living."

She let out a happy shriek and tried to wrestle me down to the mattress, but I was ready for her this time and I held my ground, pinning her and then bending down to kiss her. She stopped struggling, giving in to the kiss and I felt her body relax beneath me. I lay on top of her and allowed my hands to explore her body.

"I love you," I murmured against her skin as I closed my eyes and worked my way from her lips down over her jaw and the soft, warm flesh of her neck.

"I love you, too," she said, then her hand slid between my legs and a whole world of pleasure bloomed behind my eyelids.

We made love for two days.

Let me just say that again, because it wasn't an exaggeration.

Cass and I did not leave that room, nor did we manage to keep our hands off each other, for two full days. It was forty-eight blissful hours at the end of which we both felt exhausted, overwhelmed with happiness, and just the slightest bit dehydrated.

When we finally came up for air amid a room full of delivery pizzas pilfered from Tank, Talia and Bree, who'd had the restraint to go on living their lives in all that time, it felt like being born into a whole new world.

I'd told Cass all the ugly details of what happened with Donnie, and she told me about how she suspected

Henry had given her up to the police. We had nothing tying us to New Vernon anymore, but it didn't matter. We had each other, we had about a million dollars each from the heist, we each had fake IDs and passports ready for just such an occasion, and there wasn't a single other thing I could think of that we would need.

"What next?" I asked as she held me in her arms and we watched the sun rising through the window to mark the start of our third day in the safe house.

"The world's waiting for us," she said.

27

CASS

EPILOGUE

White sand stretched as far as the eye could see on either side of me as the sun set behind a row of palm trees lining the beach. The water, blue as sapphires, lapped at the sand. In the distance, a pod of dolphins surfaced, shooting water into the air.

A beautiful redhead clad in a bikini lounged next to me, drink in one hand, book in the other. I was sucking down my own fruity cocktail, some mix of pineapple, banana and tequila. I drained the liquid and swirled the fruity remnants along the bottom of the glass for better access to every last drop.

Another one bites the dust.

That day, Madison and I had already built a sand-castle and snorkeled with the dolphins. We'd made love on a blanket in a secluded grove of palms. We'd had a lunch I could never dream of at home, and then we'd made love again.

Theoretically, given the amount of times we'd both orgasmed, I should have been a very happy and very satisfied woman.

Not to mention, I was sitting in paradise.

I pulled out my new smartphone and scrolled aimlessly through the nothing on the screen. Then I typed "paradise" into the search bar.

I turned to Madison. "Did you know the word paradise is as old as the Bible?"

"Mmm. Makes sense." Madison flipped a page in her book, a brief smile flashing across her lips.

"It's defined as an idyllic place. A place of bliss and delight."

This time, Madison didn't respond. Only her eyes moved, scanning across the page.

I tossed my phone onto the straw chair and sat up. "Some people would call this paradise, you know. Why, I'm not sure. There's so much sand. I could make a child's sandbox with just the sand I wash out of my butt crack every night."

Madison lowered her book and leveled a look at me over the tops of her sunglasses. Not even a flicker of a grin played at her lips. "You're not enjoying yourself?"

I shrugged, my shoulder emerging from the muslin wrap. I covered it back up to protect my already burned skin from the last rays of the sun. "I wouldn't say *that*. I'm just saying that paradise is subjective, you know? That maybe my version of paradise is actually, oh, I don't know—the mountains. Somewhere without so much bright sun."

Or that moment right in the middle of a heist where you have everything on lockdown but there's a chance—just a chance—that you won't get out and the adrenaline is pulsing through your veins. Everything around here was just so damn *calm*.

"Do you want to go to the mountains? We could try the Alps or the Andes. Though I'm not thrilled about the potential lack of oxygen, or food. I don't want to have to eat you for sustenance, Cass Hartley."

"No. You're right." I settled back in my chair and closed my eyes, trying to relax. "Plus, I like it here."

"Then what are you saying?" She looked sleepy in the sun, her eyelids dragged down from the heat and the alcohol, and it seemed like the conversation was requiring a lot of effort on her end.

I couldn't blame her. I was barely following my own train of thought. I couldn't expect her to magically understand it. I squinted, one eye open in her direction. "I'm sorry. I should let you read."

She picked her book up again and I tried to let it go. I didn't want to ruin her afternoon. I could see, plain as anything, *she* was enjoying herself, relaxing and totally immersed in whatever romance novel she was reading.

Still, there was this niggling feeling. It was the feeling I got when something was about to go haywire in a heist. My sixth sense. What was it? What could possibly go wrong now? No one knew where we were. According to the internet, the hype around our escape had died down somewhat. Talia was off traveling Asia with Tank, which apparently was something she had always wanted to do, and I could trust Tank to take care of her. Hell, I could even trust Talia to take care of herself nowadays.

Bree was in Bermuda.

Spider had, according to the news, been nailed on unrelated forgery charges, so he couldn't bother us.

There was Henry, of course. He was a loose end I hadn't been able to tie up. In the light of day, once I'd secured our freedom, I didn't *really* believe he had turned me in. He *had* tried to warn me when I came over to his apartment and I stupidly hadn't listened. I missed him. A lot.

It had been almost two months—56 days exactly—since we left the States and everything was good. We were in *paradise*. I was imagining things. My sixth sense was firing because there was nothing exciting left to do here.

I stood abruptly. "I'm going for a walk."

"Okay," Madison said, dragging her hand along the sand absently. I stood, watching her. *Please come with me, please come with me, please come with me.* She ignored me for a heroic amount of time before lowering her book. "Do you want me to come with you?"

"Not if you don't want to."

The smile I loved appeared and she closed the book, setting it on her lounge chair. "Of course I want to. I was getting sleepy sitting there anyway."

I offered her a hand and pulled her to her feet. She had fair skin but it tanned well and that, paired with her body rocking that skimpy bikini, made me want to put her right back down to the sand, laying her on her back. But that niggling doubt was bothering me, so I didn't.

We started walking in silence along a path just wide enough for the two of us to fit. The birds were twittering and animals scurried ahead of us. *If someone was lurking in the palms, it would be silent*, I reassured myself. No one was here.

I tried to put my mind off of whatever was bothering me and focus on *her*. Madison was what mattered. As my focus turned, however, I sensed something about her. Maybe this was what was bothering me. This slight weight, like a blanket had been laid over us.

I let go of her hand and wrapped my arm around her waist, pulling her close. Then I did something that had only recently become something Cass Hartley did. I asked her a direct question. "Do you miss Donnie?"

She took a couple steps before answering. "I spent so much time missing him, I don't think I was even missing the real Donnie. When I met him in that diner, it was like talking to a stranger."

"I'm sorry," I whispered, tucking her hair behind

her ear. We walked for a few steps before the words that had been brewing for months bubbled out of me. "I feel responsible for how all that ended."

Madison frowned. "You're not responsible. Donnie didn't want a relationship with me—simple as that." She kissed me, then asked, "What makes you bring it up now? After all this time?"

"When we're quiet together, I can sometimes feel your sadness."

Madison pulled away and stopped walking. "It's not... I'm not sad. I hope that isn't what you think. You make me so happy. It's just... you and I can never show our faces back in the States. All I need is you, but we left a lot behind without much thought to the consequences. Are *you* happy here?"

"Yeah," I fibbed. "It's paradise."

I'd go anywhere to make Maddie happy, even if I was getting stir-crazy on this tranquil beach. I took her hand in mine and ran my thumb over the back of her palm. This was something I'd learned from Madison in our months together. Sometimes, especially if you didn't know what to say, it was best to just show you were there. Strong. Quiet.

"I was thinking..." Madison said. Then she paused, shooting me a glance.

Let her speak, I reminded myself.

"When I went to meet my brother, the cops showed up before I had a chance to give him the map," she said. "I stuffed it in the booth where the back and the seat meet."

"The Verne treasure map?"

"Yeah." Madison glanced at me coyly. "You know some people think the treasure is real."

I scoffed and rolled my eyes. "Urban legend, probably. Those things are, most of the time."

"But what if it isn't?" Madison asked, light coming into her eyes.

I raised an eyebrow. I had to be sure she was saying what I thought she was saying. But I couldn't let myself think it. It was too exciting. The hope bubbling in me was too strong. If she didn't mean what I thought she meant, well, I probably wouldn't handle it all that gracefully. It was better to find out for sure.

"Are you saying—" I started, but she didn't let me finish the sentence.

"I'm thinking we should get our hands on that map."

"And then?" My throat was dry, my voice came out hoarse.

"Find the treasure."

A laugh spilled out of my mouth. The birds called out, echoing my cackles. I laughed so hard a stitch developed in my side, bending me in half.

Madison set her hands on her hips. "What's so funny?"

The laugh made my cheeks ache. I gulped in air and choked on it. Apparently it was contagious because Madison let out a quick chuckle before regaining her self-possession. "What?"

"You want to go hunting for treasure. Like... like pirates?"

"No, not like that." She tipped her head sideways, a smirk drawing up one side of her mouth. "Maybe a little like that. We'd be incredibly hot pirates, don't you think?"

The laugh died in my throat as I realized she was serious. "You want to find the treasure."

"I want to... look. I have to confess, I'm getting a little bored sitting around here, doing nothing but soaking up the island life. I'm not made for that life-style long-term, you know? And I can tell you aren't, either. What do you say?"

Tears burned behind my eyes. I'd gone from laughing to near crying in minutes. Why? Because, since meeting Madison, I'd somehow become an emotional sap. "You'd leave this place?"

Madison scoffed. "In a second. I'm bored out of my mind."

"We might get caught."

"It's us you're talking about," she said with a laugh. "We're unstoppable."

"What about going straight?"

"It's overrated. And, like I said, boring. Who wants to be straight?" she asked with a wink.

My eyes flicked back and forth between hers. She was serious and not only that, she seemed to have been considering it for a while. I was the one who always made rash decisions. Madison was the one who thought everything over carefully. There was a serenity behind her eyes that told me this wasn't a rash decision for her. Maybe she *had* been bored here, just like me. How had I missed that?

That hope started to bubble in me again and, this time, I let myself feel it. "If you're pulling my leg right now, I swear—"

Madison grabbed both my hands in hers. "I'm not, I promise. Let's do this."

"You really would?"

"I would go to the ends of the earth with you."

Tears stung and blurred my vision. How did I get so damn lucky? That wasn't supposed to happen to a Hartley. But here I was, in paradise, so I let the tears flow. I broke my hands free and put one on either side of her chin, placing a kiss on her lips, soft and sweet. I hoped it told her everything. How thankful I was, how much I loved her, how much I wanted to be with her. Everything I couldn't tell her in the moment.

As I pulled away, I couldn't help but smile. "Well, then let's go to the end of the earth."

———

As we were packing for our new adventure, my phone rang with a strange number. These days, most of the numbers were strange since I'd had to ditch my old phone and start over, plus my mind was nothing like Talia's. The numbers just ran right through. This one was from an area code I didn't recognize.

"Who is it?" Madison asked.

"I'm not sure."

"Are you going to answer it?"

"Might as well." The only people who had this number were Tank and Talia. It was unlikely that the feds or New Vernon police had tracked this phone to me, so it was either a friend or a telemarketer. Either way, harmless to answer.

I slid my finger across the screen and put it on speaker phone so Madison could hear. "Hello?"

"Is that my girl?" cracked a familiar voice across the line.

Henry. My whole body paused in response, and a thousand scenarios flashed through my mind. *Henry was working for the feds and he helped them track me down. That had been his job with my parents after all. Or maybe he was in trouble. Or maybe he was calling to apologize.* I licked my lips and glanced up at Madison. Her eyebrows were raised, but her face didn't betray much more. This time, I wasn't going to act rashly.

If he asks where I am, I'll know for sure he's working with the enemy.

"I understand if you're angry with me," he said into the silence. "I only noticed them lingering outside the restaurant just before you arrived, and I tried to warn you—"

"I know," I said, my voice barely a whisper.

"Your parents wanted me to make sure you were okay. Are you okay?"

"I'm fine," I said.

I waited for him to ask me the bombshell question, *Where are you?,* but he didn't. "I'm glad to hear that," he said. He paused, waiting for me to extend an olive branch, but I let the line go silent for a few beats. He said, "Well, I better be—"

"Henry, wait," Madison said.

"Is that Madison? Hi! I'm so glad you two are together. I should have asked, but I didn't want to stay on the phone too long just in case. Not that I'm using *my* phone, but still, you can never be too certain."

"Yeah, it's me." Madison sat on the bed and reached out her hand to me, pulling me to sit beside her. I did and she asked Henry, "I was wondering if you could help us out with something."

"Sure, anything."

"There's this diner," she started to explain and I widened my eyes at her. Sure, we trusted him, but maybe not *that* much. Madison squeezed my hand in response and nodded. *Trust me*, her eyes said. "A couple months ago, I hid a document there. It's not safe for us to come back to the states, so do you think you could get it for us?"

"That shouldn't be a problem," he said. "Just give me an address to mail it to."

Madison grinned, looked at me and asked, "How does Paris sound? I hear France is beautiful in the fall."

"I'm sure it's beautiful any time of year as long as you're there," I whispered, burying my face against the soft curve of Madison's neck. We got rid of Henry, then I wrapped my arms around her and pulled her backward onto the bed with a bounce.

"Ready to become treasure-hunting pirates?" I asked.

"Aye," Madison said, collapsing into a giggling fit the likes of which I'd never seen on my serious, somber queen. My fingers found her ribs, tickling her and prolonging the sweet moment. Before long, my hands began to venture down over her hip bones, then between her thighs, going on an adventure of their own.

ABOUT CARA MALONE

Hello and thanks for reading!

Anna and I had so much fun writing *Thick as Thieves* - we hope you enjoyed it!

I'm Cara Malone. I write contemporary lesbian fiction with drama, depth, and plenty of heat, including the Amazon bestselling medical romance Lakeside Hospital series and Rainbow Award honorable mention *The Rules of Love*.

If you'd like to be notified when I publish a new book, sign up to my newsletter at https://bit.ly/2LPRHXI or connect with me on social media using the icons below.

With love,

Cara

facebook.com/caramalonebooks

twitter.com/caramalonebooks

goodreads.com/caramalonebooks

bookbub.com/authors/cara-malone

ABOUT ANNA COVE

Hi friends,

I'm Anna Cove. Thanks for reading our little book! It came about at the suggestion of some awesome readers (you, maybe? Thank you!) and it has been one of the best things to happen to me over the past year. Writing is fun, but writing with a friend is a blast.

If you don't already know me, I write contemporary lesbian fiction that's sexy, sweet, and always has a lot of heart. If you'd like to hear more about me and my books, join my email club by visiting my website, https://www.annacove.com/. You can also connect with me on social media by checking out the links below.

Anna

facebook.com/annacoveauthor

twitter.com/annacoveauthor

goodreads.com/annacove

bookbub.com/authors/anna-cove

BEFORE YOU GO...

Can we ask you a quick favor?

If you enjoyed this book, please take a moment to share your thoughts by leaving a quick review. They help other readers decide what to pick up, they keep diverse books visible, and they make a huge difference for independent authors like us.

Thanks, and have a great day!

Cara & Anna

Calling all lesfic lovers!

Join us for a monthly book club, talk to your favorite lesfic authors, check out our growing community of published and aspiring writers, and hang out in daily chats with fellow lesfic lovers.

In fact, it's where the idea for *Thick as Thieves* was born!

Check us out at http://tinyurl.com/lesficlove

40974200R00179

Made in the USA
Middletown, DE
02 April 2019